W9-BHZ-763

"EVAN, WE AREN'T COY TEENAGERS.

"The last time we met, you said you couldn't wait very long, so...here we are," Sara concluded breezily.

Firmly gripping her shoulders, Evan spun Sara around. Her face was a rigid mask. Slowly and deliberately he took in the sight of her before he spoke, pausing to stare at her breasts beneath the lacy camisole before concentrating all the power in his eyes on her face. "I said I wanted to make love to you, Sara. Not that I wanted to have sex. That's always available."

Sara opened her mouth to respond, but no words came. Her heart constricted as she looked at him.

"How do I prove I love you?" he asked, his voice anguished. "How do I make you believe I think of you every minute of the day?"

ABOUT THE AUTHOR

Jane Worth Abbott is really two very talented ladies—Intrigue, American and Superromance author Stella Cameron and Superromance writer Virginia Myers. The two Seattle-area women are fast friends as well as collaborators, and both are active in networking with other West Coast romance writers. *Choices* is the long-awaited spin-off from their first book, the popular *Faces of a Clown*.

Books by Jane Worth Abbott

HARLEQUIN SUPERROMANCE
192–FACES OF A CLOWN

Books by Stella Cameron

HARLEQUIN SUPERROMANCE
185–MOONTIDE

HARLEQUIN AMERICAN ROMANCE
153–SHADOWS

Books by Virginia Myers

HARLEQUIN SUPERROMANCE
105–SUNLIGHT ON SAND

These books may be available at your local bookseller.

Don't miss any of our special offers. Write to us at the following address for information on our newest releases.

Harlequin Reader Service
901 Fuhrmann Blvd., P.O. Box 1397, Buffalo, NY 14240
Canadian address: P.O. Box 603,
Fort Erie, Ont. L2A 9Z9

Jane Worth Abbott

CHOICES

Harlequin Books

TORONTO • NEW YORK • LONDON
AMSTERDAM • PARIS • SYDNEY • HAMBURG
STOCKHOLM • ATHENS • TOKYO • MILAN

Published August 1986

First printing June 1986

ISBN 0-373-70223-X

Copyright © 1986 by Stella Cameron & Virginia Myers. All rights reserved.
Philippine copyright 1986. Australian copyright 1986.
Except for use in any review, the reproduction or utilization of
this work in whole or in part in any form by any electronic,
mechanical or other means, now known or hereafter invented,
including xerography, photocopying and recording, or in any
information storage or retrieval system, is forbidden without
the permission of the publisher, Harlequin Enterprises Limited,
225 Duncan Mill Road, Don Mills, Ontario, Canada M3B 3K9.

All the characters in this book have no existence outside the
imagination of the author and have no relation whatsoever to
anyone bearing the same name or names. They are not even
distantly inspired by any individual known or unknown to the
author, and all the incidents are pure invention.

The Superromance design trademark consisting of the words
HARLEQUIN SUPERROMANCE and the portrayal of a Harlequin,
and the Superromance trademark consisting of the words
HARLEQUIN SUPERROMANCE are trademarks of Harlequin
Enterprises Limited. The Superromance design trademark
and the portrayal of a Harlequin are registered in the
United States Patent Office.

Printed in Canada

For Nancy Roher,
who thought Evan deserved a story of his own.

CHAPTER ONE

"HEY, SARA. Hold on a minute!"

Ben Murphy, the big sandy-haired man who was her sister's husband, loped across the wet cement floor of the fish cannery. At the sound of his voice, Sara Fletcher turned and waited impatiently. Behind Ben puffed Chick Enderby, security man and world-class pessimist. She forced herself to smile in greeting.

"Hi, Ben. Chick. I can't stop. I have to get this stuff over to the boss. Grant's at the main office for a meeting." Sara's voice was tight, and she let the shiny black curtain of hair swing forward to partly hide her face. *Don't ask me any questions,* she thought in panic, *because I don't know the answers anymore.*

"Just one quick question, Sara. Who's that Mc-Grath guy? Chick says the night man said he and the boss were roaming all over the plant last night."

"That's Evan McGrath," she said smoothly. Old well-meaning fussbudget Chick must be starting rumors again. She looked past the two men out over the loading dock into the hot muggy August afternoon. "He's a consultant. Grant needs his advice, that's all. Grant's new at the business. You know that. Mc-Grath is an engineer, an inventor—a robotics expert." She tried to sound knowledgeable. *And all I know,* she said to herself, *is what I read about him in*

Business Who's Who. *Grant never tells me anything. He's shut me out completely.*

Sara shifted her briefcase to the other hand and rested it on her hip. Since Grant unexpectedly joined the company and took over Jarvis Foods from his ailing father, things at work had been slipping away from her. She had thought—everyone had—that when Homer retired she would take over the reins, but then Grant had arrived on the scene. The only thing she'd got out of the move from the Vancouver waterfront to the expensive executive offices in town was the need to dress better. She glanced down quickly to make sure that her costly gray dress-for-success suit was still immaculate.

"Here, lemme hold that briefcase for you. It's as big as you are," Ben said, reaching out.

Sara shook her head and held it more firmly. "No, thanks, I've got to go." She wished everyone wouldn't refer to her size, or lack of it. Small women were never seen as authoritative. Peanut-size people got peanut-size respect. Her careful smile turned a little wintry.

"Robotics," Chick said suddenly. "Well, if he's thinking to fill this place with robots doing the work you know what that—"

"Now, *Chick*," she cut in sharply. "Don't you start any wild rumors about layoffs. It's nothing like that! Grant's got more sense! Ben, you talk to him, I've got to run."

"Sure, Sara, sure. Now, you cool it, Chick, until we get something more definite to go on." The pair turned and walked away, Chick still talking. Sara gazed after them for a moment. Her sister, Christine, was in her comfortably disorganized home, happily spinning her life around Ben and their two sons. It had always seemed such a waste of a college education to Sara, but sometimes—like now—leaving the rat race behind for a home and family didn't seem such a bad idea.

It was almost four o'clock. The homebound traffic would be getting heavy, she reflected. Now she'd never make it back to the office on Burrard Street before the board meeting broke up.

Sara was right. When she entered the executive suite of Jarvis Foods, Limited in the Daon Building, she saw Grant's smooth red head, bent over his desk reading. She glanced through the half-open door of the boardroom, seeing empty chairs pushed at angles away from the polished oval table, littered with pencils and crumpled paper.

She felt a stinging in her eyes, and blinked, remembering how she had used to sit in on all the meetings.

Why hadn't Grant been content as he was? For thirty-five years he had dedicated himself to having a good time. Now, all of a sudden, he wanted to be a tycoon. She could feel her mouth setting into a grim line.

"You found them?" He saw her and rose from his desk. He was too elegant looking, Sara observed, recalling she had always thought so.

She opened her briefcase and spread fat file folders out over his desk.

"All rejected plans?" he asked.

"All rejects. For one reason or another. Too much. Too little. Too expensive. Too something. Your father kept up on everything."

Grant started leafing through the folders. "Good. This is good," he was saying. "This is what Evan wants to study."

So it was "Evan" now. They were already getting buddy-buddy.

"I see everyone's gone," she said flatly.

"Yes. We finished a few minutes ago. And I see you're giving me that frosty stare again. I just figured out what it is that makes your eyes look chillier than any one else's. The color. Not blue, exactly. Not gray. Both." A faint grin turned up the corners of his mouth, and his dark eyes held what she privately called his little-boy-pleading look. She ignored him.

Someone was still in the boardroom. She could hear the steady murmur of a masculine voice. There was only one voice with an undertone of laughter running through it. The speaker was talking to a friend somewhere, taking his time, obviously at ease. Without wanting to, she found herself straining to hear, oddly attracted to the sound of the man's voice. With an effort she brought her attention back to Grant.

"Let's not kid around. I have a million things to do. Can you give me a rundown on what's been decided about Mr. McGrath?"

"All right, I'm sorry if I've annoyed you again. I seem to do that a lot lately. I wish you and I could sit down and talk sometime—away from the phones and office hassle. Have dinner or something? You think we could manage that?" He lifted his hand and pushed aside a strand of her hair that had fallen forward over her face. She moved back just enough to indicate rejection, and he retreated instantly.

"We'll have to do that sometime," Sara said, hoping her tone conveyed an unspoken *over-my-dead-body* message. Grant had made it clear that he'd like their relationship to take a different turn. Grant was too sophisticated to let any situation become awkward, but the invitation had been there. "I'm sorry you force me to dig information out of you, Grant," Sara continued. "I hope your secretary took plenty of good notes because it looks as if I'm going to need them. Since the policy you adopt affects my job, I need to know what that policy is." She saw something near anger wash over his face, but went on anyhow. "I need to know, one, what is Mr. McGrath's ambition for Jarvis Foods? Two, are you backing him? Three, is the board backing you?" There. She had said it.

"To answer your third question first, yes, the board gave its blessing to anything I want to do with Jarvis Foods." His tone was as cold now as hers had been. "And to save you the trouble of saying it, I'll say it for you. I knew they would. My father, bless him, is a believer in family businesses and had the wit to pack the board with relatives who always vote in the affirmative. Now, what else was there?"

"McGrath?"

"Somebody want me?"

They both turned to see an exceedingly handsome man leaning nonchalantly in the entrance to the boardroom. *Evan McGrath.* Sara unconsciously smoothed her straight skirt and wondered how much of her sharp exchange with Grant had been overheard.

Grant was the first to recover, though he still seemed tense. "Come in, Evan. I want you to meet our director of personnel and the boss behind the scenes around here. Sara, this is Evan McGrath. Evan, Sara Fletcher."

She extended her hand and Evan crossed the room to clasp it firmly. Just a shade shorter than Grant, but more solidly built, he was one of the best-looking men she had ever met, with even, almost classic features. He had well-cut, light brown hair with a hint of curl and dark brown eyes that glinted with humor. She got a very clear feeling of strength, disguised by an easy, warm self-confident manner. She felt herself returning his smile, unable not to. *He's an athlete,* she thought. *He shouldn't be here in an expensive charcoal business suit—marvelous as he looks. He should be in shorts, with his tanned skin gleaming and a sweatband around his head.*

"Hello, Sara." He grinned a little, obviously enjoying her scrutiny and released her hand.

She drew back slightly. "Hi, Evan. It's nice to meet you."

"Let's go into the boardroom," Grant said, gathering up the folders she had brought him and striding ahead. Evan bowed slightly and stood back for Sara to pass. "We can spread this stuff out on the table," Grant suggested, and dropped the pile of files, fanning them on glistening rosewood. "Sara's a wonder, Evan. She went over to the plant and located what seems to be the complete past history of Jarvis's enterprises."

"Just the dead ends and blind alleys of old equipment studies," she corrected, smiling to take any sting out of her words.

But Evan McGrath had glanced up from the folders quickly. Their eyes met, and she sensed he had recognized an adversary and was now alert to deal with any threat she might represent. She felt just the faintest flicker of panic, but didn't let it show. She must put him at his ease, keep the peace, until she found out exactly what he and Grant intended.

"I understand you've been working in the States, Evan." She made her voice sound light and interested.

"Yes, the West Coast mainly—Seattle, San Francisco. But this is my hometown, you know." He was cordial, but tentative, taking her measure. "I did my undergraduate work at the University of British Columbia. Is that where you went?"

"No." Her smile took more effort this time. "I was too eager to get into the business world. I went to Vancouver Community College for two years and got a job."

"And then did ten years hard labor for Jarvis Foods," Grant said. "As I mentioned the other night, my father's health has been failing, and I guess Sara's been running the whole show for the past couple of years."

"Hardly." She spread her hands in a deprecating gesture and laughed. "This company is your dad's pride and joy. He was always on top of everything—still is, actually. He's on the phone to me at least once a week." That much was true. What she couldn't add was that she never worried him with office troubles or

Grant's latest projects. Homer had his own battles to
fight. At home in retirement, old, frail, sick, he was
struggling gamely for just a little more time; one more
week, one more month, one more autumn. And he
had achieved something like success at the moment, a
sort of holding pattern against death. Never would she
trouble that dear old man with business worry now.
She was Little Mary Sunshine each time he called.

"How are things going down there, Sara?" he'd
ask.

"Oh, fine, Homer, just fine."

"Good. That's a relief. You were always my right
hand. I can count on you. Hundreds of workers depend on Jarvis Foods, Sara. You keep Grant in line.
Don't let him make a hash of things."

"Oh no, Grant's doing fine," she would say. "He
inherited your brains, didn't he?" And he would always laugh.

Sara folded her arms against a shiver. There must
never be any showdown with Grant for Homer's sake.

She sank down on one of the chairs. She was on her
own, and she might as well face it. Both men sat down
on the other side of the table.

"What kind of work were you doing in the States?"
she asked, feeling a dim sense of pride that her voice
was pleasant and controlled.

"The last thing I did down there was designing some
machines for an aircraft factory."

Grant gave a hoot of laughter. "Here that? What
modesty. Sara, he designed a whole room full of machinery that completely manufactures an airplane
wing. For one of the big jetliners. The whole thing.

From beginning to end. I've seen pictures and drawings. It's fantastic."

"That sounds pretty impressive," Sara said. "What kind of money was involved? Maybe we're outclassed a bit. Jarvis Foods isn't exactly a giant industry."

"We're talking about a few million dollars, American," Evan said pleasantly. "That wasn't the cost of the equipment. That's what it costs now to build each wing. Those babies are expensive."

"But the point," Grant interrupted, "the point is that *without* Evan's robot machines, each wing came in at a million or so dollars more. So you see what he accomplished." He was looking at her eagerly, deeply excited.

She stirred, crossed and uncrossed her legs. "Yes," she said remotely, "he accomplished a great deal, certainly." Her slight motion toward Evan, half nod, half bow, was intended as a genuine tribute. She respected excellence anywhere she encountered it, but she was suddenly picturing her brother-in-law, Ben, worried, running across the slick cement at the plant. And her sister, Christine, and Ben and Christine's two boys. How many husbands and fathers, wives and mothers—people—had lost their livelihood because Evan McGrath's quick brain had seized on an idea and made it work—without them.

"What in the world makes you interested in a fish cannery after a success like that?" she probed. "Why didn't you go for something bigger, more important—NASA, for instance?"

"I'm not sure myself." Evan studied the back of one long, tanned hand resting on his knee. "I think it started because I got a little homesick. I've been in the

States a long time. Anyway, maybe *this* is bigger. How do we know until I get into it? In the long run, maybe streamlining fish-processing equipment will turn out to be more important work than making cheaper airplanes. Don't they tell us on the TV every day that half the world is starving? Fish is food. What's more important than food in a hungry world?''

Sara quelled an immediate flash of empathy with what he said. ''And in the short run,'' she interjected smoothly, ''say you streamline the processing at the plant, what happens then? At the people level?''

He took in a quick breath. ''You're worried about the workers' jobs.''

''Bingo. Personnel's *my* baby, remember? And one of Homer Jarvis's main concerns has always been full employment at the plant.''

Grant interposed firmly. ''Give me some credit, Sara. I researched this pretty well on my own before I even got in touch with Evan. I care about our people, too. This will *benefit* the Jarvis work force.''

''How do you conclude that?'' she asked steadily.

''To oversimplify,'' Grant said, ''Evan finds ways to speed things up. We create more product for less labor.''

''That means lay off workers,'' she cut in, beginning to stack folders on the table for fear her hands would tremble if they remained idle in her lap.

Somehow she had to stop Grant's plan.

''No! Not at all,'' he protested. ''I'm not planning to sit around looking out the window in the meantime, Sara. While Evan is increasing the production with less labor, I'll be identifying new markets. Sales will increase, don't you see?''

"Sara," Evan broke in. "Grant knows that if the workers are going to keep up with the increased sales generated, they'll need streamlined equipment and updated techniques. You may even need to hire more people. But my job is working the technical end, and I intend to give it my best shot." He was trying to reassure her, even placate her. Maybe he meant to be kind, but he didn't know what he was talking about.

She looked at him helplessly. What did he know about wholesaling fish products—this robotics expert, inventor, solver of puzzles. Well, what would happen when Grant was proved wrong—as he had been with a couple of other brilliant ideas? Evan McGrath had no idea how inexperienced Grant really was.

Somehow—and soon—she was going to have to get rid of this Evan McGrath. "But, *how*?

"Let's take a look at some of this," Grant said abruptly, flipping open a folder and spreading out its contents. Both men bent their heads over it, shutting her out, isolating her. She gripped her hands into fists beneath the edge of the table. What should she do, go or stay? She made a slight move and Grant looked up.

"Don't go yet, Sara. We may have some questions." He was so used to asking her questions that it was said almost absentmindedly.

Sara tried very deliberately to relax, mentally counting to a hundred. *Concentrate on something else,* she thought, *something good.* Unbidden came the image of Michael shortly after he had finished his residency and started his surgical practice. Michael's fair head bent over case histories late at night. The early days of Michael's career—his brilliance, his dedication. And the way he had loved her so much.

She let her eyes droop shut, thinking of Michael after they had moved into the old house left to him by his grandparents. It was summer and he was balanced on a ladder, stretching to paint the kitchen ceiling, the morning sunlight dappling patterns on his broad, naked back.

"You know, love," he'd said, wiping a hand over the hip of frayed cutoffs but not looking at her, "we can get married any time now. It's part of our master plan, don't forget." He'd paused, holding position, waiting for her answer until she walked around to stare up into his serious gray eyes. "Remember?"

And she had said, "You mean as soon as we can both get some time off together. We'll have to give it some thought. Feel like an early lunch today?"

So the years had rushed by, good years, full, rich years, until one day four years ago Michael was dead.

The only thing she could remember clearly of those few days was that the medical director of Michael's hospital came personally to the cannery to tell her, and she'd had tried—inanely—to argue the point. She distinctly recalled saying, "Michael's health is excellent. He's only thirty-eight." It had seemed vital to get that point across. "Thirty-eight," she had repeated firmly. It was unbelievable that Michael's beautiful athletic body—which had delighted her so—could have been concealing all along a faulty heart.

Sara moved restlessly in her chair. *No, don't think about that. Don't think about the bad times.* But the bad times remained in her mind. She wished now more than anything else that they had married. And she wondered if the sadness about not marrying Michael would haunt her always.

Sara often wished she could tell him about Donna. Children had been another part of their incomplete master plan. *I have a little girl,* she yearned to tell Michael. *She's been with me a year, and you would have loved her as much as I do. Single parents are acceptable now at adoption agencies. Especially if the child is older or of racially mixed parentage. They call them hard-to-place children. Her name is Donna and she's beautiful. Half Chinese, half Caucasian. She's got dark dark eyes and straight black hair, and her skin is as pale as a lotus petal. She'll be thirteen this Saturday.*

Sara could feel herself smiling slightly, thinking of the birthday party—she'd never given a children's party before. Then in the midst of the reverie she became aware of being watched and her glance lifted. Evan McGrath's eyes were intent upon her. Suddenly they were looking into one another's eyes. She turned her head quickly.

Evan leaned back and smiled. "You were a million miles away, weren't you?"

"Not quite a million," she said, trying to speak lightly. Evan McGrath was a nice man, but he was in the wrong place, doing the wrong thing. "Grant?"

Grant lifted his head from the folder he'd been reading.

"I really think we should talk this over seriously. I can get you more data." She indicated the folders. "We don't want to make too hasty a decision—"

"The decision's already made, Sara," Grant said, an edge to his voice. "I've already put Evan under contract. That's what I was reading when you came back from the plant. He's going to start immediately. And that's where you can really help."

"*I* can help?" she echoed blankly. Things were going too fast. Grant should have . . .

"Yes, Evan's going to need some briefing, some support, especially at the beginning. I'd like to do that myself, but I think you could probably do it better. So I want *you* to help him, Sara." His angry eyes challenged her. "I'm assigning this to you as your special project. Understood?"

Comprehension dawned slowly. Then Sara was filled with disbelief and, finally, rage. She clenched her teeth, willing her features into a smooth mask. Grant had figured out a way to win on every front. He'd railroaded through his decision to retain McGrath. Now he was going to rub her nose in his own power by tacking her to the man's side. And, while she was playing pickup for McGrath, Grant would be flexing his inexperienced executive muscles without the guidance he plainly resented.

"Will you do that, Sara?" he repeated, a twitching muscle beside his mouth betraying his irritation.

"Yes," she said carefully. "Of course I'll do that. From now on, Evan's work is my special project."

CHAPTER TWO

"EXCELLENT," GRANT SAID. "I knew I could rely on you, Sara. I'll leave the two of you to get acquainted while I give my father a call from my office. I like to keep him up to date. He'll be eager to hear what went on at the board meeting."

Evan saw the loaded look that passed between Sara Fletcher and Grant Jarvis. The atmosphere in the boardroom continued to vibrate for seconds after Grant closed the door to his office.

Awkwardness with a women was an unfamiliar sensation to Evan. But there was something very different about this Sara, this raven-haired little creature who appeared so smooth and businesslike. And the difference went beyond the inner turmoil he was too sensitive not to identify in every change of expression, every move of her diminutive body. Figuring out the lady might take time, which wasn't such a depressing prospect.

He'd already identified one potential handicap to working with her, maybe two. One, she definitely didn't agree with her boss's decision to hire him. Two, she was physically fascinating. The first fact was a disturbing problem, the second could become one if he wasn't careful.

"Well, Sara," he began. She had stood and moved to his side of the table to finish straightening folders. She slid papers rapidly back inside and showed no sign of having heard him. The files were supposed to be for him, yet he'd barely been given a chance to touch them.

Evan leaned back in his chair and waited. Sooner or later she'd have to acknowledge his presence. He didn't intend to waste energy on one-sided conversation.

As though she heard his thoughts, Sara rested a hand flat on the table and hooked her satiny hair behind her ears. For seconds she remained still, her shallow breathing scarcely moving crisp tucks on her white blouse. Evan scooted his chair sideways until he could put an elbow on the table and prop his head. His gaze wandered to her feet, back up shapely legs and past a tiny waist to her breasts. She was small in every respect, but perfect, trim.

"Was there something you wanted to discuss now, Mr.... er... Evan, or can we get started on Monday?"

Her words were like a slap. Evan's head jerked up, and he met her penetrating eyes. He recovered quickly enough to sound unaffected. "We should talk now, Sara. I'd like to make a dent in the preliminary stages of this project over the weekend." God, she was something. Those eyes were a knockout; pale, clear— early morning summer's day sky clear—with a hint of dusk's gray deep inside. Silken lashes, as thick and dark as the jaw-length curtain of hair, cast curving shadows on high cheekbones.

As he watched, faint pink color swept over her face. "Will it take long?" she said, the tendency he'd noticed for her husky voice to break more pronounced. "I've got several hours of work ahead of me when I get home."

Of course, she had a life outside this office. Evan stirred. Why did he have a tendency to become interested in a woman either for the wrong reasons or at the most bizarre times? Like now. "We'll keep it short." He pulled out the chair closest to his own. "Sit down, please. I'd just find it useful to get a few facts from you—then perhaps you'd leave the folders with me."

She hesitated before she came. The pause was only for an instant, but it was there and he felt her reluctance to be near him. Could some of her tension be sexual—as his was? He covered a smile by leaning to pat the arm of the chair. He was a fool. It must be time to spend less time on business and more on his social and physical needs.

Sara crossed her legs as she sat down. Evan conquered the temptation to study them and concentrated on her face. *Business,* he reminded himself, *stick to business.* "Good," he said affably when she was settled. "Maybe we can get some coffee, or something."

"I . . . Yes, of course. I'll order some."

She picked up the phone, but Evan knew her immediate instinct had been to refuse. While she spoke into the receiver, he studied her mouth. It was full and soft, smooth, displaying glimpses of small teeth as she spoke. He blew into his closed fist. Oh, but the lady was more than fascinating—and a challenge. Evan liked challenges; they were his life.

"Done," Sara said, hanging up. "It'll take a few minutes. Now, how can I help you?"

Her cool approach riled him. "You could start by telling me what your main objections are to what I intend to do." He smiled mechanically, aware he'd come on like a carbine.

Her eyes fixed unwaveringly on his. The features were smooth, emotionless, but he saw her throat move convulsively. Damn. This was going to be difficult, particularly if she wouldn't be open with him.

"Sara," he coaxed. "I heard everything you said to Grant about the people who work for Jarvis. If the market expansions he proposes come off, there won't be any layoffs, I assure you."

"If!" she exploded, and the pink in her cheeks flared bright red. "If they come off? You don't know—you haven't lived through the fiascos of the past year. First these ridiculous and totally unnecessary offices. They cost a fortune—do you realize that? A fortune! Then we *had* to have television advertising because that would increase sales. After all, everyone knows television advertising's all it takes. Another expensive bomb. Now this. And this may be the final—" She stopped, lips slightly parted, a horrified expression widening her eyes.

He wanted to grab her hand and say it was okay to blow—healthy, and helpful in fact, to him since her words put him more clearly into the picture. Instead he nodded sagely and averted his eyes to give her time to recover composure.

"I'm sorry," she whispered. "That was unforgivable—and unprofessional. Grant's been through some tough times getting to know the ropes, and the last thing I have a right to do is undermine him. Particularly with someone outside the firm.

"I don't have any excuse except to say we've all had a lot of adjustments to make lately. And I'm worried about Homer—Grant's father. I feel a sort of trust, I guess, a responsibility to make sure what he started, and loved, doesn't get thrown away. And I *am* worried about the men and women who depend on Jarvis Foods for their livelihood. Please forgive me."

Evan ran a hand through his hair. "There's nothing to apologize for. I'm glad you let off a little steam. It lets me know where you're coming from. But, Sara..."

A knock on the boardroom door interrupted him. The blond woman who was Grant's secretary carried a tray of coffee into the room and set it on the table.

Sara smiled up at her. "Thanks, Margaret. Time you were on your way home."

The secretary grimaced. "This is going to be a late one. Grant's enthusiasm is in full swing, so I guess I'll be around for a while. Oh, I almost forgot." She turned to Evan. "There's a call on the line for you, Mr. McGrath. A Mark Hunt from San Francisco."

"Mark Hunt?" Evan's heart leaped. He snatched up the phone. "Mark? Evan. Any news?"

"It's a boy!" Mark Hunt's normally calm voice broke with excitement.

"Fantastic!" Evan yelled and sent up a whoop. "Is Laura okay?"

"Marvelous. Boy, Evan—she was terrific, but I'm glad I'm a man."

Evan tipped back his head and laughed. "Me, too, friend. Were you there for the whole thing, or did they have to carry you out?"

"I resent that crack," Mark said with mock affront. "I only lost consciousness twice—when I forgot to breathe."

"Seriously?" Evan frowned.

"Good, Lord, no," Mark said, laughing. "It was wonderful, Laura's wonderful and the baby's wonderful, too. You should have heard him yell."

"I wish I had," Evan said, and meant it. A sudden wistfullness speared him, and he bit his lip. Mark and Laura Hunt had become the most important people in his life. He collected himself and caught Sara Fletcher's assessing, blue-eyed stare. "Now," he started again, "I've got to remember all the right questions. I haven't had much experience at this. I start with congratulating the father, right? Did I do that yet?"

"In a roundabout way, I guess." Pride shaded each of Mark's words. The guy really did love Laura, thank God. And he was obviously besotted with fatherhood.

"Good." Evan said, and thought furiously. "What comes next?"

"You're impossible, Evan. Talk to Laura. She keeps trying to take the phone from me."

"She can't..." Evan began, panicking. But he heard other noises and knew Mark hadn't heard his protest. Laura couldn't be ready for telephone calls. When last he'd checked, less than an hour ago, the baby hadn't been born.

"Evan?" Her voice sounded soft and sleepy, and very far away, but held traces of Mark's excitement. "Evan, you there?"

In the background came the sound of a newborn baby's cry. Evan was unnerved to feel tears well in his eyes. "Here, old buddy. Always here—remember?" He dropped his head. Some shred of caution reminded him he didn't need to have Sara Fletcher see him cry. "How's it going, Laura?"

"Fine, Evan. He's gorgeous—absolutely gorgeous."

He swallowed. "He was bound to be." *If he's anything like you,* he wanted to add. "Mark sounds like a steam engine about to bust its boiler."

He heard a muffled noise. Laura was crying. Evan wanted to rush to the nearest airport and get to San Francisco. "You okay, Buff?" The old name from their early times together came naturally. "You're crying. Do you hurt?"

"Oh, Evan, it's just that I'm happy." The next sob turned into a laugh. "You know me. I always cry when I'm happiest. I've never been so happy—never expected to be so happy. Oh, Evan . . . it frightens me sometimes."

"Don't let it, lady. You earned it. And you married a man who earned it, too. Watching the two of you these past three years has given me something to hope for. Maybe some of the magic the Hunts make together will rub off, huh?"

She didn't answer immediately, and he was afraid he'd tired her. Then he heard her sigh. "You always knew the right things to say to me, Evan. And your shot at the magic will come. You're too special for it not to."

A deep warmth spread rapidly along his veins. He loved this friend so much. For a long time he'd believed it to be a romantic love—he'd never known any other kind existed between a man and a woman. But he'd been wrong. She would always be his best, his very best friend. "Now," he said briskly, covering a sniff. "About this son of yours. Mark wouldn't remind me of the questions I'm supposed to ask about him. He's unreasonable, that man of yours—but I'm glad you've got him."

"Evan—"

"No." He cut her off. "I can manage without prompting. How heavy was he?"

The old Laura giggle wound into his heart. "Six pounds, seven ounces."

"Length?"

"Nineteen inches."

"Nineteen inches?" Evan repeated. "A shrimp! No one starts life at nineteen inches."

"Shows what you know, McGrath," Laura retorted. "That's exactly how long Mark was at birth, and he's six-foot-two, remember?"

"Mmm. If you say so. Can the kid do a double backwards flip yet?"

"Of course."

Evan grinned into the phone. "No hands?"

"You idiot." Laura definitely sounded tired. "He can wait for his Uncle Evan to teach him some of the fancy stuff."

He instantly remembered Laura as Buffo the clown, her satin-clad body turning rapid somersaults across an emerald lawn in Seattle. It seemed so long ago, yet, in some ways, it was only yesterday. She was an outstanding clown—he hadn't been so bad himself, for a part-timer. "He'll have several teachers. Sam Dobbs will probably find a way to get in on the act. And Mark can teach him to ride the unicycle. Buff, I want to talk to you forever, but you should sleep."

"I will, Evan, I will. But you've forgotten the most important question."

His mind blanked. "I have. Oh, good grief. You have to remember I'm new at this game. What's his name?"

She cleared her throat. "Evan William."

For a moment he thought he would come unglued. He covered his eyes and took deep breaths through his mouth. The name Evan would have been enough to undo him, for it was totally expected, but William had to be in honor of Mark's father who had died beneath the wheels of a car Laura had driven.

"You still there, Evan?"

"Yes," he managed. "Yes, Laura. I just don't know what to say, except, how could you saddle a nice kid with a name like Evan?"

"He's the second nice kid I know of with that name. I like it. And Mark and I thought it would be appropriate for him to have his godfather's name."

His brain was definitely on overload. "Whoa. Are you saying you want me to be the baby's godfather?"

"Naturally."

"I don't know how. He needs someone more . . . he needs someone a bit more holy than me."

Muttering sounded at the other end of the line. "Evan?" Mark came on again. "Laura's whacked, says she'll call you again tomorrow at your condo. We've already told young Evan you've agreed to be his godfather, and I know you wouldn't disappoint the little guy—or Laura—or me. Right?''

Evan smiled despite himself. "Right, you operator. Just as long as I don't have to change his diapers, too. Wait—when is this going to be? Not next week or something?''

"You really don't know much about some things, do you?'' Mark sighed. "It'll be weeks. And we'll give you plenty of notice. Now I'd better go. I'll send you a cigar.''

Before Evan could think of a suitable comeback, Mark had hung up.

"Evan,'' he muttered. "Young Evan.'' He slid back in his chair, smiling, and immediately remembered he wasn't alone. Sara Fletcher's curious gaze moved away as soon as she saw him looking at her. She poured coffee.

"Cream or sugar?'' she asked matter-of-factly.

He shook his head. "My friends.'' He indicated the phone. "They just had their first baby, and they named him after me.''

"You must be thrilled. Did you want anything in your coffee?''

"I . . . no.'' He stood and paced. "I'm going to be a godfather. How about that?''

Her softly expelled breath brought his focus sharply back to her. "I think it's wonderful,'' she said quietly, and gave him a genuine smile. "Children are special creatures. They always bring so much happiness.''

It was the first time he'd seen her relax, even for an instant. She was so beautiful, elfin but all woman in a way that made him want to hold her. A rush of longing to express his joy in physical contact engulfed him, and he shoved both hands in his pants pockets.

"I know exactly what I need to do," he said at last. "I need to go somewhere where I can buy a wildly expensive bottle of champagne and drink it."

"Sounds like fun." She bit her bottom lip while humor shone in her eyes. "Also sounds like a good way to wake up with a headache in the morning."

"Ah." He raised one brow. "Not if I share it with someone. I don't suppose I could persuade you to come with me?"

Without looking at him, she lowered her head. "Thank you. But no. I must get on."

"We could discuss business while you help me celebrate," he coaxed persuasively.

She kept her face hidden. "It's really nice of you to invite me. But I have to pick up a cake for my daughter's birthday." The sleek hair swished back when she looked at him again. "She's having a party, and nothing's been done about it yet."

The force with which his muscles tensed jolted Evan. He looked at her left hand. No ring, but that didn't have to mean anything anymore. Why had he assumed she was unmarried? A sinking inside was easily identifiable as disappointment. Then he felt like a fool.

"How old will your daughter be?" he made himself ask.

"Thirteen."

The answer surprised him. "You must have married young." She couldn't be more than twenty-nine or thirty.

"I'm not married," she said shortly. "This coffee's getting cold."

He couldn't think of a reply, except that he was glad she wasn't married, which would only confuse her. Silently he took the cup and saucer she offered him.

"How old are you, Evan?"

She knew how to get a man's full attention. "Thirty-two." If he wasn't careful she'd control every phase of their dealings.

"I'm thirty-seven. Quite old enough to have a thirteen-year-old, wouldn't you say?"

"I didn't intend to—"

"To pry, Evan?" she broke in. "I didn't think you did. But I always think it helps if people know a little about each other's backgrounds, including some of the personal stuff—if they're going to loosen up and work well together."

She was smooth. "I couldn't agree more."

"Good. By the way—Donna, my daughter, is adopted. She's been with me a year. This is the first birthday party she's ever had and the first one I've ever given. So you'll understand why it's so important—to both of us."

"I understand. And I'm sure you'll have a ball," Evan replied. Her age surprised him. She looked much younger than thirty-seven, not that it made any difference to the effect she had on him. She was becoming more interesting with every tiny piece of information she dropped. And he wasn't fooled. She was keeping the personal facts to the minimum, ensuring a basis for professional respect with him, while engineering her own escape from this building as soon as possible.

"Sara." The secretary, Margaret, poked her head around the door again. "Grant would like a word with Mr. McGrath, and this box was just delivered for you from..." She pushed the door wider and came in, carrying a large package and reading a card. "From 'Czar Nicholas and the Toad'? Is that for real?"

"It's a children's shop," Sara said. "Must be Donna's party dress." She took the box and picked up her shoulder bag as if preparing to leave. "Thanks, Margaret."

As soon as the other woman had left, Sara turned to him. "Grant may take a while, so I'd better cut out. Please feel free to use the files and we'll talk on Monday."

Even before he replied, Evan knew he was going to be difficult, and that he was unlikely to make points. But he couldn't let her go, not yet. "I'm sure Grant just wants to make sure we're on the right track so he can leave himself," he said firmly. "If you wouldn't mind waiting, I'd appreciate a few more words before you go home. I'll keep it short with Grant."

He avoided looking at her as he went to join Grant Jarvis. She did mind waiting—very much—but maybe he'd come up with some miraculous way to change that.

"Close the door, would you, Evan?" Grant said. He stood before the wall of bronze-tinted glass overlooking the dozens of other modern skyscrapers that made up downtown Vancouver. "This view is something. Look at those mountains."

Evan joined him. "I've got an even better view from my condo on English Bay. But, as you know, I grew up looking at these mountains, Grant. Not that I ever tire of them." Something in the other man's rigid posture made him wary.

"How's it going with Sara?" Grant asked abruptly.

"Fine," Evan said, without knowing why. Why should he feel protective of her with this man?

An abrupt twist of the head brought Grant's dark brown eyes boring into his. "She was my father's right hand. A damn good one. I want her to be mine—if she'll ever stop thinking of me as some sort of subintelligence where the business is concerned. While my father was here he preferred to run things alone. He didn't want me around then. Sara doesn't realize that, and I can't tell her. She's important to me—" he paused and loosened his tie "—I mean, it's important to me to get along with my staff members, particularly someone as valuable as Sara."

"I understand," Evan replied evenly. He was getting the idea he understood a lot more than Grant intended to convey. A crystal insight into the true conflict between Sara and Grant, at least as far as Grant was concerned, shook Evan. The man wanted Sara Fletcher as more than an executive assistant, and she didn't return the interest. If Evan was to try a guess at her feelings for Grant, he'd say they approached comtempt. *Poor devil,* he thought with genuine sympathy.

Grant had sunk into deep, contemplative silence and returned his attention to the skyline.

"Was there something else on your mind, Grant? It's been a long day, and Sara evidently has a pressing engagement."

The corner of Grant's mouth twisted down. "I'm sure she does." He straightened and turned a brittle smile on Evan. "We could all probably find something more exciting to do than hang around a dull office building. How about joining me at my club later?"

Evan forced himself to smile. Spending an evening with Grant was far from what he'd rather do. But he had to attend to business. "Sure. I'll finish up with Sara and get home to change. I've got your home address. Why don't I pick you up at, say, eight?"

"Bachelor Cove's too far out of your way. I'll swing by your place instead," Grant said, then hesitated. "You don't suppose Sara would come...we could clear up a few things? It always seems easier to do that in relaxed surroundings."

Odd, Evan thought, to hear insecure pleading in the deep voice of a man who appeared so confident. He glanced away. "I wouldn't think so. She's getting ready for her daughter's birthday party."

"Good, God," Grant barked. "Little Donna's a year older already? Seems like yesterday when Sara got her. She's an angel, Evan. Half Oriental and like a dark-haired doll. Sara adores the girl, and I don't blame her." He picked up his briefcase. "Of course she'll want to get home. I'll see you a bit later, then."

"Later." Evan watched him go and tried to sort out his feelings for the man. Unrequited love made people behave strangely and do even stranger things; Evan knew that only too well. Grant cared for Sara, and there was also no doubt he'd responded to the mention of Sara's daughter with unaffected interest and understanding. And there was some undercurrent about the relationship with his father: "My father preferred me to run things alone..." Evan pressed his lips together. It was a puzzle. The situation at Jarvis Foods was a potential minefield for the unwary.

He rejoined Sara, congratulating himself on his own rapid assessment of the potential hazards that confronted him. He simply wouldn't get involved in anything here beyond the work he had to do.

"There," he said brightly to her back. "I told you we wouldn't be long."

"Mmm," she muttered, concentrating on something in front of her. Then she glanced over her shoulder at him, frowning slightly. "I don't suppose you'd like to fill me in on what was so important and so confidential I couldn't be included."

Evan experienced a swift desire to make his own escape. "Grant wanted to make sure we were communicating," he said honestly. "He cares about you and obviously respects your opinion. He wanted to make sure I understood that."

"That's considerate of him," she said without inflection. Evan couldn't decide if she was truly expressing gratitude or being sarcastic.

"He's a good man, I think, Sara. The business seems very important to him, and he's probably going to make it a success. He's certainly got the energy and enthusiasm it'll take to do it."

"Yes," was all she said. She was leaning over the table again.

Evan walked to her side, stood where he could look down at her face. No, Grant's club or his company weren't at all what he wanted this evening. He took a deep breath. Sara Fletcher's perfume reminded him of wild roses—and petal-like softness. He ran a finger beneath his collar. "What's so interesting?" He'd expected to see one of the folders; instead Sara was smoothing the folds of a lavender organza child's dress. "May I see?" he added quietly.

She looked up at him, so tiny, the top of her head barely reached his chin. "You wouldn't be interested," she said shortly, and reached for the box lid.

"Yes I would." Evan stilled her hand and didn't fail to notice it was smooth and cool, or that it was completely enveloped by his own.

He lifted the dress from its tissue cocoon. A mass of ruffles fluttered, row upon row, beneath a narrow purple satin sash. The bodice was plain, but another ruffle edged a rounded collar and short, puffed sleeves. Any little girl's dream dress, he thought. Any *little* girl's dream dress.

"It's a beautiful thing," he said. "Looks like it should be eaten with a long spoon."

Sara's laugh was pleased but nervous. She was far from ready to trust him. "Think she'll like it?" Immediately she covered her mouth in a surprisingly childlike gesture Evan found irresistible. "How would you know?" she said, chuckling. "You're only a year less of a novice at this game than I am. And you certainly don't spend your spare time evaluating childrens' dresses."

He smiled and felt his lips tighten as he restrained an urge to touch her cheek, run his fingers over her hair.

"I guess I don't. But I know pretty things when I see them. And this is lovely. How old did you say Donna was going to be?"

"Thirteen," she replied happily, carefully folding the delicate garment into its box.

Evan cast his mind to picture other children he'd noticed at that age. They weren't really children anymore he supposed, but starting out toward young adulthood. He'd performed his mime act at enough parties, when he and Laura worked together during his clowning phase, to have retained a clear picture of early teens in faded jeans and happy sweatshirts. Mostly they giggled and blew chewing gum bubbles. The frilly little number Sara had chosen for Donna to wear at her party was unlikely to thrill the kid, particularly in front of a group of her peers.

"Now." Sara had retied the string around her package and turned to him. "You said you needed to discuss one or two more things with me. Could we make this quick, do you think?" There was a definite softening in her. Discussing the child and the dress had achieved that.

He sighed, rubbing his eyes. "Y'know, Sara? I think I've about had it for one day, too. But I just had another idea. This is my hometown, but I'm a stranger here now and the weekend is going to get long. How about having dinner with me tomorrow night? You'd be keeping me company, and we could really get down to nuts and bolts."

She shifted the parcel from one arm to the other. She was going to refuse, but she wasn't happy about it. That was a slight improvement, he acknowledged. Evan waited.

"I'm really sorry, Evan. Really. But the party's tomorrow afternoon, and the girls are staying overnight for a slumber party." She tilted her head, causing her hair to fall away from a pale, slender neck. "Some other time, maybe?"

"Some other time," he agreed. "There's nothing I can help you with, I suppose?"

"No, thank you." Her posture was awkward. "I just have to get organized. Buy party favors and think up some games and so on. I thought I'd get a book on that from the library."

Evan curled up inside. It took every ounce of control not to tell her thirteen-year-olds didn't want favors, and the only entertainment they needed was a stereo and a place where they could giggle and talk about boys all night. This was one mother who really had a lot to learn. He found himself desperately wishing he could help her.

"Go to it, then," he heard himself say. What else *could* he say? "Donna doesn't know me, but wish her a happy birthday on my behalf anyway. And whatever you do, stay calm—particularly if they're still talking at five in the morning."

She stared at him. "How do you know what little girls do at slumber parties?"

He shrugged. "I've got a brother who lives in Ottawa. He and his wife have a daughter about the same age as Donna, and my sister-in-law has moaned about the evils of slumber parties." He grinned. "But the main thing is, the kids love them."

"I see." She edged around him to the door. "See you Monday, then? Unless you decide you want to eat hot dogs with five thirteen-year-olds tomorrow night."

Grasping the package in one arm, she managed a wave that gave him a view of a blue eye through splayed fingers.

His gut twisted. "Yup. See you Monday."

Then she was gone.

Evan dropped, bemused, into the closest chair. What a hell of a job he was likely to have ahead of him. How was he going to persuade this woman to open up and work with him, to at least give him a chance to prove that once solidly grounded, his ideas would work—and benefit—rather than hurt all these people she was so concerned about? His ideas always worked, but she wasn't to know that, yet.

He arched his neck and took a deep breath, then gripped the edge of the table. More important at this exact moment; how was he going to be around Sara Fletcher and not long to feel her in his arms?

CHAPTER THREE

SARA DECIDED THAT IF she could make it through this evening without having a nervous breakdown, she could probably field any curve life chose to throw her way.

Five girls, Donna being the only one not tall enough to look down at Sara, lounged around her elegant living room, trying valiantly not to appear bored.

The late afternoon hot-dog barbecue had gone over well. And the cake, also shaped like a hot dog, complete with frosted bun, weiner, ketchup and mustard, was also an instant hit. From that point, the event had slid steadily downhill.

Sara's mind flitted errantly to Evan McGrath's dinner invitation. About now, it would be wonderful to sit among adults, in a sophisticated restaurant—even with a man who represented possible threats to her peace of mind. He was certainly handsome, and charming...and...very handsome. She felt herself blush. She was thinking like a silly adolescent. A hundred times—most of them in the night—she'd remembered the way he had covered her hand on the boardroom table. His fingers were hard and masculine, capable. Michael had had such capable hands. Confusion washed over her. She was reacting to a man—as a man—for the first time since Michael had died. And her choice of subjects was lousy.

A loud pop startled her. Amy Dross, the blue-eyed blond girl who lived next door, was peeling a gum bubble from her nose. Amy was a nice kid. She used to follow Michael around the garden when she could hardly toddle and her hair was a short mass of pale curls. He'd explain every move he made as seriously as if he was discussing surgery with a student. Sara got a fleeting mental picture of the two blond heads bowed close together during the careful examination of an earthworm. She roused and stood up. These past two days had been one long round of emotional beatings, both with memories and with new experiences.

"Donna," she said quietly. "Let's play another game. One I read about in a book sounded great. Could you find something for a blindfold."

"Sure, Mom." Donna's long braids were flipped back over her lavender-clad shoulders, and the girl ran up an open staircase winding from one side of the living room to the bedrooms.

Sara grinned engagingly at her young guests while they waited. She should have borrowed a library book on communicating with sloppily dressed almost-women, who wore more makeup than she did. But, regardless of her own taste, Donna's organza dress was all wrong. The child should be more like her peers: relaxed, casual.

"This is a super house, Ms Fletcher," Amy said, looking around at nubby-textured couches and chairs in shades of beige and honey. Sara had echoed blond oak paneling and a soaring marble fireplace in the colors and lines she'd chosen for her geometric furnishings. Amy went to stand beneath a screen depicting a lion. "I always loved it here. My mom says you have better taste than anyone she knows."

Gratitude toward the girl for breaking an awkward silence warmed Sara's heart. "Thanks, Amy. Your mother's no slouch in the interior-decorating department."

"I like the pictures, too," another girl chimed in. This was Jennifer Cadogan who lived some distance away, but attended the same school as Donna. "They all sort of go together, don't they?" Her green-shadowed brown eyes underscored the question.

"Yes," Sara concurred. "Japanese screens. Start over there." She pointed to a screen by a corner window. "Then move around. Left to right. If the six were joined they'd make one big wildlife scene."

"Gee," Jennifer marveled, following Sara's instructions. "Like one of those movie machines with cards that flip quickly."

Sara liked her pictures, too, but she was glad to see Donna's flying figure skim downstairs. She was struck afresh at how immature the girl's body was beside her much bigger friends. As usual, when she studied the new miracle life had given her in Donna, she quelled both tears and an urge to hug the child. She'd read it was wrong to suffocate kids with too much physical display of affection.

"Will this do?" Donna held up an old scarf, and Sara knew it had been carefully selected to preserve any she might consider important.

Donna was always so good, such a well-behaved considerate girl, old for her years, despite her slight build. Docile—that was Christine's term for Donna.

Sara didn't think she liked the word, or its inference. Could the girl be so quiet because she was insecure, or unhappy? This wasn't the time to struggle with deep questions.

"That's perfect," she said quickly. "Sit around the coffee table."

All five, Donna in her softly feminine dress, the four others in jeans and sweatshirts, immediately circled the table and sat cross-legged.

Sara put a plate on the middle of the glass top and unwrapped a block of chocolate, then she set down a knife and fork. "Now. You take turns." She surreptitiously checked her book of games. "Each player is blindfolded, then gets five minutes to eat as much chocolate as possible with the knife and fork. No fingers allowed."

A nervous giggle rippled around the table. A tensing of muscles in Donna's back and the flooding blush that blotched her pale skin didn't go unnoticed by Sara. She was making a mess of this, yet she didn't know how to put it right. Instinct told her she'd chosen the wrong activities. But how was she supposed to have guessed at the right ones?

After a short silence, Amy picked up the scarf and turned to Donna, "You pick who goes first."

Donna lifted her head and nodded at Kelly Spring, another, but very recently arrived neighbor. "Kelly's the chocolate freak. Better give her first shot in case we run out."

They all laughed as Kelly submitted to being blindfolded, protesting in a high-pitched wail for her hair not to be "destroyed." The tow-colored French braid had taken "forever," she moaned.

Kelly had speared the chocolate, with deadly accuracy, sending a lump flying across the room, when the doorbell rang and Sara ran into the hall.

At the door she paused to straighten the waistband of cream linen pants over a brilliant magenta silk blouse. With any luck, it was a parent who'd discovered one of the girls *had* to be home for the night after all. The wish made Sara feel intensely guilty.

She swung the door wide and squinted into the setting sun at the extraordinary figure that stood before her. "What..." she began. "Who...who are you, and what on earth do you want here?"

The person was definitely male. The solid chest and muscular arms were encased in a tight red-and-white striped T-shirt. Baggy black pants, a little short and held up with suspenders, revealed several inches of white sock above black dancing slippers. Sara was afraid to study the face. And he hadn't said a word.

Cautiously she checked dead-white features that appeared flat. Arched brows had been drawn on several inches above black-ringed eyes. The mouth was also outlined in black and filled in with brilliant red greasepaint. A vertical black slash from quizzical brow to an inch below each eye gave the man a doleful expression—if he had any expression at all. Sara had seen mimes at a distance, but never close enough to realize exactly how the face was made up, like a blank wall, to paint reactions upon.

Must be a sales gimmick. She should have used the peephole in the door. "There's nothing I want," she said politely, and began to retreat.

The mime said nothing, only thrust a card into her hand and bowed deeply, doffing a battered top hat.

Sara got a brief impression of curly brown hair before he replaced the hat. Silently she read the card.
Evan McGrath

Apart from the name, address—altered from somewhere in Seattle to a Vancouver location—and a phone number, the card would have been blank. But several words had been added in neat block printing beneath the name: "Mime—children's parties a specialty. Former member of the world-renowned Benevolent Association of Fools."

"I don't understand." Sara checked the back of the card, then the mime's face. "What does this mean? Did Mr. McGrath send you?" The idea seemed preposterous, but it was Evan's card. She craned her neck to scan her driveway for a car. An empty Mercedes, a silver sedan, was parked on the far side. A plush car for a door-to-door salesman, Sara thought. "*Did* Mr. McGrath send you?" she tried again.

The white face shook violently from side to side, and one floppy-gloved finger jabbed at the name on the card she held.

"Yes," she said. "Yes, Evan McGrath. Did he send you? Look, I know you aren't supposed to talk or something, but could we dispense with all that, at least until I understand?"

There was another shake of the head.

Sara expelled an exasperated breath. "This is all I need. Five bored little girls in my living room, and some nut at my front door."

Immediately the man began to caper, waving his hands nodding, pointing past her into the house. Then he stepped very close, staring into Sara's eyes.

She took a half step backward and stopped. "No!" she exclaimed and peered back. "You've got to be kidding. No, it can't be." But it was Evan McGrath himself, in the flesh, and a few innovative cosmetic aids. She'd know those glinting brown eyes anywhere.

"Speak to me, Evan," she pleaded. "A hint. That's all I ask. A hint of why you turn up at my house like some sort of clown—and how did you know where I live anyway?"

He made airy gestures, crossed one foot over the other and pursed his lips into a soundless whistle. The sky seemed to interest him deeply.

Sara began to laugh. He was funny. Really good, in fact. Where the devil did a highly successful production expert learn to put on an act like this? And when had he found the time?

"Okay. So keep it up. But either you let me know why you're here or I'm shutting the door—with you outside. I've got enough on my hands right now."

The speed with which he grasped her wrists shocked her. He backed her into the hall, turning the corners of his painted mouth sharply down. With one hand, he smoothed her brow as if removing her frown, then he smiled and pointed to Sara's lips. Her answering grin was involuntary. He shut the door with a slippered foot, lifted his chin high and gestured for her to follow him along the hall.

The party. She looked at the card in her hand once more. "Children's parties a specialty." He knew she was having a party for Donna today—she'd told him. For some reason she'd probably hate when she found out, he'd decided to turn up and put on a show for the kids. For one wild moment she was tempted to grab his broad back and twist him around for a sound kiss. A diversion had been exactly what she needed. And he'd certainly be that. Later she could explore his motives—and the other questions steadily mounting in her brain.

Just outside the living room, he paused and motioned Sara ahead. She was to introduce him somehow. Improvisation had never been her strong point. Numbers, facts, logical deductions, were Sara Fletcher's specialties—not outrageous little efforts like this.

"Here goes," she muttered as she passed him. "But, boy, are you going to have some explaining to do later."

She thought she saw a slight narrowing of his eyes, a flicker that deepened their laughing quality, but dismissed the idea. He was jamming his hat firmly down, almost to his ears.

"Girls," she cried, striding into the room. "Off with the blindfold. We have a surprise guest. I don't suppose he'll be staying long, so be kind and give him your full attention."

What happened next left her gaping. Evan exploded from the hall in a series of handstands and flips. Forward and backward he leaped, bounding over furniture that got in his way. He toured the room, cartwheeling, spinning in the air without touching the floor, and all with no apparent effort.

Sara collapsed into a leather love seat and held the neck of her blouse. Yesterday, when she'd first laid eyes on the man, her thought had been that he was an athlete. This was more than even her fertile imagination could have concocted.

It took the girls several minutes to stop staring and react. Jackie Scott, daughter of the orthodontist who tended Donna's braces, was first on her feet. "Ms Fletcher," she squeaked, "you're something else. *Nobody* ever came up with something like him. He's *fan-tas-tic*."

Without a pause, Evan came to a stonelike halt in front of Jackie and made one of his deep bows. As he came up, he handed her a stick from one of his pockets. When her fingers closed around it, a bouquet of feather blossoms burst from one end like a multicolored dandelion puff. The feathers collided with her delighted face, and all the girls laughed in unison.

Evan appeared to sink into deep thought. Sara covered her mouth. Evidently he was prepared to do anything to win her over—even spend time that must be worth a fortune entertaining a bunch of giggly kids. But she'd enjoy his efforts and thank him afterward. He was wonderful. A lifesaver. Maybe she could persuade him to change his vocation. He shouldn't waste his definite flare for the fantastic among boring old machines.

The next five minutes passed with Evan alternating gymnastic feats with magic tricks, each one leaving a girl with a prize. There were sequined freckles for Amy, and a spiky, striped wig that made Kelly forget her French braid. Donna soon sported two-inch-long green fingernails.

Between each burst of activity, Evan returned to his trancelike state while the girls waited in breathless anticipation.

Almost an hour had passed when he began teaching them flips. First he demonstrated a simple somersault, then pointed to his prospective pupil, carefully and repeatedly guiding each one through the move until the others applauded a feat that appeared easy with Evan's help.

Finally, only Donna hadn't had a turn. She'd sat on the rug to watch. Long, exaggerated steps, took Evan to her feet. He offered her a hand, and she took it. Hauling her up, he pointed to her dress, then scratched his neck, clearly puzzling. In a lightning motion he revolved to stand on his hands and took several steps, then returned to his spot before Donna. He pointed to her, then to himself and repeated the handstand.

When he vaulted to his feet again, he put both hands on slender hips and studied her hard, a heavy frown drawing the raised brows down.

"He wants you to do the handstand," Amy said breathlessly. "But you can't in your dress. Go put on pants." She leaned to see Sara. "She can, can't she, Ms Fletcher? Just so she can learn the trick. They're going to love this at school. Wait till Monday."

Sara nodded, unable to stop her lip quivering. The dress had definitely been a terrible mistake. "Quickly, Donna. Find jeans. Mr.... our guest can't stay much longer."

But Evan didn't leave. Donna, happily dressed in patched jeans and her own red-and-white striped T-shirt, quickly learned not only to walk on her hands, but to spring from hands to feet, and back like a bucking pony. Sara noted how Evan assessed her movements more carefully than the others', dropping his studied pose for a moment.

The immaculate living room was steadily reduced to chaos. Then he moved to the kitchen, where he introduced his willing imitators to the delights of theatrical makeup. His large box of greasepaint had been stashed outside the front door, ready for the right moment.

Sara watched, and worried thoughts revolved in her mind. Sticking to a purely business relationship with Evan McGrath would be more difficult after today. She sighed. His calculated reason for being here, no doubt. The disappointment that followed the idea annoyed her. Let him get through whatever he intended to try at the plant. Let him see Grant's idea wouldn't work. Then wave goodbye to Evan and hope there were enough pieces of Jarvis Foods left to pick up. She didn't have time for a romantic involvement, neither did she want one.... Or need one? *Hell*...

"Do we have to?" Jennifer's voice, raised in a wheedling tone, snapped Sara back to reality.

The makeup had been creamed off and the residue removed over her now color-spattered sink. Evan was making sleepy motions, resting his head, eyes closed, on his hands, then pointing to the girls.

When he took over, he *really* took over, Sara thought with a sliver of resentment. How come this man, who supposedly knew even less about children than she, was able to organize a party no kid wanted to end?

Kelly took one of his arms, Donna the other. "Can't we do just a couple more stunts?" Donna asked. She laughed and tipped her head into one of his own quizzical attitudes.

Sara frowned. Donna had never looked so totally happy—so spontaneous and so very young. Sara chewed a fingernail, then realized what she was doing and shoved the hand into her pocket. There had been too much tension in the past few days.

Evan held up one forefinger and walked back to the living room, his knees skimming the rug with each step as if his legs had turned to rubber. Sara couldn't help laughing.

Another ten minutes and all five girls trotted in a satisfied, obedient line down to their sleeping bags in the basement. Sara heard the door at the foot of the stairs close with a firm thud. A moment later, rock music filtered up.

One glance around the mess that had been her orderly living room, and Sara plopped into the corner of a couch, overwhelmed. She didn't even want to consider the mess in the kitchen. Evan came to sit beside her.

"They liked it, didn't they?" he said.

Sara jumped. She'd gotten used to his silence. "Yes," she said, scrunching deeper into the corner. "They're crazy about you."

"How about you?"

"I . . ." What kind of a question was that? "You're very good at all that stuff." He couldn't have been asking how she felt about him personally. "You really shocked me. Jekyll and Hyde. Where did you learn to mime? And how *did* you know where I live? What made you decide to do something like—"

"Stop!" He cut her off, laughing. "You're as bad as the kids. Questions, questions."

She tried to frown, but failed. "And you're something else, Mr. McGrath. You saved me. But you can't blame me for being just a teeny bit curious."

"I guess not," he admitted. "Sit there while I start picking up the junk, and I'll tell you whatever you want to know."

He made it very hard not to be entranced. "Leave everything, please," she said. "The housekeeper comes tomorrow, and she'll do most of it. I'll tidy up a bit before I go to bed."

"No you won't. You must be exhausted. I made this disaster. We'll fix it together if you like."

Sara opened her mouth to protest, but shut it with a snap. He wouldn't take any notice of what she said, and she couldn't help liking him for his disarmingly concerned manner. The sensation of being looked after was an almost forgotten memory—one she could get to like again too easily.

They started cleaning up, and Evan again became silent while he worked. Sara wasn't going to let him get away without the answers she wanted.

"Do I have to repeat all those questions?" she said, and stuffed handfuls of streamers into the garbage sack he held open. "Where did you—"

"Clown school," he broke in. "That's where I learned. Mime is natural for me, and my preferred method of expression. Clowning's a great way to forget your problems while you help others do the same thing. I needed the outlet once. And now I still enjoy it on the rare occasions when there's an excuse to show off—like today."

"I see." She wasn't sure she did.

"Remember the people I spoke to yesterday? The couple in San Francisco who just had a baby?"

Sara reached for the remnants of a popped balloon. "I remember." She leaned into the trash bag to press down its contents at the same moment as Evan. Their fingers meshed, her shoulder pressed into his arm. His fingers tightened, and her face came up slowly. It didn't matter that he wore the ridiculous makeup—she saw only his eyes, and this time there was no doubt about what she read there. Gentle interest—and desire.

Fear snaked into her belly. She wanted to hold him, to feel his arms around her. This was madness; the man was a stranger. True, he was a stranger who'd taken over her home in the past few hours, but a stranger nevertheless.

His attention had moved to her mouth.

"The people in San Francisco?" she prompted, pulling her hand from his, feeling his fractional hesitation in letting it go.

"Mmm?" A deep breath expanded his broad chest. "Oh, yes. Mark and Laura. Just Laura, really. She's a clown—the best. We met in a clown class at a community college in Seattle. Within two years she'd formed her own troupe."

Her skin prickled. She could feel him, almost hear his heartbeat. "And you were part of the troupe? That's hard to swallow, Evan. All of this has been a bit much...."

"Believe it," he said easily. "I just performed occasionally while I worked on my projects. Those were good times." A wistfulness had entered his tone, and she glanced at him sharply. His eyes were averted, and the white face betrayed nothing.

"What does Mark do? You said Laura's a clown. Is he one, too?"

"No! Not Mark." Evan laughed, the full, unself-conscious laugh she'd heard yesterday, and again to-day, with the girls. "Although word has it he's a whiz on a unicycle. I've never witnessed that. Mark's the head honcho in a giant firm of corporate lawyers—Fenton and Hunt. Fenton was Laura's name before she was married. She and Mark grew up together. Her uncle and Mark's father were partners." He seemed to miss a beat stacking plastic glasses together. "That's a long story, though. The main thing is, Mark and Laura ended up together—where they belong. Mark takes care of my legal business in the States."

"You're fortunate to have friends you care about so much." She ducked her head. The comment had sounded envious, and she hadn't intended that it should. If she had few friends—almost none outside Christine and her family—it was of her own choos-ing. There wasn't time. She was grateful Evan didn't seem to notice what she had said.

"I think we've just about made it through in here," he said, sweeping green glitter from an end table into the palm of his hand.

The living room was almost back to normal. A quick round with the vacuum and some dusting would do the rest. "Looks great to me now." Sara pushed back her hair. "Mrs. Beamis will manage everything else in a jiffy tomorrow morning."

He was tying the garbage sack closed. "There's still the kitchen. We really did a bang-up job there. My fault, too, I'm afraid. Your housekeeper will prob-ably quit if she's faced with that."

"*I'll* do it," she insisted firmly. "And again, I don't know how to thank you."

"Trusting me might be a good way." He straightened.

Sara ignored the comment, but her heart began to hammer at her ribs. This could get sticky. "Why did you go to all this trouble?"

"Because I'm good at it. And I was lonely. And I knew you were having a kid's party for the first time and might appreciate some help...." He swallowed audibly. "And I wanted an excuse to see you again. I didn't get here in time for the hot dogs—but you did invite me, remember?"

Heat suffused every inch of her body. "Not exactly. Who gave you my address?"

"No one."

"No one?" She was finding it harder to breath. "Are you clairvoyant as well as a magician?"

"I looked up your address in the personnel files after you left the office."

"You..." Sara whirled away, irritated. "You didn't have any right to pirate those records. The only papers you need concern yourself with are the ones you're given—the ones you need. But you're a pretty good snoop, aren't you?" Banging through the kitchen, she thought of Ben and Chick's comments about Evan poking around the plant at night. Now he was trying to use the loneliness he must have detected in her to win points at the executive level. And she'd almost fallen for the ploy. Her own malleability and weakness infuriated her.

She heard Evan enter the kitchen but didn't turn around.

Sara concentrated on sprinkling cleanser into the sink. She heard him clattering jars and cans together in the makeup kit, but willed herself not to look. How could she get him out of here gracefully? They had to work together whether she liked it or not. She owed it to Homer not to give up now. And if she was honest with herself, even without him her job was just about the most important element in her life. She'd made a success of her career and intended to keep on making it a success.

"Sara." Evan's voice could be so tearingly soft. She didn't answer.

"You don't have to say anything. But I *am* sorry if I've upset you. I guess I shouldn't have rifled the company files, but I really did want to find a way to be here today. You said children's party, and an old light came on in my head. I needed this." He paused. "And if I *was* devious, the way you say, I wouldn't have admitted how I found your address, would I? I could have lied and said Grant gave it to me, or his secretary—or that I looked it up in the telephone book. All perfectly feasible."

She closed her eyes. Was she looking for reasons not to like or trust him? Was she afraid to let go and enjoy another man for fear of being hurt again? Sara locked her elbows against the sink. That excuse for her reticence wouldn't wash. She had never been truly hurt because the deep, deep love she'd shared with Michael never went sour. "Forget it," she said clearly. "I'm a bit touchy right now, I guess. Overprotective of the company. We've been through some rough months."

"I can relate to that," Evan replied. "Can we set Jarvis Foods aside for a few hours—at least until Monday? Then we'll start afresh."

The full meaning of his words might be better left unexplored, but Sara decided she was willing to grab at a chance for peace. "Sure. Sounds like a good idea to me."

"This stuff goes on a whole lot easier than it comes off," Evan said. He came beside her to throw away greasepaint-caked tissues. "Soap and water finishes it off pretty well, though."

Calmly he pulled down the suspenders and shucked his striped shirt. Sara felt the blood drain to her feet. Her head was light. He leaned around her to turn on the faucet, and, fascinated, she watched his tanned biceps flex, solid muscle ripple beneath dark hair on his chest.

"Would you mind getting the bag from the back seat of my car?"

Sara backed away, hands dripping.

Evan bent to take off the slippers and socks. "I didn't lock it."

The cool night air whipped her cheeks before Sara realized she'd followed his directions like a zombie. At least the basement was silent, she thought gratefully. The girls must be asleep. If they awakened, there was a bathroom down there. How would it look if Donna or any one of the girls found Evan half-dressed in the kitchen? What would the other parents think if they heard about it—secondhand and embellished?

Her hands fumbled uselessly for seconds before she managed to open one of the Mercedes's rear doors. The bag was exactly where he'd said it would be, in the middle of the back seat. She grabbed double handles and retraced her steps. Outside the kitchen, she paused and lifted her chin. Time for *her* to take control.

"Here, Evan." Sara opened the kitchen door and walked in. "You can use the shower off my room. I put clean towels in there this morning."

After a skipped beat, Evan said softly, "Of course. Thank you."

She fastened her eyes on the point between his collarbones, where fine hair sprinkled tanned skin. "I'll show you the way."

"Right." He eased the navy canvas bag from her fingers and followed her from the kitchen.

They didn't speak. Sara felt his solid bulk behind her on the spiral staircase, smelled the faint scent of after-shave mixed with greasepaint as they walked along the hall leading to her bedroom.

"This is nice of you," he said, passing her noiselessly on deep-pile umber rugs. "Sorry for the strip-tease act. I tend to forget not everyone's used to people whipping off their clothes just anywhere. You get used to that when you're performing."

He reached the foot of the circular bed and faced her. Sara managed a wobbly smile while she clasped and unclasped her hands. "You aren't the first man I've seen without a shirt." She winced. *Of all the dumb things to say.*

"I'd be very surprised if I were." Evan's broad grin made it impossible not to smile in return. "In here?" He ducked his head toward the bathroom.

"Yes," Sara crossed her arms tightly and watched Evan turn away. His back was broad and sharply tapered to slim waist and hips. She noticed every aspect of the man as if he *were* the first she'd seen.

"Won't be long." He closed the door behind him.

Sara drew in a long, uneven breath. She probably ought to offer him coffee or a drink before he left.

She made it as far as the doorway before looking back. Her room was the upper floor of a tower at one corner of the house. Like her bed, it was circular. But she hardly saw the familiar trappings. The sound of running water came from the bathroom, and an unmistakably male voice raised in rumbly, tuneless song.

Michael had sung in the shower. No man had been in this room since he died—until tonight.

Sara covered her mouth with a shaky hand. She really was dangerously vulnerable. She wished, almost violently, that Evan McGrath didn't have to leave.

CHAPTER FOUR

HOW THE HELL COULD HE have been such an ass? Evan rotated the faucets hard to turn off the water and leaned one forearm against steamy tile.

He'd already identified Sara Fletcher as emotionally fragile beneath her smooth, professional veneer. But he'd still come roaring into her home, taking over, catching her off guard. The mime act would have been fine if he'd left it at that. Allowing himself to behave as if they were old and familiar friends was a tactical error that made him cringe. Unless he could pull them back onto even footing, he had blown it.

She was so lovely. Evan gritted his teeth and slid open the door. He was one lonely guy, and he hadn't even realized it until Sara Fletcher's small presence insinuated its mind-stunning influence into his life.

"Damn." He'd forgotten to put down a bath mat, and now he was dripping all over her immaculate white rug. Hopping from one foot to the other, he reached a huge black towel from a gold-toned rail and rubbed his skin vigorously. Cool. That was it. He'd be pleasant, but cool. She'd hit an old cord and sent all his suppressed male responses into full gear. She made him want to be near her and in this situation, giving in to that kind of reaction would be poison.

He dressed quickly, suddenly acutely self-conscious about the climate he'd created. The last place he should be right now was Sara Fletcher's bathroom. *Damn! He had no comb.* He swore softly under his breath and ran his fingers through his hair. Maybe he should borrow one of hers and explain— No! Lord, he was behaving like an adolescent suffering a first crush.

His insides churned, and he sat on the toilet lid with a thump. This was a class A example of overreaction. He didn't even know the woman, and she clearly wasn't hot to know him. He looked at the gilt-edged mirror over a double sink, at uncluttered glass shelves reflecting subdued lighting. This house was big and expensive for a woman who'd been alone until a year ago and who'd started her career cold with nothing but a community-college education behind her. There had to be more to Sara's story than she'd revealed in her little "openness" spiel the day before.

Evan scrubbed at his face and got up to stuff his mime outfit into the bag. The timing for romantic interest was off—and probably his instincts, too. He laughed self-derisively. Good timing and an instinct for choosing the right woman for the right reasons hadn't exactly been his forte.

He reached for the doorknob, then hesitated. Slowly he picked up a bottle of perfume, unscrewed the top and held it to his nose. Those marvelous wild roses— winter roses, again. Oh, he was smitten all right, but his instant infatuation was going nowhere. After Laura, he wasn't about to risk another emotional debacle. And this feeling, this squeezing of his heart or whatever that sensation was, was uncomfortably familiar. Thinking Laura Fenton would be his for all time, only to discover they'd never been intended to touch as more than friends, nearly finished him for a while. When he'd first met Laura she'd affected him the way Sara was doing now. *Time to retreat, buddy,* he thought. No way would he willingly go through more of that kind of pain.

Stalling now would only make his position more awkward—and increase Sara's discomfort. Evan closed his eyes for an instant, then set out resolutely for the living room. The way he'd unsettled her; that's what he was going to hate most about all this later, when he was forced to remember each little cameo in living color. And he would live and relive every second of the past hours—and feel like an inconsiderate fool. He'd never learned not to care what he did to someone else.

Sara heard Evan's muffled footsteps on the stairs. "Hi," she said, smiling up at him. "Feel more human again?"

"Oh boy, do I." He jogged down the last few steps, his bag slung over one shoulder. "The paint's fine as long as you're moving. Afterward it feels like cold mud."

She tucked in one corner of her mouth. "I'll have to take your word for that." In casual clothes he looked different, even more appealing. Crew-necked tan sweater, beige shirt and well-cut brown corduroy jeans accentuated his leanly athletic build. Yes, Evan McGrath was an unnervingly attractive man.

They were staring at each other, silent, unmoving—uncomfortable as hell, darn it. And it could never be any other way between them. "I made some coffee.'' She waved at a tray on a low glass and bronze table. "Least I can do after you bailed me out." If she kept the conversation light, there would be no repeat of their earlier tension, or, she hoped, of her traitorous urge to keep him with her somehow.

"Thanks," Evan said. He bent his head to finger comb his hair. Beads of moisture glistened on thick wet curls. "But I'd better get going. You probably have other plans, and I should be slaving over those folders you gave me."

An achy tightness drew Sara's insides together. He'd been kind, reached out. And she'd managed to embarrass him with her infernal reserve. "I have no plans," she said, and cleared her throat. "And you shouldn't spend all your time working. Please, if you don't want me to feel like an ungrateful heel, let me give you some coffee—or a drink—or both. Humor me." She smiled, received his answering grin and looked away, intoxicated by the warm openness in his face.

"Twist my arm," he said lightly. "The coffee smells great."

"Sit." She waved to a love seat. "How about something in it? Kahlua? Drambuie?"

"Do you happen to have brandy?"

His bag flopped to the rug and Evan sat on the edge of the love seat, leaning forward, hands hanging between his knees.

"Brandy," Sara repeated. He had marvelous hands. "Yes," she said slowly. "Brandy, of course." And she went to pull a bottle of Courvoisier from beneath the marble-topped wet bar. "I hope this is okay. I think Michael . . ."

Her mouth dried out.

When she looked up, Evan was staring at her. His nostrils flared, white lines spreading from nose to the corners of his mouth. He hadn't missed the slip, but he wouldn't probe.

"I hope it's okay," she continued lamely. "This is an old bottle."

"Best kind," he said evenly, and she knew he followed every move she made.

Carefully, afraid he'd see the trembling she felt inside, Sara poured coffee into two cups and added brandy to one. She hesitated and dumped an equal amount of liquor into the second cup. Alcohol had never been big with her, but tonight she'd try anything that might calm her jittery nerves.

"Tell me if that's okay." Her hand did jerk as she offered him a cup and saucer.

Evan took the drink, but captured her hand before she could withdraw. "Sit beside me, Sara." His voice was controlled, yet she felt an undercurrent of tension—and the unyielding pressure on her fingers.

Awkwardly, unwilling to make a scene, she reached across her forearm to set down the bottle of cognac and allowed him to guide her to the seat. "Try the coffee." She sounded breathless. None of this should be happening.

He placed her hand between them on the couch and took a sip of his drink. "Not bad. Pretty good, in fact. Michael had good taste. How's yours?"

There had never been another time like this. Since Michael, no other man had sat here alone with her—except Homer when he'd come to lift her from the self-imposed pit she'd chosen after Michael died. And after that, no one had threatened the peace she'd made. She wouldn't allow Evan to do so now.

"Where do you live, Evan?"

"Sara, Sara," he said quietly. "Did I get too close to something? Are you running for cover?"

Goose bumps shot out on her arms, and she hugged her ribs. "Maybe I shouldn't have asked you to stay for coffee after all."

"I think you did the right thing. We all suffer a few failed relationships. I certainly have—one at least."

Sara opened her mouth, then closed it. She was going to... no, she wasn't going to cry in front of him... she never cried. "Evan." The breath she took burned. "This is wild. I don't even know you and probably never will. I do like you in a way, and that may make it easier for us to work together. If we let this evening drop now. Please, don't probe into my private life. It wouldn't do either of us any good."

"If you say so." He settled farther back into the couch. "Laura Fenton Hunt was more than a friend to me for a long time."

She stared at him, nonplussed. "Why are you telling me this?"

"We weren't lovers. She'd never let it go that far. But I wanted her enough not to care if I lived or died for a while after I knew we could never be together. Now I know we weren't meant to be more than friends. Surprisingly, life went on. Quietly for me, but not totally empty. Maybe we have to let go of what's past and grab at new opportunities."

Every nerve ending in her body felt sanded. "I'm sorry you had a disappointment, Evan. But I don't know what it has to do with me."

His saucer met glass with a crack. "This is terrific stuff. Drink some." He lifted her untouched cup to her mouth, held it until she folded her hand over his and took a long swallow. "Good, right?" he insisted.

"Good," she agreed in a small voice.

"Should I leave now?"

Tell him yes. Tell him to go. "Finish your coffee."

"What happened to you, Sara?" He held very still, his hands under hers. "What made you so afraid to let go, even a little? This Michael . . . is he still in town?"

Damn, damn, damn. She wouldn't cry. She would *not*. She turned her face away, anguished.

"No." Evan's voice was miles away. "No, Sara. Hell, I'm sorry. I didn't mean to do this to you. Please. I'm sorry."

The cup was taken from her hands, and she unconsciously made fists. A strong arm slid around her shoulders, but she sat more rigidly. He didn't understand. No one would ever understand. She'd failed Michael, and it was too late.

"Sara—"

"I'm fine," she said, opening her eyes wide. "This has been a weird day. And a lot has happened to me lately. Don't worry. I'm not going to break down and weep. I'd appreciate it if you'd forget any of this ever happened."

Distress turned his flashing eyes to deep brown velvet. "What would I say? That I pushed myself in here and upset you? Don't worry about that angle. But, Sara... I know we're strangers...but I can't leave you like this." Muscles in his jaw flexed.

Sara looked at his mouth, the neck of his shirt. She smiled wearily. "Michael and I were together for ten years. We always intended to be married and have children. The house—" Her hand fluttered and fell to her lap again. "We worked so hard to make it like this. It was his and he left it—" It didn't matter what Evan thought anymore. "Michael left this house to me. He died of a heart attack a few years ago. He was a surgeon. It happened at the hospital. He was—he was thirty-eight." She'd said it all aloud for the first time in all these years. The comparative anonymity of this stranger had made it possible to voice her so ordinary, so common little story. Only it wasn't little, or ordinary for her. She missed Michael, always would.

Evan cursed under his breath. He tilted her chin toward him. "And you've kept to yourself ever since, haven't you?"

She nodded, pressing her lips together.

"I don't know what made you decide to spill everything to me. But I'm glad you did. For what it's worth, I've never told anyone else about Laura, either. We must both be pretty lonely I guess, but if you'll agree not to say I ran off at the mouth, I'll keep what you said to myself, as well. How about it?" One thumb stroked her pointed chin.

"Okay. But I can't believe this happened." She straightened, moving away from him. "I really think it would be best if you went now, Evan, and forgot everything we've said. Attending to business is the main thing, and I promise you, you won't see the mournful side of me again."

Evan studied his splayed fingers. "Sure," he said. "Business is always the main thing." His dark eyes met hers steadily. "We'll work just fine together."

After her behavior tonight, any dealings with Evan were bound to be strained. She'd just have to keep their involvement to the minimum while still doing what Grant had asked her to do.

Her own cup skittered in its saucer when she set it down. "Of course we'll work fine together," she said brightly. "We'll make a great team. A lot hinges on what you do in the next few weeks, and I'll do my best to support you." Right now, she simply wanted to be alone.

"Christine Fletcher—" He leaned toward her, snapping his fingers.

"What?" Sara frowned. "What did you say?"

Evan grabbed her wrist and looked closely into her face. "You're related to a Christine Fletcher, aren't you?"

"My sister?" she gasped. "You know her?"

"Yes. We were in college together. At least, I remember her from a few classes. She looked a bit...no, a lot like you, only bigger. I mean—"

Sara shook her head, smiling. "I know what you mean. Christine's a lot taller than me. I was the runt of the litter. She's Christine Murphy now. Married with two boys. Her husband, Ben, is one of our foremen at Jarvis. You may have met him at the plant already. Big man. Sandy hair. Kind of quiet, but nice."

"I did meet him," Evan said. "This is strange. School seems like part of another life, something that happened a century ago. Now there's you, and you bring it all back. Chris was a nice girl."

"She still is. And she's my kid sister. You two should get together for a chat. You'd have something in common. Education, age..." Her voice trailed off.

Younger men had never appealed to her. "It would do Christine good to talk to someone who used his education."

"Meaning?"

Sara met a piercing gaze. "Meaning nothing really. Christine married right out of school. She's never had a job."

"Looking after a husband and two kids isn't a job?"

A violent blush suffused Sara's face. Something had gotten reversed here. "Of course it is. I didn't mean—"

"You didn't?"

"Well." She stood abruptly. "I'll tell Christine you're in town. She's a fantastic cook. Maybe she'll have you over for dinner, and you can talk about old times."

"Do your folks still run the grocery store downtown on . . . what street was it on?"

"There's a hotel on that whole block now. Progress, y'know? Mom and Dad moved to Alberta to farm." She edged around the coffee table.

"Sara . . . ?"

"Don't forget your bag, Evan. And thank you more than I can say for showing the girls a good time. I'll be expecting Donna to want gymnastic lessons."

Evan's expression closed. He picked up his grip. "The kids were wonderful. Good for my soul. Donna would be worth a few lessons. She's going to be a natural." He turned on his heel and headed into the hall. "Please do remember me to Christine. I'll get her number from Ben and give her a call."

Stay, she longed to call after him, *stay with me. I don't want to be alone tonight.* But she followed him silently to the door and watched him open it.

He faced her. "Are you okay?"

"Of course." She forced a grin. "See you Monday. My time will be yours for as long as you need it."

"Really?" Two long fingers passed fleetingly over her cheek. "Yes, of course it will be. I only wish you didn't dread every moment."

He slipped outside, closing the door with a solid thud. Cool air and the scent of damp leaves rushed into the house.

Sara leaned against the wall, her arms crossed. Grant's attitude, the party for Donna, the mounting uncertainties that had crowded in since Homer had left the firm—the constant battering at her spirit in recent months had left her fair game for almost breaking down this evening. There could be no repeat performance.

A click brought her to attention.

The basement door opened, and Donna stumbled upstairs pink and sleepy. "Mom?" She gripped the banister at the top. "Watcha doin'?"

"Nothing, sweetheart. Can't you sleep?" Her heart still expanded when Donna called her Mom.

"Uh-uh. I wanted to see if you were okay."

Sara closed her eyes as the girl came into her embrace. "Like to come into my bed for a while?" The bony arms loosened their grasp, and Donna's breathing became shallower. She was still uncertain, insecure. "Just till I get to sleep," Sara added quickly. "I'm a bit lonely tonight. Then you can go back down to your friends."

They climbed the stairs together. Sara remembered the dishes on the living room table. They could wait. She'd made one mistake in her life when she hadn't proved to Michael how much he meant to her. She wasn't going to flunk another chance at love. Donna was all she needed.

In bed, she pulled the thin little body close. Her daughter was all she'd ever need.

Sara closed her eyes but sleep wouldn't come. *"I wish you didn't dread every moment,"* Evan had said. But she didn't, and there was the danger. Heat flashed over her skin, and she stared into the darkness, totally awake.

CHAPTER FIVE

SHE'S NERVOUS AROUND ME, Evan thought as Sara entered the office with too quick a step, her manner too brisk. He'd noticed the same jumpy guardedness about her in the few minutes they'd spent together yesterday. She had met him at the Daon Building, told him he was to set up base here, in the cannery, then been unavailable for the rest of the day. Lengthy conferences with Grant had made it impossible to get down to the waterfront until this morning. He had only just arrived. Sara must have been downstairs watching for him.

"What a racket," she said, shutting the door behind her, dimming the rattle and roar from below.

"I'm used to working in noise. I tune it out," Evan said, making a production of putting down his armload of folders and rolls of drawings. He'd start right in talking business, give her a minute to become at ease, to see that he wasn't going to make any reference to their meeting at her house.

"Well, that's good," she said crisply. "One thing I can say about the new offices—they are quiet. Well, what do you think of this place? Will it do?"

"Admirably," he said, looking around, hands on his lean hips. "Admirably. I just need a private spot to brood over my drawings and notes and a secure place to leave them when I'm not here.''

"This office has the best lock of any in the building,'' Sara answered. "It was my office.'' There was a slight catch in her voice.

"Was it?'' He glanced at the Spartan room, massive ancient desk, bare wooden floors, lopsided slat-blinds that had seen many years service, stained plaster walls. A naked cork bulletin board, scattered with a few stray pushpins, covered part of one expanse of peeling green paint. He met Sara's eyes again.

"Homer wasn't one for show,'' she said, and turned away rather quickly. "Now some of these file drawers are still full. I hope you won't mind that. But the two I emptied when we moved have foolproof locks, so your stuff will be safe enough.''

"Good. Two is more than enough.'' He risked a longer look at her now. She was composed, the efficient smooth mask she wore at work in place. Wryly, he waited for and experienced the sensation he was already coming to expect each time he saw her. *Watch it, old buddy,* he cautioned himself.

She took a small envelope from her handbag and opened it. "Here are your keys. They're new. I had them made from my set, so you'd better try them and make sure they work. This big one is your office door, the two small brass ones are the file cabinets and this one is for the men's room at the end of the hall. Nobody from downstairs uses it.''

He took the keys and bounced them in the palm of his hand. "Who else has the office key?'' he asked.

"Nobody. That is, I have. And there is a master set used by whoever is on for security. And, of course, the janitor has a master."

"Of course." He grinned faintly. "Absolutely foolproof arrangement."

A reluctant little smile curved her lips. "I guess our security isn't exactly perfect," she admitted. "But just remember to put your stuff in the file cabinets, and you won't have to worry. Lock them, of course." She was definitely smiling now.

He considered and rejected the idea of asking for a lunch date. It would be better to take it more slowly. "I'll do that."

"Will you need anything but what's already here?" she asked. "Or is there something you want taken out?"

"No. The desk is fine, so we'll leave it. I like a big desk." He passed a hand over its scarred top. Sara must have looked awfully tiny sitting behind it. "I'll need some surfaces for my computer setup, though. But I can get those when I select the components."

"Computer?" There was a sudden definite wariness in her tone.

"Yes. You sound alarmed. Have you got a thing against computers?" Good grief, he thought, were they going to cross swords again? They'd started out so well today.

"Only against the cost. May I ask if you already *have* computers to bring here? Or are you going to purchase them?"

"Of course, I have a good deal of my own equipment," Evan said tentatively. "I do a lot of my think-work at home, and I need to keep the main outfit there. But there must be a terminal here and a few other components. So, yes, I do have to purchase what I'll use actually at Jarvis.'' The way she had said "computers" told him she didn't know much about anything beyond standard office equipment that businesses used. "Are you familiar with computers?" he asked carefully.

"Oh, yes," she said confidently. "There's a computer downtown. We keep our perpetual inventory in it and some other things. Naturally, I've never entered personnel records, because several people have access and the information must be kept private."

"Of course," he agreed, feeling relieved. He was right; she knew practically zero about the subject. He did already own the major part of the necessary equipment, but she was still likely to overreact if she had any idea of the costs involved in getting the sophisticated peripherals he had to have for design work.

"When you make your selections, let me know," she said, frowning slightly, "and I'll get you a purchase order. Is there any possibility you could rent what you need?"

"Not really," he said apologetically. "And I... uh...already have a purchase order." *Damn*. He watched delicate color sweep into her face. He'd stepped on her toes again.

"Oh, of course. Grant gave you one yesterday, didn't he?" She was all business again.

"Yes. That is, he had his secretary do it." No need to tell her that Grant had signed half a dozen blank purchase order forms and handed them over when they'd discussed equipment.

He sat on the edge of her massive old desk and crossed his legs at the ankles. "Incidentally, what's a personnel director doing worrying about purchase orders?" he asked, smiling. *No, that was the wrong note.* He cursed himself. She wasn't the kind of woman you could jolly along. Sara was much too sharp for that.

"Because I wear several hats and do a lot of other jobs in addition to personnel." She stopped, leaving something unsaid, and her lips came together firmly.

"Would you like me to...uh...clear everything with you?" he asked, hoping fervently she'd refuse.

"No, no," she said quickly. "If Grant okays the expenditure, then it's certainly in order." Her tone was a bit still and grudging, but her ethics were first-rate, he thought. He had given her an opening to second-guess her boss, and she'd turned it down. His opinion of her went up another notch. And it was already pretty high.

With an awkward half wave, she went, leaving a hint of her perfume in the air. He remained sitting on the desk for a moment, watching the door that had closed behind her with a decisive click. Then he moved to squat and examine the lock, grinning to himself. A determined little child with a toothpick could cope with this lock. So much for security. Well, it was just a fish cannery. He had worked too long in high tech, where industrial espionage was a real problem. Who could possibly care what he did here at Jarvis? He felt a sudden easing of tension. It would be nice to work for a while where he didn't have to use plastic entry cards to get into every room and watch each word he said. He set about busily making himself at home.

He was stuffing folders into a file drawer when the phone rang. It took him a moment to remember where he'd put it. Ah. In the space underneath the desk. He lunged over the top, scooped up the receiver and answered, lying across the desk on his stomach.

"McGrath."

There was a clearing of a throat at the other end and a somewhat timid voice asked, "Mr. McGrath?"

"Right. What can I do for you?"

"Mr. McGrath, this is Donna Fletcher. Did you get them?"

Donna Fletcher. That sweet kid of Sara's. The image of her black braids, black eyes and perfect oval face sprang to his mind.

"Just the person I wanted to hear from," he said, "tell me how it feels to be thirteen. I've forgotten."

There was a delighted giggle. "It feels great, Mr. McGrath. Mom raised my allowance again. But what I wanted to know is, did you get them? The cards and stuff?"

"What cards and stuff? No, I guess I didn't get them. What are we talking about?"

There was another breathless laugh and the sound of coaching from the background. So she wasn't alone. She probably had the whole party crowd with her. He visualized five thrilled girls. Well, he was batting a thousand with the early-teen set. Maybe some day he could graduate to someone a bit older—like this one's mother.

"Oh darn. We spoiled the surprise. We all got you thank-you cards. You're going to love them. They're so *funny*. They're *wild*. We spent the whole of Sunday morning in the card shop reading them all to get the best. We really broke up. We took the bus clear down to the post office to mail them. Maybe your mail hasn't come yet. Maybe you'll still get them today.''

"Maybe I will. I'll look forward to it. How did you get my address? I haven't been back in Vancouver long enough yet to be in the phone book. You hired a detective didn't you?''

There was a cascade of giggles as Donna relayed this question to the others.

"We sent them to your *business* address. The cannery. Mom said you would be working there.''

"Oh, that's great. I don't have to wait until I get home, then. You want me to thank you for them when they come? I'll thank you for the thank-you cards, and then you can thank me for thanking you and then I can thank you for—'' A veritable explosion of mirth cut him off. Boy, he was in good form today.

He hung up in a couple more minutes, feeling good. There was nothing like a happy kid to lift the spirits. And the nice part was, he really did like Donna. He wasn't just trying to charm her to get to Sara. Not that it would do any harm.... *McGrath, you're a devious devil,* he told himself with no remorse at all.

It was almost noon before he got his work space arranged to his satisfaction. He enjoyed this settling-in stage when he was preparing for a challenging job. He was beginning to feel the underlying excitement with which he always worked. He'd learned enough about the plant operation to get at least a preliminary idea of the way to go. It was like the start of a race, just before the gun sounded.

Leaving his office, he clattered down the stairs. Deafening noise and the smell of fish enveloped him.

In a moment now, the noon whistle would blow and the workers would break for lunch. He made directly for the end of one of the double conveyor belts as they jiggled along. The lower belt had its load of wet, shining, headless and tailless fish. A row of uniformed, rubber-gloved women at the side of the belt fitted the fish expertly into cans, drained, then weighed each container. If the weight was right, the can went into a wet wooden tray on a shelf above.

The man they called the "stacker" saw Evan approach and gave him a reserved nod of recognition. These people were suspicious of him. He expected that. It would take a while for acceptance. Evan stood watching the man lift off the loaded trays of still-open cans and stack them on a hand truck. As he watched, another man hurried up with an empty truck to replace the filled one. The operation was smoothly accomplished, without either man missing a beat. Once again the stacker turned to lift a tray. Evan studied the twisting, bending motion of the man's torso.

Low-back pain, friend, Evan thought. *That's what you're going to have in a few more years. And you're probably going to blame it on your bowling. What you really need in this spot is a robot. Robots don't get low-back pain.* He sensed someone beside him and turned his attention away from the stacker.

"Hi. Ben Murphy, isn't it?" He held out a hand.

The sandy-haired foreman wiped a hand down the side of his jeans and extended it. Evan liked his handshake.

"Yeah. Mr. McGrath, right? We were introduced when you first came around."

"Name's Evan. Yes, we were. I found out since then that you're Sara's brother-in-law. Incidentally, I know your wife—knew her, that is. We met in college," Evan explained tentatively, and was pleased to see Murphy's expression of sudden, open friendliness.

"No kidding? You know Christine?"

"Well, we had some classes together...she may not remember me." Evan had to smile in return.

"Oh, she'll remember," Murphy said confidently. "Mind like a steel trap, that girl. Wonderful memory. Say, you got to come out to the house for dinner. I mean—" He was suddenly awkward, as if he had been too forward. "That is, if you want to."

Evan laughed. "You bet I want to. I'm remembering a couple of parties I went to where Christine cooked the food."

"Oh, yeah?" Ben's rumble of laughter joined his, and he slapped his stomach. "She's always after me to watch my weight and how can I? Look, I'll tell her you're here. I'll give her a call on my lunch hour."

"Do that. I'd really like to see her again."

As he finished speaking, the noon whistle shattered the air, and there was a short interval of expectancy while the noise diminished, conveyer belts slowed and came to a stop. A few final cans were filled and weighed and placed on trays. There was a rising of conversation, broken by laughter and a few shouts. Women and men began peeling off gloves, taking off aprons on their way to the washrooms. Just beyond the open main doors, a catering truck had pulled to a stop. The driver jumped out and began lifting metal sides to reveal rows of prepackaged foods.

"Ben." Evan watched workers file outside. "Answer a question for me, will you?"

"Sure, if I can."

"The guy who works at the end here, the one who takes the trays off the belt, does he work long at the job?"

"As long as he can," Ben said, laughing. "It pays more."

"Why?" Evan asked.

"Why? Because a guy's got to have his wits about him doing that job. Got to be fast, pay attention to what he's doing. He can't fool around like the truckers can. Yeah, every trucker in the place would like to stack. It increases the old paycheck."

"But how long does a man keep doing the stacking job?"

Ben looked thoughtful, suddenly realizing Evan wasn't just making conversation. "I don't know," he said finally. "Some workers stay and some come and go in the business. It's hard to pin down."

"Oh, we don't have to pin it down," Evan said easily. "Is it months or is it years?"

"Years," Ben answered promptly. "Marty—the guy you were watching—has been stacking for four years now. He's a nice steady fella. I figure him to be real permanent. He'll stick."

At least until his back gives out, Evan thought. "Well, you'll want your lunch, so I won't keep you," he said. "Is the stuff on that truck any good?"

"Sure. First-rate."

"Good. Can I get you anything?"

Ben laughed, a little sound of pride in his voice. "Hell no, Christine makes my lunch. But thanks anyway."

Later, Evan was hunched over his desk making a sketch, deciding that he would bring down the extra drawing board he had at the condominium. He might as well economize where he could. He grinned slightly at the ridiculousness of the idea. He'd save a few dollars on getting a drawing board and spend megabucks on the computer components—at least, Sara would think their cost was a fortune.

"Mr. McGrath?"

He glanced up to see the day watchman, Chick Enderby, poking his head in the door.

"Hi." Evan leaned back and stretched. "Come on in. Chick Enderby, right? Security?"

"Yes, *sir*. Chief of security. I'm in charge of the other guys." Enderby came in and shut the door behind him.

"Sure. I remember. Sara told me. What can I do for you?"

"Oh, not a thing. Just wanted to bring you your mail. Happened to be there when the mailman came up. We don't usually get a delivery at the plant anymore. But these here are addressed right to the street address instead of our postal box."

Evan suppressed a grin. It was clear Enderby had examined the mail. It did look interesting enough to have aroused his curiosity. Two of the envelopes were brightly colored, one a violent violet, the other a brilliant chartreuse. Two others were oversize. These had to be the thank-you cards from Donna and her friends. He held out his hand and Enderby passed

them over. Evan dropped the envelopes on the desk
without looking at them further.

"Thanks a lot."

"Wasn't anything." Enderby dithered by the doorway.

"Was there something else?" Evan asked politely.
Clearly, the little man wanted to say more.

"Oh, no, nothing. That is, I just happened to hear
you talking to Ben before lunch." He paused.

"And?" Evan felt a sudden wariness.

"Well, I mean asking about the stacker's job and
all. They get good money, stackers do."

"So Ben said," Evan answered noncommittally.

"Not many high-paying jobs in a place like this,
though. Very few, in fact. It's all scut work. Labor,
you know. Very cheap mostly, you see. Well, I got to
get cracking. Lots to do. Enjoy your letters." Enderby touched his cap smartly, did a somewhat mili-
tary turnaround and left the office.

Now, what was that all about? Evan wondered, as
he reached for the top envelope. He spent the next half
hour chortling over the crazy cards the girls had picked
out. He'd have to do something with them. They
mustn't go to waste.

He thought of Sara's bulletin board. He'd put them
there and brighten the place up! And it wouldn't hurt
to have her see them there next time she came in,
either. *Look, lady, see what a nice guy I am? Kids love
me. Old ladies smile at me. I'm kind to dogs. And I'm
probably falling for you.*

About five o'clock he turned on the lights. Septem-
ber was still a week away, but already the days were
getting shorter. He stood at the window for a mo-

ment, making a mental note to have stronger bulbs put in so that he would have the best lighting for his work. Outside, the waterfront was still teeming. In front of the cannery, the catering truck had long since been replaced by an assortment of other trucks and vans. He watched a few of them come and go, bumping over derelict railroad tracks. This place had been on a freight line once. Now everything was hauled by truck. He wondered how old the cannery was. Sara would know. Or Grant would. He was getting more interested in the project, in the place. It was a good feeling.

He was still working at seven, concentrating deeply on a sketch, when he heard the decisive click of Sara's heels on the uncarpeted hallway outside his door.

"Sara!" Surprised, he dropped the worn eraser he'd been absently rolling between his fingers. "Two visits in one day. Great! Come on in."

"Thanks. Do you realize you're working overtime? Can't you hear the silence?" She opened the door wider, and he noticed for the first time that the remote roar of the plant had ceased.

"Trying to make a good impression on the boss," he said, grinning.

"What in the world have you got on the bulletin board?" She walked toward it, and then turned quickly. "Those girls!" she exclaimed. "Well, you certainly did make a hit."

He joined her laughter. "I sure got a kick out of those today. They came this afternoon." Ah, things were finally open and friendly. *Thank you, girls,* he thought fervently. Sara laughing, her beautiful eyes alight, made a heart-stopping picture. How would she feel in his arms? How would she look stretched out on that marvelous round bed of hers....

Hell, she'd better not read minds. "Speaking of working overtime, you're a little late getting away yourself," he said, gathering up his sketches. He tried not to move too obviously, but he'd rather not have her see what he was working on just yet.

"Christine called me this afternoon. She's all agog because an old classmate has turned up. Wants to roll out the red carpet."

"I love red carpets," Evan said, opening a file drawer and sliding a role of sketches inside. "What does she have in mind?"

"I have no idea. I'm sure at least a ten-course dinner. I gave her your home phone number—was that okay?"

"Absolutely. I'll love seeing her again. I like the guy she married, Ben. I had a kind of get-acquainted talk with him today. Nice guy. Obviously thinks the world of Chris."

"Yes, he does." There was a tightness in her tone now.

Evan turned slowly from the file to look at her. He could have sworn they were having a friendly chat, but suddenly there was a chill in the air. He was right. The exquisitely shaped face was expressionless.

"I said something wrong? What'd I say wrong?" He turned the key in the file drawer, locking it.

"No, of course not. But I *am* in charge of personnel, Evan. Grant said to give you all the support you need and I will. If you want to know anything about wages and salaries, just ask. I'll give you the information. You don't have to go skulking around getting it out of the employees."

Evan felt the rising of a slow anger. "I'm sorry, but you lost me," he said stiffly. "You lost me at the word 'skulking.' I haven't *skulked* for years."

"I'm sorry. I guess that was uncalled for. But you were talking to Ben about wages this afternoon. Evan, if you want to know about wages, I wish you would ask me. Employees get upset and rumors fly. The current one is that you are locating the highest-paying jobs so you can replace them with robots."

"Good grief!"

"So, after this, would you please—"

"Thank you. If I ever want to know about employee wages, I will ask you. But in passing, let me compliment you on the efficiency of your company grapevine. It's impressive. And I wasn't talking to Ben about wages. I was talking to him about that...what's his name...Marty's job."

"What about Marty's job?"

"The way he does it. Forget the wages. Let me ask you about industrial insurance claims. I'm talking about every insurance adjuster's nightmare, the 'bad back.' Marty—anyone who works for several years doing what Marty is doing, is slowly but surely messing up his spine. Ah, that struck a little chord, didn't it? Are you mentally reviewing insurance claims?"

"There are always insurance claims. That's what we pay premiums for, to protect the workers."

"You 'protect' them by seeing they get an income when they're too disabled to work? How kind. Why can't you see they don't get injured in the first place?"

"Now, what's *that* supposed to mean?" Her tone was level, but her eyes were bright with anger.

"Look, Sara, let's not cross swords again." Evan began to temporize. He mustn't make her angry. He'd lose whatever ground he'd made. "Actually, Marty's problem isn't why I signed on in the first place. I just happened to see him work and realized what's happening to him. So I thought that it was one place where a machine would do better."

"What do you mean, 'do better'?"

"Well, without too much trouble...and without too much money, either...I could design..." At the withdrawal in her expression, he let his voice trail off. They were adversaries once more.

"You're telling me you could design a machine to stand at the end of the conveyor belts and stack trays? Is that it?"

"Uh, yes. More or less."

"It does Marty's job?"

He cleared his throat. "Right. And Marty doesn't louse up his back."

"And Marty doesn't have a job, either. And don't tell me we could transfer him to some other job, because that would mean displacing someone else. You see, it's like dominoes. A job eliminated, is one job less. One *person* less. Or is that too simplistic for you?" Her voice was faintly unsteady.

He turned and stood staring unseeingly out the window. She cared about these people, perhaps too much. He'd have to watch it when he talked with Ben after this. He might have known Ben was a direct pipeline to Sara.

And in the meantime...

He faced her again, but she was at the door.

"I only stopped by to see if everything was okay. You're doing all right in the office? Need anything?" She was a total professional again, remote, untouchable.

"I might use a few more pushpins," he said jocularly, but he knew as he spoke that the little effort at lightness would fall flat.

"Pushpins," she said tonelessly. "I'll see you get some more tomorrow."

He watched her go out and shut the door behind her. It gave him a sinking sensation. She'd moved even farther away from him.

CHAPTER SIX

"Night, Miss!"

Sara jumped and stared unseeingly at a guard by the heavy glass door of the Daon Building. She hesitated before answering. "Yes—good night." Everything in this new place was so slick and perfect. Oddly, she missed old Chick Enderby and his haphazard security efforts.

Sara smiled absently and walked outside, past shedding maples and angular planters filled with petunias. No wonder she was preoccupied. Her plan to try talking sense into Grant would never work and could, very probably, make her position at Jarvis impossible. But she had no other choice. At every turn she met more evidence that Evan's proposed improvements would put people out of work and even if it cost her job, she must try to head off disaster.

Still, Sara reflected, she shouldn't have suggested Grant meet her for dinner. He'd undoubtedly arrive bristling, expecting opposition and also hoping for some change in her personal attitude toward him. If she allowed him to relax, he would turn on the charm. Grant at his most persuasive best was likely to be a formidable obstacle to her resolve.

The distance along Hastings to the restaurant, "1066," seemed too short. When the yellow tables and folded Cinzano umbrellas in the forecourt of the restaurant came into view, Sara moved with increasing reluctance. Across the street, she stopped. For a wild moment, she considered not turning up at all. But that was out of the question.

She crossed between dense traffic, flinching at blaring horns, dodging a cycle messenger bent on self-destruction.

Sara's mind turned to Donna. Lately she longed to spend more time with the girl, just puttering around the house. This urge had to be because she was worried about her child. Suzy Homemaker was the last role she'd ever fit into easily.

Christine would say she was fractured. Chris invariably had neat little terms for Sara's frame of mind. Regularly her sister dropped hints about the satisfaction she felt in being available whenever the boys needed her. "One job's enough, Sara. I don't know why you want all that pressure in the business world when you could be with Donna. It isn't as if you need the money—Michael left you everything he had." Well, Sara wasn't Christine, and she'd worked too hard to give up her job. Besides, Homer still needed her, and Mrs. Beamis was at the house every day when Donna came home from school. Everything was under control.

She smoothed her hair and passed beneath hanging ivy above the door into the restaurant's darkened interior.

The place reminded her of a converted wine cellar, with its stucco walls, brick pillars, polished oak railings and walls covered with wine racks.

A hand on her elbow startled her. "Hi, there, Sara. We're over by the fireplace." Grant, looking tall and striking in a dark three-piece suit and glistening white shirt, smiled down at her. "I know you like fires."

She walked slightly ahead of him, trying to relax and accept the pressure on her arm naturally. Had she ever told Grant she liked open fires? She never remembered discussing anything personal with him. "This is nice," she murmured. He'd pulled out a high-backed damask chair and she sank down. The warmth from the leaping flames beside her felt good.

"Sure it's okay?" Grant hovered at her shoulder. "Not too hot? I can arrange another table if you are."

"I like this one." Sara straightened her suit skirt and slid her briefcase out of the way. "Sit down, Grant. I'm fine."

He did as she asked, unbuttoning his suit jacket and hitching at his cuffs. They were both apprehensive.

"Talked to Dad today," Grant announced suddenly. "He sounded in high spirits. How about a drink?" He looked away and signaled a waiter. "The usual?"

Sara bit back the temptation to ask how he'd have any idea what her usual was. She was allowing herself to become prematurely antagonistic. "I'm glad Homer's doing okay. I'll just have a tonic with a twist of lime."

He smiled and a muscle twitched in his cheek. "Right. But I think I'll have another martini. I only have to go as far as English Bay tonight—unless..." He trailed off, his eyes fixed on hers. He had beautiful eyes, soft and brown. Grant was a handsome man many women would line up to be with. But she wasn't one of them.

Sara ignored the veiled hint that he would like to spend the entire evening with her—and his comment about English Bay. No doubt he had plans to visit Evan, but she wouldn't give Grant the satisfaction of asking why.

The waiter, who took their order for drinks, then returned quickly, provided a welcome diversion. Sara made no attempt to break the awkward silence. She'd initiated this meeting, but there was no reason not to allow Grant to sweat a little. Let him fumble an entry into their discussion. That way he was more likely, unwittingly, to open doors he'd rather leave closed.

He cleared his throat. "How long is it since we did this?"

Sara was caught off guard. "I . . . well, a while, I guess." Surely he didn't truly believe she was trying to set up some kind of personal relationship with him.

Her right hand rested, clenched, on the table. Grant rubbed a broad forefinger along a flexed tendon, from knuckle to wrist. "I'm glad you suggested it. I've been counting the hours all day."

Sara ran her tongue over the roof of her mouth and willed her hand not to move. He did have the wrong idea—or he'd decided to pretend he did. "Yes. Good. I thought it was about time we had a little talk away from any distractions."

He covered her hand now. "How's Donna? I haven't seen her for a while. Maybe I'll come over one day. She's a lovely girl."

"Donna's fine." The air seemed suddenly thinner. She mustn't be sidetracked, and she couldn't talk about Donna . . . to anyone.

"What is it, Sara?" Grant tightened his grip, leaned across the table. "Something's wrong. I can feel it."

"No." She pulled her hand away and drank some tonic, concentrating on smoothing her expression. "You're like your father. Always imagining things."

"I like to think I *am* like my father. Coming from you, the suggestion's praise indeed. But you can't fool me, Sara. You've got a problem. Let me help you, please. Is it something to do with Donna?"

Suddenly despair swept into Sara. Donna was the last subject she'd intended to touch with Grant, but she needed someone to talk to. "Yes," she whispered. "Her. . . her mother. . ." She paused because her voice had gone wobbly.

"Hey, hey." Grant held her wrist, shaking it gently. "*You're* her mother."

A lump formed in her throat, and she swallowed around it. "I am now—in a way. But I can't forget that Prairie Crawford gave birth to her. And . . . oh, Grant. . . I'm sorry. This isn't why I asked you to meet me. I never had any patience with wimpy women who bring their troubles to the office. Forget I mentioned it. I wanted to talk business."

"Sure," he said, his voice low, even. "And we will if you like. But first, you're going to tell me what all this is about Prairie Crawford. I thought the woman had gone back to San Francisco, or wherever she's from."

"She did. She is. I mean that's where she is. But she called yesterday to wish Donna a happy birthday."

Grant gave a hard little laugh. "Ten days after the event?"

Sara's answering smile was wan. "It didn't matter to Donna how late Prairie was or that she's heard nothing from her in months. Grant—" she sucked in the corners of her mouth for an instant "—Donna was thrilled. She looked so radiant. I...damn, I can hardly breathe."

"Ssh." He reached to smooth back her hair. "Hold on. Give yourself a couple of minutes, then tell me the rest."

She took deep gulps of air through her mouth, but her heart still thumped hard. "Afterward. An hour or so later, I found her crying. She said she was okay, just worried about something in school, but she wouldn't say what. Then she was like a quiet shadow, doing things for me—fussing. She's always so good I didn't think too much of it for a while."

"Maybe she just sensed you were upset."

"No, Grant. No. Prairie told her she's coming up to Vancouver to see her soon. Finally Donna told me that. She was trembling and gripping her hands together so hard I could see every bone. In her way, she'd been trying to make sure I wouldn't object, appeasing me before she dropped the bomb because she knew I wouldn't be happy. She felt guilty about letting me know she still loves her biological mother. Thirteen years old, and she's got to balance relationships too complicated for a lot of adults. I feel like such a failure."

"Here." Grant pushed his own glass across the table. "Take a sip. If nothing else it'll burn your throat and divert you. I can always drive you home if you get tipsy." His expression was one of concern.

Sara did as he suggested. "Thanks." The drink did burn, but she took a second swallow. "I wish I had . . . children need two parents. I never thought I'd say that, but sometimes it's pretty lonely." She'd almost said she wished Michael was with her, and she did, but Lord, could two sips of a martini turn the tongue completely loose?

Grant regarded her silently for a long time. "You never got over what's his name, did you? Winston? He's who you were thinking about just now, wasn't he?"

"I guess." It was definitely time to change the subject. "This'll pass. I need to spend more time with her, that's all."

"Everything's going to be all right," Grant consoled. "Donna's lovely, and she *loves* you—who wouldn't?" He turned abruptly sideways in his chair and hailed the waiter again. "Take some afternoons off. You need a break now and then, too. You work too hard, always have."

Sara studied his clear-cut profile, the arch of his brow, the strong line of his jaw. Grant had so many fine qualities. He was a kind man under that studied casualness. Too bad he wasn't her type.

"Oh, good grief," she said, grimacing. "I just remembered the present you sent. Donna loved the headset and cassette player. The pile of tapes was outrageous. You spoiled her, but thanks. She'll be writing a thank-you note. How did you know what little girls like?"

"She's not a little girl, Sara. Thirteen's a teenager, remember? I'm glad she liked the gift. I see all the kids with those things. A boy in the store helped me with the tapes. I told him to pick out everything he'd buy if he could have what he liked."

Sara shook her head. "I'd never have thought of that. You're her current hero."

Grant gave a pleased grin. "It pays to keep your eyes open."

"How did you know it was her birthday, anyway?" Sara asked.

"Evan. He mentioned it that first day you two met at the office."

"Ah, yes. He was quite something. Saved the party. Without him, I'd probably be in a mental institution...." Her teeth came together with a click. What a stupid slip! Grant's eyes had darkened.

Silently he passed her a menu and opened his own. "What looks good to you?"

She'd never learned to watch what she said closely enough. "Whatever you're having. Grant—"

"I'm having steak and kidney pie. I enjoy that English stuff sometimes, and they do a good job here."

"Grant—"

"Let's have a bottle of wine."

"I'd have to be carried out of here. Grant, will you listen...?"

"Carrying you anywhere would be heaven to me, Sara. I think you know that." His gaze bored into her now. "What was Evan doing at Donna's party?"

She wouldn't, *couldn't* explain about the mime act. Grant probably knew nothing about Evan's hobby and might laugh. She didn't like what Evan was engaged in for Jarvis, but she did like the man—there was no denying how much she liked him. If only she could take back this whole day, including her impetuous invitation to Grant.

"Sara?" Grant said sharply. "Don't go into a coma on me. How did Evan McGrath happen to be at your house on Donna's birthday?"

It was on the tip of her tongue to snap back that what she did and who came to her house was her own business. Instead she ran a fingernail around the rim of her glass. "He'd started going through the folders we gave him."

Grant cocked an eyebrow. "At a teenager's party—at your house?"

"No, dammit," Sara flared. He was pushing, and she wouldn't be pushed. "But he needed to check out a few things so he came over."

Grant narrowed his eyes disbelievingly. "Why didn't he come to me? Particularly since you two didn't exactly hit it off on the subject of his proposed project."

Clear thought was imperative. She must go more slowly. "I think he hoped to smooth the way between the two of us."

"Well, he certainly seems to have managed that." The sarcasm in Grant's tone irritated her. "In fact, I'd say the two of you feel more than smooth together."

The arrival of their dinner provided another brief respite, but it wasn't long enough and Sara quelled a desperate urge to flee.

"How did Evan 'save the party,' as you put it?" Grant went on as if they'd never been interrupted.

"Did he persuade you to leave the kids to their own devices while you two got to know each other?"

"Grant!" He always managed to make her lose her temper. "I resent that implication. Evan McGrath is someone *you* brought into the firm, not me. On your orders I have to work with the man. 'Make him my special project.' Remember saying that? Don't make something out of nothing."

"Well, I'm sorry." He was suddenly sheepish. "I guess that was out of line."

"To put it mildly. Now, can we discuss what I invited you here to talk about?"

Grant lowered his head and firelight made red highlights in his thick hair. "Shoot, buddy. As usual, I've managed to get you mad at me. Sara." He met her eyes squarely. "I like you. I respect you—you know that. But you also know I'd like to be more than your boss and a very occasional confidant. Could you give some thought to that maybe? There's no hurry. I've waited a long time, and I can wait longer."

The food in Sara's mouth turned tasteless. "Don't complicate things, Grant." She didn't like hurting him, or anyone. Fate played some pretty lousy tricks sometimes. Until a couple of weeks ago, no man since Michael had made her want to be held and loved as a woman. Now one had, but Evan was just passing through. If she achieved her purpose this evening, he'd be gone very soon. And here was Grant, so accessible and willing to fill the empty spaces in her life, yet he didn't arouse a shred of longing.

His features had set hard. "I won't mention it again unless you bring up the subject, Sara. Sorry if I've embarrassed you."

"Let's forget it. Like I said, business is what I want to discuss."

Grant's knife and fork clattered to the plate. "Drop all that about business will you?"

There was several minutes of heavy silence while they both pushed food around their plates. "We don't have that much time, Grant. Or that much money to play with. And while you're playing the great tycoon, I can see our people's job security getting more and more tenuous. They *know* something's going on and they're rattled. I want you to stop this thing before we go too far."

"*You* want?" Grant's fist hit the table and Sara blushed, feeling a sudden still watchfulness at nearby tables.

"I shouldn't have put it that way," she mumbled. "What I meant was—"

"What you meant is perfectly clear," Grant said, cutting her off furiously. "You want to be back where you were when my father was in my chair. You want to be running Jarvis the way you did when his health was failing, and the way you hoped you'd do permanently when he retired." He rested his forehead on one fist.

"That was unforgivable, Grant," Sara whispered. "Yes, I used to have a lot more authority when Homer was around. And yes, I was disappointed at first. But I also know it means the world to Homer to have you there and that makes it okay with me. I just hope to God you manage to keep this company afloat as long as he's alive. If we go down the tube, it'll break his heart."

"Hell. Forget I said all that. It was a low blow. I'm sorry." Grant bowed his head, a weariness deepening every line in his face. "Dad knows what I'm doing. He's given me his blessing. It's for him I want to succeed, too, can't you understand that?"

She stared at him. Of course, that's exactly what this was all about. Why had it taken so long for her to see it?

"I think it's time we left." Grant pulled his wallet from an inside pocket.

Her scalp tingled. "So do I."

"People aren't going to lose their jobs over this."

Sara moved her briefcase an inch. "And I say they will."

"They won't, dammit. Get behind me and give me the support I need. Don't undermine me." He was furious, more furious than Sara had ever seen him.

She wouldn't back down. "Where are all the new markets you said you'd identify? Give me facts, Grant, hard, backed-up statistics." Her chest rose and fell rapidly.

Grant's face was like granite. He wasn't going to give her any facts at all. She felt that a door had been slammed in her face.

"This is my firm, Sara, not yours. Together, we could make quite a team. But if you're not with me, it won't mean I'll give up what I'm determined to accomplish."

She watched him place a credit card on top of the check. "I invited you," she said mechanically. "That's my bill."

"Over my dead body," he replied.

The only thing to do was make one last-ditch effort, then get out. "Forget me as anything but a business acquaintance, Grant. But do allow me to be part of that team you mentioned. Please, for all of us, let's not go any further with this expansion idea. We've still got time to retreat and come out strong. Smaller than you'd like, maybe, but solid. We'd have something we could slowly build on."

"I don't understand you." Grant hooked one arm over his chair back. "Oh, I know you don't like what McGrath's doing. But for a while there I could have sworn you had a thing for the guy. I know damn well what I see in his eyes when he looks at you. I'd have thought you'd want to keep him around."

What did he see in Evan's eyes? Sara wondered, unaccustomed heat flashing through her body. "I respect him," was all she said.

"I'm not turning back," Grant stated flatly. "Are you with me or not?"

This was it. He was offering her an alliance or a declaration of war. "I can't support you, Grant," she said quietly, and stood. "Thanks for dinner—and for being kind to me earlier."

"I'll always be as kind to you as I can. I . . ." His throat convulsed before he stood, too, looking down into her face with thinly veiled pleading in his expression.

"Thanks," she repeated, and turned away.

Grant's hand on the back of her neck stopped her from leaving. He turned her slowly around. "I didn't ever want to say this, but I've got a business to run and I intend to make a good job of it. I've *got* to make a good job of it."

Hyperventilation must feel like this. "Yes," she managed to say.

"If you can't live with my decisions or support them, you should do some thinking about your job. It's not the same one you had with my father. So do you really want it? I'm serious, Sara. *Think* about it."

CHAPTER SEVEN

SHE DID THINK ABOUT IT, not really wanting to. Suddenly, at odd times in the night Sara would wake up wondering how her life would be if she no longer focused almost solely on her career. Would things be better? Or would she feel at loose ends?

She and Grant pulled apart. They seemed to avoid one another by mutual consent, as if both knew they'd gone too far. Both knew what a final confrontation might do to Homer. Grant was on thin ice, too, Sara realized, because of Homer's regard for her. Grant had his father's wishes to consider in any decision he made concerning her. It was, in a way, a kind of security.

More and more she wondered if she could talk to Evan. Then, one evening, after work without making a conscious decision about it, she was on her way toward English Bay.

All the stores were closed. Streetlights were beginning to come on. Sara walked along Denman Street, her head bent against the rain. Discarded newspapers lay in sodden coils against walls and in doorways. Her feet squelched in her shoes. She had left her car in her parking place at the office. She hadn't wanted to drive. The energy spent in walking provided a little relief from building tension.

At Pacific, she turned right past the Hotel Sylvia and headed along Beach Drive toward Stanley Park. The rain fell more heavily, plastering her hair to her head. On the other side of the promenade, waves crashed off English Bay, sending spume high into the air. She tilted her head and inhaled its salt scent.

Sara wandered across the deserted street and stood pressed to the railing above the beach, watching a sea beautiful in its anger.

The time had come to do something about her fears. At least to try to impact what was rapidly unfolding around her. She'd seen the steady installation of expensive computer equipment in Evan's cannery office—and listened to the growing unrest among the workers. Poor Ben. Her uncomplicated brother-in-law had haltingly passed on progress reports of Evan's constant streams of questions, the way the robotics expert sometimes stopped a man or woman from working while he studied a certain function of the equipment and took detailed notes. Everyone was frightened, and she was increasingly certain they should be.

She turned to scan the buildings along Beach Drive. Immediately opposite was a modern, square block of condominiums. Sara took a crumpled scrap of paper from her pocket, stared from the address she'd written to the building and back. Evan lived inside one of those rows of lighted windows. If she was honest with herself, she'd admit this was where she'd half intended to come tonight.

Dragging her feet, she looked each way and headed for the sidewalk in front of Sea Crest Place. Evan's sleek Mercedes was parked at the curb. She made patterns with her fingers on its dripping hood. If she had any sense she'd turn back now. A violent gust of wind slapped her skirt and coat against her legs. She was fresh out of sense.

By the door, a row of buttons flanked a speaker. Each button matched a name and number. *Mc-Grath—4a.* Sara stepped back and gazed upward. There were only four floors. Two condos on each one, she guessed, and Evan's must be on the top level. It figured. He was the type of man who'd spend time enjoying the fantastic view he obviously had of the bay and the city's lights.

She was going to see him, to tell him everything that bothered her. They'd be open with each other, and then the chips could fall where they might. She jabbed the black button and waited, an uncomfortable thumping in her chest.

"Hello."

Sara gritted her teeth. She was past the stage of ringing bells and running away. "Hello, Evan. This is Sara. I—"

"Sara!" He cut her off. "Come on in." A loud buzz sounded, and the plate-glass door clicked open beneath her tentative push.

She was still staring at the elevator when it bumped solidly and the doors slid open to reveal Evan, slightly disheveled but smiling broadly. "Great to see you, Sara. What a surprise." He ushered her inside, and they rode to the fourth floor. She still hadn't managed to speak when he waved her into his rooms.

"Good Lord!" The shock in his voice brought her attention sharply from Evan's elegantly modern decor to his startled face.

"I'm disturbing you, I know." She edged back toward the closed door. "I don't have any right to interrupt your evening. Forgive me. We can talk in the morning."

"You're soaked." He touched her arm. "Sopping. Where's your car? How did you get so wet?"

She took a deep breath. "My car's still at the office. I decided to take a walk and got caught in the rain."

"You walked all the way from the Daon Building?"

"It's not far."

"Not in nice weather—or in daylight. It's rotten out there, Sara. Has been for hours. Give me your coat." He moved behind her to take hold of her collar, and she had no choice but to undo the buttons. "Who's with Donna, Mrs. Beamis?"

"She's spending the night with Amy Dross. My little mouse is becoming a social butterfly. I've got a lot on my mind, Evan. If I didn't, I wouldn't wander in here like an idiot. Do you have time to listen to me for a while?" She faced him.

"Of course. I always have time to listen to you. All I wish is that you'd talk to me more often. I'm not blind, Sara. I know you're worried and I'm the reason." He regarded her levelly before looking at her feet. "I'm going to hang this coat in the bathroom. Take off those soaking shoes before you get pneumonia."

Sara couldn't stop a faint grin. "You sound like my mother. And I'll tell you what I always told her—rainwater doesn't give you bugs."

"Regardless." He wasn't smiling. "Getting cold and wet and staying that way doesn't do anything for your health."

He stepped from the stone tiled hall into a sunken living room and disappeared through a door on the far side of a formal dining area.

She yanked off her shoes and searched for a place to set them where they wouldn't ruin a surface. The floor in a gleamingly modern and immaculately clean kitchen to the right seemed the only spot.

"There you are. Thought you'd sneaked out on me again." Evan waited when she returned to the living room. He immediately went to a glass and rosewood bar tucked into an alcove beside a soaring stone fireplace and produced a bottle of brandy. "This is what you need. It'll warm the cockles of your heart as my old grandfather used to say."

Deep discomfort settled into Sara's bones, as chilling as the soggy clothing she tried not to notice. "You seem more like a man who was hatched—all grown up—than someone who had an old grandfather."

He looked reproachfully at her. "Are you trying to say I don't seem to have had a childhood. I'm wounded. Donna wouldn't agree."

She took the glass he handed her. "You do have a way with thirteen-year-olds."

"But not with their mothers?" He tilted his head to one side.

She ignored the question and went to the window. Crystalline specks of rain sparkled on the glass. The ocean was an obsidian mass slashed by the white edges of combers. Beyond the water a million lights wavered jaggedly in the city. "You have an incredible view."

"I like it."

This wasn't going to be easy. She swallowed some brandy. "I'm overstepping my position by coming here."

"Oh?"

Why should he try to help her, even if he knew what she wanted to say? "Grant wouldn't like it. He'd say I was meddling—and he'd be right, I suppose."

She felt Evan at her shoulder. "Whatever you choose to say to me will remain between us. Believe that."

Did it matter anymore what Grant thought of her? With each day she got more of a feeling of hanging on to her job by her fingernails. Sometimes she longed to let go and become the full-time mother she increasingly longed to be. Perhaps she would soon—after Homer's death. She leaned her forehead against the window and peered at the tops of cars below.

"Sara," Evan prompted quietly. "Open up. Help me to help you. I can't if I don't know what's on your mind."

Abruptly she swung away and walked to the center of the room. Overhead, a mobile of delicate, perfectly formed wooden airplanes drifted gently. "That's lovely." She glanced at him. "Did you make it?"

An odd closing settled over his features. "Yes. It's like another one I used to have. It broke, so I made this."

She puffed upward, causing the balsa models to jiggle faintly. "You're good at making things."

"I guess." Over the rim of his glass he looked not at the mobile, but directly into her eyes. His gaze caused a hot little tightening low inside her.

"Making things and then making them better is everything to you, isn't it?" She recognized the effect he had on her only too well, but knew their attraction could never go anywhere.

He swirled the liquor. "I'm fascinated by technology and the way it can improve labor systems, if that's what you're getting at."

"It is what I'm getting at." Her skin felt stretched tight over her face. "Your *improvements*. Are you so sure they're always improvements? Or is it just progress at any price because doing things faster for less money is what turns you on?"

Evan quelled rising irritation. "No. I don't think that's what 'turns me on,' as you put it. Sure, I'm into cost-effectiveness, but only as a by-product of robotics."

"I don't understand all that." She began to pace. "I've been reading up on robotics," she said after a moment.

"And you think there ought to be a law against it?" he asked, a smile touching his lips.

"No. I don't think that. But it's pretty unusual in fish canneries. This is what you intend to do at Jarvis, isn't it? Different, but the same? Make machines that will do things without human help? Machines one man can press a few buttons on and then leave to do the work?"

"Not exactly."

"Then what exactly?" Her eyes were blue fire. Her hair had started to dry and caught the light with each toss of her head. "Evan, explain to me the benefits you see in what you're doing. In your robotics. Will they help the people you put out of work?"

He spread his hands. No matter what he said, she wouldn't listen. The woman was impossible.

The phone gave a shrill ring, setting every nerve in his body on edge. He wasn't expecting anyone to call.

Sara put her hands on her hips. "Aren't you going to answer?"

"No. There's no one I want to talk to right now— but you." They both listened to five rings, then silence.

"You're overreacting about my work, you know."

"I am not," she almost shouted. "I'm worried, that's all. Until Grant kicks me out, I'm going to do anything I can to make sure not one man or woman loses a job to—to a *machine*—at Jarvis. There's nothing I can do to stop Grant from pouring money away, but if he ruins the company, and I'm still around, I want to be able to tell our people they have to go because we're closing down, not because some hunk of metal and wire is going to do what they've done well, and reasonably, for years."

She was taking short breaths. Evan flopped into a leather chair and watched, fascinated, more excited than he cared to acknowledge, while she used her hands and body to stress every word. Sara Fletcher was, without a doubt, the most alluring woman he'd ever laid eyes on. And he wanted her.

"If you'll let me," he said carefully. "I think I can put your mind at rest."

"I'd like that." The arch of one brow suggested she doubted he could say anything to allay her fears. Suddenly she downed the last of her brandy and sank heavily onto a couch. She had drunk too fast. He should have stopped her.

"You're exhausted." And wet to the skin, he thought.

"That doesn't matter. Tell me whatever's supposed to stop me from worrying."

It was time for him to take charge. "Not until you get out of those soggy clothes and relax."

Her stare showed amazement. "I don't think you need concern yourself with my comfort or my state of mind."

"Don't worry. I don't have any plans to make a pass. I just don't want to be responsible if you collapse from exposure to the elements. I'll get you a robe. Your things will dry out fairly fast in the bathroom. It's warm in there."

The phone's raucous jangle split the air again. He half rose to answer, but changed his mind. "Ignore it," he muttered. "Someone wants to clean the rugs or sell me insulation. I'll get you that robe."

She waited for the phone to stop ringing, then shook her head. "No. Thanks anyway. I should leave."

"I thought we were going to sort a few things out." He moved closer until he could see the dark flecks in her blue eyes.

She looked away. "Maybe this isn't the time," she mumbled. Her eyes looked tired, and the lids drooped.

"Will there ever be a better one?"

A deep breath lifted fine cream wool over her breasts. "No. No there won't. If you're sure you don't mind, I'll borrow that robe."

He left without another word. The less he said the better. The white terry-cloth robe he brought her was the short kind, but it would still fit three people her size.

She left for the bathroom and returned in record time. Clearly, she'd combed her hair and washed her face, but made no attempt at applying makeup. He liked her even more for her ability to dispense with the shields of artifice so many women were lost without.

"Your bathroom looks like a laundry." She wrapped the robe tightly around her slender body and sat on the couch she'd used before. "I should be horrified at this spectacle, but it is necessary. As soon as possible, I'll get out of your hair."

Evan suppressed a sigh. Swathed in what seemed to be yards of terry cloth, she was an irresistible scrap of a thing any man would want to gather up and carry away. Yet she spoke like the tough executive, as poised as if she was dressed for a boardroom. While he waited for her to speak, he kept his attention on her small bare feet and narrow ankles.

"Okay, Evan. Put my mind at rest."

He started slightly. "Ah...yes. Well, I won't do anything...actually implement things, I mean... without evalutating every angle first."

"You'll evaluate? And on what basis will you make a final decision?" She crossed her arms, and he noticed an abrupt shudder. She was chilled.

"On a broad base, actually. Taking cost into account, first, of course." The phone rang again. He snatched up the receiver, depressed the cradle and shoved the instrument away. "That's standard procedure."

"Of course." She regarded him narrowly. "Then?"

"Sara." He closed his eyes for an instant before going to sit beside her. "Look at me, please. And try to listen with an open mind.

"Robots, machines—technological devices produced by men—are just that, the products of people. Machines don't make themselves or program themselves. People will always be needed."

Her freshly scrubbed face was tilted up to his. She had the clean, open look of a beautiful young girl just out of the shower. "You're talking about highly trained people, Evan. Not the Bens and Martys of this world. They can't design computers—or even operate them." A frown drew her fine brows together.

Tentatively he took her hand, fully expecting her to pull away. She didn't. "The people you're concerned about won't have to do anything but change a few work habits. Robots aren't people. They can't do what men and women do. Ben and Marty and the others may be doing slightly different jobs, that's all. And they'll be producing more for less money in the end. At the simplest level, it takes a human to make raw material into a form a machine can handle. The machine just does the scut work—faster. Does that make sense?"

"I don't know...I..." Sara covered her face with both hands. "It's so simple to you and so damned complicated to me. Think what a puzzle this is to some of our people." She rested her head against the couch, her eyelids drooping.

"Maybe a few diagrams would help?" Evan suggested.

Her eyes had closed entirely. Now they flew open. "Evan—" Involuntarily she twined her fingers in his. "I guess I was out in the rain too long. I can't seem to concentrate." Faint pink spread over her cheeks. "Maybe if I sit here quietly for a few minutes, I'll wake up. This is embarrassing," she finished indistinctly.

He murmured for her to take her time, and in seconds her hand went limp in his.

What were the real motives behind each project he undertook? Sara's lips had parted fractionally, showing a glint of very white teeth. Had he immersed himself in work to keep from thinking too deeply about himself as a man, about his needs—his disappointments? Why else would he have cut himself off from the things he'd once been sure he wanted—a wife, children—if not out of fear of being hurt again? Losing Laura had torn him apart.

He looked at the clean line of Sara's jaw as she slept, her slim, pale neck, the V of soft skin where the robe had gaped. Faint shadow suggested the swell of her breasts. She was probably naked underneath the loose garment. Heat—the best, most insistent kind—flooded his body. She was alone. So was he. He could carry Sara to his bed almost without waking her. And when would she awake . . . ?

Carefully he sat upright and eased her toward him until her head rested in the hollow of his shoulder. She stirred and drew up her knees, snuggling comfortably beneath his encircling arm.

Evan smiled. If he'd ever had a playboy image, this tender little scene would destroy it. He rubbed her back, making absentminded circles. Had he ever related his complicated puzzle-solving to the real people it affected. Oh, he hadn't lied when he said human input was always needed, no matter how sophisticated the procedure, but was he fooling Sara, and himself, when he said no one at Jarvis would lose a job to a McGrath invention?

Moving cautiously, he reached to flip a switch on a console by the couch. The room became dim except for silvery reflections from wet rivulets on the windows.

He couldn't get out of his contract with Grant. Would he, even if it was possible? His belly tightened. He wasn't callous, or totally self-serving, just a scientist doing a job. That's how he must think of himself.

The woman sleeping so close to him wriggled and draped an arm over his thighs. Evan grimaced. He was *very* human, dammit. He had to be careful. Be sure. Next time, if there was going to be a next time for him with one woman, he must know she wasn't going to carve him up and leave him in pieces. That mustn't happen again.

Every object in the room became a series of clearly defined angles.

Sara muttered indistinctly and clutched his shirt. "What..." Drowsily she raised her head, but only tilted it to rest more neatly at the base of his throat.

She was absolutely exhausted, mentally and physically, and he felt responsible. Perhaps, Evan considered, he should try to back out of his work with Grant Jarvis.

Sara's lips were parted against his neck, her breath warm on his skin. Through the robe and his own cotton shirt, he felt every soft curve of her body. He held very still, but couldn't stop his growing arousal.

Who was he kidding? If he tried to back out of his agreement, it would only be to make points with Sara and, in the end, they'd both know it. Lasting relationships couldn't be built on empty compromise.

Evan eased himself away, laid her down facing the back of the couch. He tiptoed into his bedroom and closed the door.

With fevered haste, he shucked his clothes and headed for the bathroom. Cold showers probably didn't help, but right now he had to do something to divert what was going on in his head—and the rest of him.

He opened the door and stopped. The first thing he saw was a skimpy lilac teddy draped over the shower doors.

Whoever had said fate was a temptress, was right. He sat on the toilet lid and pressed a fist against his mouth to smother his laughter.

CHAPTER EIGHT

HER SKIN WAS ON FIRE. Sara lay still, slowly feeling herself rise from a dark pit. Behind her closed eyelids she saw bright speckles of light.

Fleeting pressure on her forehead brought her to full consciousness, and she stared up into Evan's troubled eyes. He stroked her hair back from her brow and temples. "How do you feel, Sara? You're hot."

She frowned and struggled to sit up. Every muscle ached. Her body was sticky inside his terry-cloth bathrobe, and a blanket he must have covered her with while she slept was twisted around her legs like an imprisoning vine.

Thin, early morning sun washed the room. She'd stayed all night. *Donna!* she thought, panicked until she remembered that Donna was safe and sound with her friend Amy.

"Are you sick?" Evan sounded alarmed.

"I..." Sara cleared her throat. It was searingly painful, and her head throbbed. "Wow. I guess I'm coming down with something."

"I'll get the car." He turned a complete circle, searching for something. "My keys...where the hell did I put the keys?"

Sara watched him tour the room, lifting magazines, shifting rolls of blueprints. Evan had evidently been up and waiting to go for some time. He must be planning to visit the Daon Building. His hair still glinted with water from the shower, but instead of the customary jeans and casual shirts she saw him in at the cannery, he wore the pants to a charcoal gray suit, the jacket of which had been flung over a chair back. A silver-and-blue striped tie hung loose from his shirt collar. She was slowing him down. How *could* she have been fool enough to come here? She'd embarrassed them both.

She coughed and immediately winced. "Sorry I've held you up, Evan. It won't happen again." Every breath ripped at her raw throat. "Don't worry about things here. I'll lock up as I go."

"Don't be ridiculous." He rounded on her. "You aren't well. I'm going to take you somewhere."

"*Take* me somewhere?" What was he talking about? She didn't have time to get sick. "Where?"

"To emergency, of course. You need a doctor." With both hands sunk in the pockets of his suit pants, he stopped pacing and stood over her. "Did you happen to see my keys?"

She almost grinned. *Men*. Always overreacting. She had a sore throat, and he was going to haul her off to an emergency room. She closed her eyes and sank back against the pillow, which also hadn't been there when she fell asleep. "Evan," she said softly, trying not to jar her head. "I'm not going to emergency. We aren't going anywhere. I've probably got a touch of flu. In a minute, I'm going to get my act together, go home and then into the office. They expect me at the plant at eleven, and I've got a million things to do downtown first."

"You've got a fever. People with fevers are supposed to take aspirin and stay in bed. Drink lots of fluids—"

"Stop!" She pressed a forefinger and thumb to each temple. "You sound like a TV commercial. *Please*, Evan. Go to work and let me do the same. My clothes will be dried out by now. I can't show up anywhere near the office until I look presentable. I'll leave my car there and take a bus home to change. Then I'll see you at the plant later—okay?"

"I don't think—"

"Okay, Evan?"

He pursed his lips. "Okay. But only under protest. I'm going to check on you. We also have a lot more to talk about. I did some thinking after you fell asleep last night. I haven't explained things to you fully enough. I've assumed too much, and if you'll let me, I know I can make you see the positive angles of what I'm doing."

Sara realized she must be sick. Concentration was almost impossible. "Sure." She couldn't discuss anything for a while. Later maybe, but not this minute. "We'll talk at the plant. Now, please will you go and let me get on with it?"

His expression closed. "I can't leave you here alone. I'll take you home, then run you to the office." He was intractable.

"No, you won't. And if you keep this up, I really will get sick. Look." She swung her feet to the floor and stood, locking her knees to stop them from wobbling. "Right as rain. It would embarrass me to show up at my house—with you—and looking like an unmade bed. Mrs. Beamis is due by nine. And Amy

Dross's mother will be dropping off Donna's sleeping bag. If I hurry, I can make it in before anyone knows I wasn't at home last night. I don't want any gossip, Evan. Neither do you, if you think about it."

"It's not even seven. We can hurry, and I'll get you there before either of them arrive." A pugnacious set to his jaw made Sara feel weak. He bent close. "Why do you have to be Superwoman?"

"I'll ignore that crack," she snapped, glowering. He wasn't to know he'd used another of Christine's favorite labels. "And just to put your mind at rest. As soon as I'm dressed, I'll call a cab." She spied a bulge in the pocket of his suit jacket. "Here." Walking carefully, she went to pat the lump. It jangled immediately. "I think these are what you're looking for."

Evan took the jacket and produced a bunch of keys. "Of course," he muttered. "I'm always forgetting where I put the things. Sara—"

"No." She cut him off, holding up one palm. "Don't argue anymore. I already feel terrible about imposing on you. I'll be at the plant at eleven. If you're there, I'll stop by for coffee. Make sure the pot's on. I'll need fortification after talking to the cannery people."

"If you're sure..."

One more stare from Sara, and Evan subsided. He was still muttering as he gathered his briefcase and a stack of computer printouts from his desk.

Sara followed him to the door, quelling rush after rush of nausea and willing her expression to remain bland. "See you later," she said.

Evan undid the lock. "If you say so. But I don't like it. Hey." He set down the briefcase. "I ought to take your temperature. I don't have a thermometer, but I can run out and get one."

"No, Evan." She straightened her shoulders.

His gaze flickered downward from her eyes. "Okay, okay. I'm leaving. But you'd better not get another chill." He pulled the lapels of the bathrobe together, letting her know they'd gaped without her noticing.

"Thanks." Sara flattened her lips. She felt flushed enough without blushing.

He tucked the terry cloth snugly around her, cinched the belt and held her lightly under each arm. The heels of his hands touched her breasts. "My pleasure, Sara. I'll be looking for you at the plant." He kissed her brow quickly and disappeared into the hall, closing the door quietly behind him.

She held her neck. There was no mistaking what she was beginning to feel whenever she was within reaching distance of Evan McGrath. Falling in love with the man would be so easy. And it would be best not to follow that line of thought. As quickly as her heavy limbs allowed, Sara straightened the couch and threw on her clothes. After calling a cab, she washed her face and tried to improve her disheveled appearance. "Impossible," she muttered just as the intercom buzzed. She looked like hell. "Coming!" Sara was pleased that the cabbie had already turned away as she left the building and followed him to the taxi.

An hour and a half later, every inch of her skin prickling and painful, she walked into her office in the Daon Building.

Her secretary, Anne Parker, immediately started shuffling a pile of memos. "Whew," she muttered. "Am I glad to see you. Grant's on the warpath. Poor

Margaret's called for you half a dozen times. Guess you're supposed to be on duty around the clock. Margaret says he's muttering about you never being available when he needs you."

Sara watched Anne's round, flushed face. "I'm an hour late—for the first time I can remember. What does he mean, I'm never available?"

"I don't think he's concerned about this morning." Anne's candid brown eyes met Sara's for an instant before she bustled toward the outer office. "Evidently he thinks he should be able to call you at ten or eleven at night. Or one in the morning. Maybe you should set him straight."

The calls she and Evan had ignored—had they been from Grant? A steady tap came from Anne's typewriter keys. Sara pushed unsteadily to her feet and closed the door to the outer office. Grant had tried to call her at home last night, then, when she didn't reply, called Evan—and again, got no reply. The conviction grew. She was being steadily tied in knots by these two men.

Grant wanted her to support Evan's work, but have nothing to do with the man. Grant knew she didn't approve of the proposed innovations or of the huge expenditure Evan represented. He'd gone so far as to tell her to support him or find another job. She'd buckled down and done her best to back him up—for Homer's sake and for the Jarvis employees who needed an ally at the executive level. Nothing satisfied Grant. Now he was becoming paranoid about her personal relationship with Evan. Why, when there never had, never would be anything between Grant Jarvis and herself? The situation was impossible.

Then there was Evan . . .

The intercom on her desk gave a harsh beep. Sara hunched her shoulders, suppressing a shiver, and lifted the receiver.

"Mr. Jarvis on the line for you, Sara." Anne always called Grant Mr. Jarvis when he was likely to hear.

Before Sara could respond, Grant's voice bellowed from the receiver. "Where the hell have you been, Sara?"

He'd been cold to her since their disastrous dinner, formal, remote even. This was a new twist in his attitude. She gripped the phone tighter and said nothing.

"Sara? Are you there? Sara?"

"Yes, Grant. I'm here."

"Dammit all, woman." Sharp breaths punctuated his words. "For days you hardly say a word to me. I've got enough on my plate without worrying about what's on your mind. Finally I decide to hang out the white flag and see if we can't bury this damn hatchet you insist on carrying around and what happens?" He paused and Sara heard him swallow. She didn't trust herself to speak. "What happens is that I can't find you. Half the night I tried to call you. Where were you?"

"Grant," she managed in a whisper. "Stop it. Stop it now. I don't know what started you off on this. But don't push me. If there's too much on your plate, you put it there. And where I go and what I do on my own time has nothing to do with you."

"You were with him. McGrath . . ."

This was too much. She sat in her chair with a thump and rubbed her aching eyes. "Listen, please."

She mustn't lose her temper. "If there's something you want to discuss with me—about business—discuss it. Otherwise, get off my back and let me do what you pay me to do—work. Is that a reasonable request?" Maybe Christine wasn't wrong about the lure of hearth and home. The business world often proved less appealing than it was cracked up to be.

There was a short silence before Grant spoke again. When he did, his voice had lowered almost to its normal pitch. "Are you going to tell me if you spent the night with Evan McGrath?"

She felt sicker with each passing second. Clammy perspiration stuck her silk shirt to her back. "Grant," she said tightly. "I'm going to hang up now."

"Sara . . ."

"Goodbye." She let the receiver drop into its holder. Grant was jealous. The man had been married and divorced, seen every high spot in the world several times over, lived with a perpetual silver spoon in his mouth, and he still had tantrums because there was one woman who wasn't bowled over by him. And he let his personal feelings interfere with work at the most crucial point in whatever sort of career he thought he was trying to build.

Sara was rocked by another wave of nausea. She checked her watch, realizing she was going to be late for her meeting with the cannery staff. If she could only relax for a few minutes. She folded her arms on the desk and leaned on them to rest her head. Grant was behaving like an ass. He'd sink, and the whole firm would go down with him. Why couldn't Evan have been Grant . . . ? She was so hot and tired. . . .

"Sara!" *Not again. Why didn't Grant give up?*

"Okay, sweetheart. Get up. We're going to find you a doctor," a voice ordered.

Sara jolted upright in the chair. Evan was sliding a strong arm around her waist, helping her to her feet. "I fell asleep, Evan." She stared at him and his face blurred. "Can you believe that? Right at my desk. It's never happened to me before in my life."

"Is she all right, Mr. McGrath?" At the sound of Anne Parker's anxious voice, Sara screwed up her eyes. "Sara, you should have told me you felt rotten."

"I'm fine, Anne. I need a little sleep, that's all." Evan was draping her raincoat around her shoulders. She was sick. And she'd worried him. Sara pushed the pile of memos on her desk together.

"Leave that." Evan picked up her briefcase and purse. "Do you have a doctor?"

"Cambie," Anne said quickly. "In the Medical-Dental Building on Robson. I'll give you the address. You take her over there while I call and say you're coming."

They were taking everything out of her hands. She hated not being able to cope. "I can make it, thanks. Call for me, if you don't mind, Anne. But you don't need to waste time on this, Evan."

"I'm not wasting time. Anne, I'll get in touch with you later. Let Grant know Sara decided to take the rest of the day off." He paused. "I saw him a little while ago. He's a busy man. Maybe you shouldn't . . . don't explain why Sara's leaving. No need to worry him. You should inform Ben Murphy the staff meeting's postponed for a day or two, though."

The ground seemed to meet Sara's feet with each step. She was burning up. Had Evan called her sweetheart?

"BOY, AM I GLAD you talked some sense into her. She's my sister, but sometimes she drives me nuts." Christine Fletcher Murphy hadn't changed much. She was a little plumper perhaps, but just as pretty. She was a larger boned, less delicately formed version of Sara. "I've got her to bed," she went on. "Keeping her there will be the challenge. She thinks she's invincible. Always did."

"I noticed," Evan said. "The doctor said she had some sort of virus. Gave it a name—type WWZ, or something. You know how they come up with a new label for every fresh flu strain?"

"Don't they just?" Christine pulled on the stretched hem of an old purple sweatshirt. Her hair was almost as dark as Sara's, but curly and cut very short. "Let's go in the kitchen and try to decide how to handle this. Kitchens are my favorite places. Sara's living room is spectacular, but I always feel I should brush off my jeans before I sit down."

She was still a chatterbox, Evan thought, smiling as he followed Christine into the kitchen. "You made it over here in record time. I guess Ben told you Sara had gone home."

"Yup." She started a pot of coffee. "I know what goes on at Jarvis before most of the people who work there do."

I just bet you do, Evan thought. "Sara's really involved with her job, isn't she?" He'd have to be even more careful from now on about what he said at the plant.

"She's too involved. And she hasn't been happy...." Christine glanced at him quickly and made much of putting two or three dirty plates in the dishwasher.

Evan sat on a stool by the mosaic counter. "She hasn't been happy? You were going to say why, Chris?"

"No. No I wasn't really. I'm not sure why. Just trying to do too much I think and..." She pulled the sweatshirt hem again and looked directly at Evan. "I think she's lonely and won't admit it even to herself. But I shouldn't be talking to you about this. Sara wouldn't like it. She's very professional. But—"

"But?"

A faint blush spread over her cheeks. "Oh, I don't know. You know me, Evan, or you used to. Always talking out of turn and putting my foot in my mouth."

"I like directness. I liked that in you, and I hope you haven't changed."

Christine gave a rueful smile. "I haven't changed. Sara would be the first to tell you that. But she'd be the last to tell a man she was attracted to him... *Damn*, I can't believe I said that."

Evan absorbed his old classmate's message and tried not to allow his elation to show. She grabbed mugs from a cupboard and rummaged in the refrigerator for cream.

"You think Sara might be interested in me?"

The cream Christine was pouring slopped over the edge of a jug. "We aren't going to discuss what I think anymore. Sara will never forgive me if she gets wind of this. You sure grew into one stunning guy, Evan McGrath. How come I never noticed what a knock-out you were all those years ago?''

He chuckled. ''Guess you couldn't see my beauty for my brains. On the other hand, I always knew you were gorgeous.'' These two sisters had more in common than he'd thought. They both knew how to effectively block a subject.

Christine passed him a mug of coffee. ''Flattery will get you almost anywhere. Now, I've got to figure out how to keep Sara looked after. She's going to have to lie low for a couple of days.''

Evan wrapped his hands around the mug. ''That's likely to be quite a trick to pull off.''

''Donna's a capable kid. Too capable sometimes. It's not natural. She'll do fine in the evening. Sara would never hear of her missing school, though. I'll come for a while in the early afternoon when I can get my neighbor to look after Jim—our youngest boy. But I've got to be back when Ben, Jr., comes home from school.''

''I can cover here.'' Evan spoke without thinking.

Chris's expression registered surprise. ''That wouldn't do, Evan. Sara would croak for sure if she thought she was putting you out anymore.''

He smiled down into his coffee. ''Maybe she's not the only one who's lonely.'' Their eyes met. ''I come and go from the plant and the downtown building. And I do a lot of stuff at home. There's no reason I couldn't work here instead of at my place. That way I can keep an eye on Sara.''

''I don't know....''

"I do, Chris. It'll work out fine. With me, she's less likely to try sneaking around and doing too much. And—and—"

"And what?" She gazed at him steadily.

Hell. "And we'd have a chance to get to know each other . . . since we have to work together, I mean."

"Sure. So you can work together better." Christine looked skeptical. She knew exactly what he was beginning to feel for Sara.

The phone rang and Christine snatched it up quickly, glancing toward the living room and stairs. "Fletcher's," she said brusquely. She listened, following the pattern on the floor with one toe. "I'm taking care of things here, Grant. No. No, there's nothing you can do. Sara has some sort of bad flu, that's all. I'm sure she just needs rest and a little space from pressure for a while. I think she'd rather not have any visitors. . . . Of course I'll tell her you called. She's bound to be in touch with you as soon as she's up to it."

Evan's attention wandered. His interview with Grant earlier had been strained. The other man had probed, not very subtly, into where Evan stood with Sara—personally. Grant had a bad case. But then, who could blame him? All Evan wanted himself right now was to be near Sara, to snatch whatever moments he could with her.

"That guy never gives up," Christine said as she hung up the phone and checked her watch. "Darn, I do have to get home. Look, I'm going to take you up on your offer—at least for a while. I'll let Sara know you're just covering until Donna gets home, and we'll take care of tomorrow when it comes."

She gulped half her coffee and emptied the rest into the sink. "Tell Donna to contact me this evening."

Evan trailed behind her into the living room and flopped onto a couch. Christine ran upstairs.

This *was* a spectacular room. He spread his arms along the couch back. Everything about Sara Fletcher was special. He was beginning to...really like her. He leaned his head on soft cushions. Christine was taking too long. No doubt Sara was putting up a fuss about his staying.

"Ssh," he heard Christine whisper loudly. "Yes, sis. I'll tell him." She rushed down the steps and grabbed her purse from an end table.

"Tell who what?" Evan roused himself and stood. He was starting to feel the effects of too little sleep the night before.

Christine was halfway to the front door. She didn't look at Evan. "Sara wanted to make sure you'd make yourself comfortable—down here. She feels pretty punk, and she's afraid you might catch something if you get too close. Talk to you later." She left, and a waft of autumn wind rushed inside as she slammed the door.

I might catch something. Evan walked slowly to the foot of the stairs, shrugged out of his jacket and hung it on a banister. He'd already caught something, and it was likely to last a lot longer than a case of flu.

The house was silent yet he felt her, listened for her. He mounted the bottom step. Part of him cursed the way they'd met, and the contention his work caused between them. A larger, more logical part, reminded him it was this commission that had brought them together.

Slowly he climbed upward, his footsteps cushioned by deep carpet. Outside her door, he stopped, fists clenched. If he could keep things light and uncomplicated between them for a while and still find a way to bring them closer, they might have a future together. If that's what he really wanted.

What did he want? Evan rolled to lean against the wall. He'd loved Laura Fenton, wanted her more than he'd ever wanted anyone or anything. Or he'd thought he did. And when she'd chosen Mark Hunt, the feeling had been like slow death, a gradual squeezing off of everything within him that laughed and breathed—and cared.

Did he feel something different for Sara? Could he simply be lonely and reaching out for the first lovely woman who'd caught his attention since Laura? He heard a cough from her bedroom. This squeezing in his gut, the slow twisting of his heart—this wasn't the product of simple loneliness. He already *had* fallen in love with Sara Fletcher, and he was damned if he'd give her up without a fight—as long and tough a fight as it had to be.

He knocked her door gently and waited. From the room came the sound of rustling sheets but no voice.

"Sara?" he whispered hoarsely. "May I come in?"

There was the sound of more rustling. "Yes."

Carefully he turned the knob and slid open the door. Christine had closed slatted wooden shades, and he had to peer to locate Sara's small form in the huge round bed. It was too big a bed for one person, he thought immediately. Just as quickly, he discarded the idea as unworthy under the circumstances.

"How are you doing?" He advanced on tiptoe until he stood beside her.

"Terrific." Her attempted smile ended in a grimace and the jerk of her throat as she swallowed. "Look." She craned to see her bedside clock. "Donna will be home in a few hours, and I know you must be frantic to get back to work. I'm perfectly fine here. Please, go to your office and don't worry about me. Chris will come back when she can, and I'm not exactly at death's door anyway."

Evan studied her wan face and colorless mouth. Her eyes were huge blue mirrors underscored with dark shadows. "I promised Chris I'd stay, at least until Donna gets back."

"Your work—"

"No." He shook his head emphatically. "Don't worry about that. I've got stacks of papers in my briefcase—plenty to keep me busy. You know I do as much work away from the office as I actually do there."

She pushed herself up in bed and tucked back her hair. "I'm feeling better already." Her hands trembled.

Evan's attention warred back and forth between her obviously weakened condition and the way her nightgown, of some mauve, satiny stuff, slid from one smooth shoulder and clung to her breasts. What would she do if he tried to hold her?

The satin rose and fell more markedly, and he flicked his eyes to meet hers. She'd probably guessed at some of his thoughts—hers were a mystery.

"I can cope here, Evan." She hitched at the gown and only succeeded in making it plunge lower in front. "Could you hand me my robe?"

He located another wisp of matching satin on the foot of the bed. Her composure was admirable. Most women would have made an awkward attempt to cover up. "Why do you need this?"

"I'm feeling better. After I see you off, I'm going to make a few telephone calls and make sure everything's running smoothly at the office."

His fingers sank into the robe, but he didn't offer it to her. "No telephone calls. And the office won't fall down if you aren't around for a while."

Unnaturally high color rose in her face. "I didn't say it would." She swung her legs from the bed, glaring at him. "But I can take care of myself. Why don't you get the message?"

"Get out of that bed, and I'll put you back." He cringed inwardly. If he'd researched the wrong approach to use with this woman, he couldn't have done better. Still, he kept his expression impassive.

"You'll what?" she snapped. "Where do you get off throwing around your weight...? Oh, shoot!" She grabbed the gown, once more sliding from her shoulders, at the same time as she noticed her bare legs were exposed all the way to shapely thighs. "This is impossible."

Her eyes closed, and she pressed a fist against her stomach.

"Are you going to be ill?" Evan went to his knees in front of her. He felt helpless. His brother the doctor would laugh if he could see this debacle. "Let me get you into the bathroom."

Sara groaned, but didn't stop him from holding her and pressing her face to his neck. "Are you going to be sick?" he persisted.

"Evan," she whispered. "You're embarrassing me. How would you like it if someone you were supposed to deal with professionally offered to hold your head while you threw up?"

"If I thought you'd do it, I'd probably arrange to get sick as soon as possible." She wasn't in any condition for his puny attempts at humor.

"I've got a stomach ache, that's all. And a head ache and muscle aches and pains in my back." She looped her arms around his neck. "I feel bloody awful, and I don't like it. I also feel like a perfect fool and a complete nuisance. You're going to have to promise me you'll forget this mess and never remind me of it again, or I'll have to wear a bag over my head when I do get back to work."

Evan laughed softly. She felt wonderful. The skimpy gown was a tantalizing barrier between her body and his hands. For a few minutes, he savored the feel of her, allowed himself to imagine he'd slid off the nightie, and his own clothes, and that they lay together in this big, big bed.

He sighed. "As long as you stop fighting this, I'll promise anything. Come on, back into bed with you." He put a hand beneath her knees and lifted her easily, placed her flat on the bed, smoothed the gown and pulled up her covers. *Saint Evan.* The more he tried to appear nonchalant, the more his hands seemed big and awkward. "Do you need another pillow?"

She shook her head, her eyes pressed tightly closed.

"Aspirin, water...?"

"*Don't* go into that routine again, Evan, please."

"Sure you don't need to go to the bathroom?"

Her head rolled away. "I'm going to die if you say that once more."

"Yes." He jerked the quilt. "Well...yes. I guess I'll go downstairs then..."

"Fine. If you insist on being here."

"I do insist. Sick people need lots of rest and..."

"*Evan!*"

"Right. I'll be downstairs if you need anything."

"Mmmm." She was falling asleep.

He watched her a few more seconds. Her fists atop the covers gradually relaxed. A frown softened from her brow. Sleep. That would fix her up. He started for the door, then stopped and looked back. She was so lovely, and so special.

On tiptoe, he returned to her side, waited, watching her eyes flicker beneath their lids and the steady pulse at her throat. Careful not to jolt her, he ran the back of a forefinger along her jaw and bent to kiss the corner of her mouth before hurrying downstairs. He was in love with the woman. All the arguments in the world wouldn't change that.

Someone was clearing her throat. Evan opened heavy eyelids and squinted up into velvety black eyes. What the...? The face belonged to Donna Fletcher. Where was he?

"Hi, Mr. McGrath. What're you doing here? Where's Mrs. Beamis?"

He'd gone to sleep on the couch. Some nurse he'd make. "I was, um...taking a nap, Donna. How are you?"

"Great. Fantastic. I just got home from school. Beamis is always here in the afternoon."

He had to get his act together. "Mrs. Beamis isn't coming today. Your mother got a little case of the flu. I was filling in for Chris—your Aunt Christine. She said for you to call her as soon as you can, and she'll tell you the program."

"Mom's sick?" The girl sat down abruptly. "What's the matter with her?" Her reaction shocked Evan. She was obviously fearful.

"It's nothing, honey." He took a bony, cold hand in his. "She's been working too hard and last night...and she picked up a bug. We just have to make sure she takes care of herself for a day or two. She'll be back to normal before you know it."

"You sure?" Black braids slithered forward over hunched shoulders. "She isn't going to die or anything?"

Something shifted inside Evan. The poor little devil was terrified she'd be left alone again. Sara must be the first secure element Donna had ever had in her life. "Your mom isn't going to die, or anything. She's tough as tacks; you ought to know that. Run in the kitchen and call your aunt."

He waited until the girl had gone, then leaped upstairs to check on Sara. She was sleeping soundly, a thin film of perspiration covering her brow and upper lip. Moist tendrils of hair strayed across her eyes and mouth. He got a wet washcloth from the bathroom and sponged her face and neck. Sara stirred, smiled drowsily up at him and sank back asleep.

Back in the living room, Donna stood, shifting from foot to foot, her eyes wide and scared. "Aunt Christine says I'm to thank you and to say I can cope now. I didn't know you two knew each other in school."

Evan gave what he hoped was a reassuring smile. "We had biology classes together, and English."

"Yeah, so she said." Her eyes stared at the floor. She still wore a bright red parka. "Thank you for staying with Mom. We'll be all right now." Movement at her throat suggested she found swallowing difficult. "I don't mind being alone at night."

He watched her carefully. "Your mother's here."

"Sure." She sighed. "She couldn't do anything if someone—well, you know, but I'd know what to do."

Evan slid an arm around her narrow shoulders. "You're a very capable young lady. But, you know, I'm pretty beat. What say you and I make dinner together? Maybe we can even get your mom to eat a little soup. Then we could watch television. This couch is kind of comfy. If you don't mind, I'd rather not drive home tonight. I'll get fresh things in the morning. Then, if it's okay with you, I'll bring some work over here to do until Chris can get back in the afternoon. How does all that sound?"

A huge grin transformed Donna's pinched face. "Great, Evan—I mean, Mr. McGrath. Absolutely super. I could do just fine on my own, of course. But if it would help you out to be here, I'm real happy, and I know Mom will be, too."

"Call me Evan. That's the way we'll do it then." He smiled. "Why don't you pop up and take a look at her. She's sleeping, so don't wake her up."

Evan hooked his thumbs into his pants pockets and watched Donna stretch to take two stairs at a time.

The kid was agile. She'd make an acrobat. He also liked everything else about her.

If it would help him out, Donna had said, she'd be happy for him to stay here. Oh, but it would help him out. She had no idea how much.

CHAPTER NINE

FROM HIS FAVORITE THINKING SPOT, by the window, Evan watched her come into the office. The mere sight of her gave him a deep sense of pleasure. Was she finding excuses to see him, to be with him? It seemed that since her illness their paths had crossed almost constantly. Certainly, the episode had forged a tentative bond between them. Several times while Sara was off work, he'd talked Christine into letting him take Donna shopping. He'd become close to Donna and slowly, Sara, too, had also begun to unwind around him.

He propped his chin and studied her, the way she riffled her fingers through the papers she held. Her concentration shut him out. Pleasure ebbed to be replaced by an uneasiness. She looked harassed. Maybe she was beginning to hear some of the bad news filtering back to him.

"Do you know what a pariah is?" he asked, grinning deliberately.

She looked up quickly. "Of course I do. It's someone being shunned by everyone else. What are you getting at?"

"Well, now I know how it feels to be one." He tried to speak lightly, but the subject rankled. He had always gotten on well with the people he worked with.

The slowly increasing antagonism he was experiencing here at the plant put him on edge. But he was steadfastly refusing to let it interfere with his work.

"What do you mean?" Her voice held sharp worry. "Has anyone been saying things to you?"

"On the contrary. It's difficult to get a response to anything even as ordinary as 'good morning.' The atmosphere here is so thick I could cut it if I had the right kind of knife. Do you know anything about it?" He didn't miss the sudden veiled look in her eyes that told him she did. He sat on the edge of his big desk, reaching to stop the printer. The dying away of its steady pattering left a thick silence in the small office that was intensified rather than relieved by the faraway noise of the cannery.

"Well, yes," she said reluctantly. "And since it concerns you, you certainly have a right to know."

"Yes, I would say so," he said gently.

"I'm afraid that Chick Enderby has been spreading some rumors about layoffs in the future."

"The security guy? How'd he get that idea?" He observed the slow sweep of delicate pink into her face.

"I'm afraid from me—in a roundabout way."

"Oh, for Pete's sake." He wanted to laugh at the idea. "If I ever knew a Company Man, it's Sara Fletcher. You'd be the last person...." He was touched by her quick honesty. "How'd it happen?"

"I guess I told Christine about your wing-assembly invention. And...I don't know this for a fact, but I'm taking an educated guess that she told Ben. And I'm afraid Ben probably let it slip to Chick. Ben's so uncomplicated and good-hearted, he thinks everyone else is, too."

"Would that be enough to start Chick spreading rumors?"

"Anything is enough to worry Chick. He's the original bad-luck kid. He hasn't had a very easy life, and I guess he always looks at the dark side."

A strong impulse to touch her shook Evan. He went back to the window and stared outside. Without knowing why, he sensed the timing was still wrong to show even a hint of how desperately he wanted Sara. He must concentrate on their discussion. *Chick Enderby*. Just what he needed, a dedicated gossip monger. "Well, what do you suggest we do?" he asked after a time, keeping his voice noncommittal. "You're the personnel department. I can talk to Chick, try to allay his suspicions. Or maybe it's your territory. What do you think?"

"I'll talk to him," she said thoughtfully. "We go back a long way, Chick and I. I can't have him upsetting the rest of the work force. He'll listen to me."

"Keep in mind, Sara," Evan said levelly, "that the wing-assembly system does get the job done with about a fourth as many people. If he's given your staff that fact, they're bound to be edgy."

"I know," she answered in a small voice. She put the papers she'd been carrying on his desk and came beside him. "I wish—"

Evan waited. She bowed her head, and her hair swung forward.

"What, Sara?" He raised a hand toward her a fraction, then shoved it quickly into his pocket. "Was there something else?"

"No, nothing. See you later."

When she was gone he remained looking at the door until a beep sounded on the computer terminal and he restarted the printer.

Sara had been about to say something. He flexed tense muscles in his shoulders. She probably wanted to add a point about the problems he was having with the cannery staff. He wondered if Grant knew how hard she worked. He'd have a difficult time getting along without her. Evan settled back into his chair and started flipping through sheets of calculations. He hoped she could shut up Chick in a nice way. He was sorry for the old geezer, but enough was enough. His own fuse was getting shorter by the hour in this place.

Just after lunch he found the drawing fragment. He had taken to having a sandwich in his office if he was at the plant during the noon hour. He'd balled up a wrapper and tossed it toward his wastebasket. He missed. The paper ball rolled into a corner, and Evan's eye was drawn to a rumpled scrap against the base-board. Absently he retrieved the sandwich wrapper and the torn bit of paper.

He rarely tore anything. It was a piece of one of his own preliminary sketches. He scrutinized it carefully, his face going grim. He had not ripped up this draw-ing. He stood there, holding it in his hand, trying to place it. Then he put it onto the desk and went to the roll file he'd had put in, looking in first one slot and then another at the various rolls of drawings. It took him a moment to realize which was gone, then the an-ger he felt was tempered by near laughter. Whoever had taken this hadn't known enough to pick some-thing important. Sara's description of her brother-in-law flicked through his mind. ''Ben's so uncomplicated and good-hearted.'' Uncomplicated maybe. Good-hearted, maybe not.

Evan became aware of a small knot of dread in his stomach. He'd have to tell her. She had too big a stake in his project to be kept in the dark, even about this unimportant act of sabotage. And sabotage it was. Who knew, maybe next time good old uncomplicated Ben—or whoever—would pick on something vital to destroy. This must have been done at night. The thought of someone poking furtively through the drawings, arbitrarily tearing one up and throwing away the pieces, gave him an uneasy feeling. And the clumsy culprit had dropped a remnant.

Reluctantly he reached for the phone to dial Sara's number at her office in the Daon Building.

Sara answered her phone, wishing she hadn't eaten her lunch so fast. As she lifted the receiver her other hand groped around inside her top desk drawer for the antacid tablets she knew should be there. This was one way to get a first-class ulcer. She had a quick longing to be with Christine. Chris was always so calm, so serene. Sara decided to stop there on her way home. Maybe some of her sister's serenity would rub off.

''Hi,'' Evan's voice greeted her, the timbre deep with a slight break that always suggested laughter. The quickening of her breathing was becoming more familiar with their every contact.

''Sara? Is that you?''

Her grip on the phone tightened. ''Yes. Sorry. There are too many things happening at once around here.''

''Thought I'd better tell you the next episode in the Evan McGrath, Boy Wonder's adventures in the world of canned fish. You want to hear?'' He attempted to sound casual, trying to hide his tension.

She felt an overwhelming sense of dread. No. She didn't want to hear it. She wanted to go home. And shut the door. Shut out everything.

"Absolutely," she said brightly. "After all, I am the personnel department. Everybody's den mother. What's up?''

When she hung up the phone a few moments later, she scrabbled around in her desk drawer for the stomach tablets. Finding them, she opened the package with shaking fingers.

Sabotage. Evan could make a joke of it if he wanted to, but that's what was happening. Somebody was trying—stupidly and ineptly—to damage Evan's work, to keep him from doing what he'd been hired to do. And on the heels of this thought was the sickening idea that she'd have to tell Grant. It would be dishonest not to. He *was* her superior. He had a right to know what was going on. She felt a swift longing for the old days with his father, Homer. There had never been any pretense between herself and the senior Jarvis. She'd have gone rushing into his office without even knocking and announced, "Homer, guess what, some jerk has torn up Evan's drawing." And together, thinking and working as one person, they'd have got to the bottom of it.

But Homer wasn't here anymore. She doubted if he even knew about Evan. And she wouldn't go charging informally into Grant's office. She'd pick up the phone and speak to his secretary to see if he had time for her.

Miserably, she slid down into her chair and closed her eyes. She was *tired*. Thank goodness Donna and her four constant companions—or at least they seemed constant these days—were leaving on their camping trip this afternoon. Evan and Donna had spent a lot of time together while Sara had been ill. She'd been surprised, and uncomfortable, when Donna had excitedly told her of his offer to take her and the rest of her friends into the mountains. Only the glow in Donna's eyes had checked an immediate protest. Sara had agreed to the expedition, but declined to go with them. Now she was glad Evan had volunteered. Immediately the nagging little guilt made itself felt. What sort of mother was she to welcome the idea of her daughter being out from underfoot for two days?

Still slouched in her chair, Sara pushed it away from the desk. She decided to see Grant. She lifted one toe and shoved the still-open drawer, slamming it shut. Resolutely she picked up the phone to call Grant's secretary.

Was Ben the culprit? The sudden question made her wince. Oh, no. He couldn't be. Tearing up a drawing wasn't Ben's kind of action at all. *Or was it?* She'd better talk with Christine.

To her further irritation, she found she couldn't see Grant until almost finishing time. When she did meet with him, he received the news somberly, but without any indication of surprise. He seemed unhappy and preoccupied, as if listening to her was an effort. He was packing his briefcase preparatory to going home.

"You don't seem too upset," she said when she had told him. "I thought you'd be roaring mad."

"Later." He gave her a strained smile. "When I get time I'll be roaring mad. Right now I've got a couple of other things on my mind."

"Are you okay?" she asked in quick sympathy. They might have their differences, but he was Homer's only son.

"Sure. I feel kind of zapped at the moment, but I...I'll come to grips with it. After I come to grips with not getting any fish from the *Nancy Belle*. We're going to run a bit short of pack this month." It was clear his mind wasn't even totally on that. Something else was troubling him.

"We always get the *Nancy Belle*'s catch," she said in disbelief. "What happened?"

"The skipper sold to some other canner. Don't ask me why. Maybe he got a better price."

"I don't believe it," she said flatly. "He wouldn't do that. He's always sold to us. For years and years."

"Well, he did sell elsewhere, Sara. And he's not obligated to do business with us, you know. There was never any contract. It was just an agreement of long-standing. That's a system we'll have to change."

She didn't know what to say. Homer had never bothered to put the fishing boats under contract. Maybe Grant was right about this one issue, at least. Perhaps everything should be signed and sealed.

"Look, Grant. Let me get on the phone first thing on Monday morning. I can probably get enough fish to complete the pack. I know everybody in the business. Let me—"

"Yes. I'll take all the help I can get on that one, but can we leave it for now. I've got to get out of here. Something's...come up."

"Of course." She drew back slightly. She didn't want to push in where she wasn't wanted. He probably had a hot date.

At the door he paused and turned. "And we can go over the other business—about Evan's trouble—on Monday. I mean, when I get back to the office."

What in the world was the matter with him?

"Certainly," she said quietly. "Give me a buzz when you want to see me."

"And, Sara—" He opened the door but stopped again. "Where will you be?"

"Where will I be when?"

"Tonight? Over the weekend? In case I want to give you a call?"

She kept her expression bland. He'd sent flowers while she was ill but made no further mention of their argument over her whereabouts the night he couldn't reach her. Surely he wasn't still trying to keep tabs on her. "I'll be at home. Later, that is. I'll stop at Christine's first. Then I'm going home. Call me either place, Grant." There, she told herself, that was cordial. She'd meet him halfway always—as long as he didn't push. She owed Homer that.

AT CHRISTINE'S, curled up in a large shabby chair, her hands warm around a cup of strong tea, she felt a little better. It seemed almost a sacrilege to mention her suspicions to her sister. This was Christine's home, her haven. Here, sunk in the deep chair, Sara could almost understand why Christine had tossed aside the idea of any career after college. Living like this would be—

"Are you going to mention it or not?" Her sister's kindly voice broke into her reverie. Christine was sprawled on the couch, her legs outstretched.

"Mention what?" Sara took another appreciative sip of the pungent tea.

"How do I know, love? You come in here fairly dripping with gloom, collapse into a chair and then...total silence for the next half hour. Obviously, something is the matter with your world. Obviously, you're mulling it over. Well, stop mulling and *talk* about it. Whatever it is, I'll help if I can. As we used to say in the sorority house, 'what are sisters *for*?'"

A shaky laugh escaped Sara, and she put her half-empty cup on a low table. Christine was always like a breath of fresh air.

"Oh, it's the plant," she said evasively. "There's always some big mess to clear up. Old Chick Enderby is busy spreading rumors and getting the workers upset at Evan McGrath. This bothers Evan, of course. Then first thing Monday I've got to, somehow or other, find a boatload of fish to complete the current pack. When we contract to sell a certain amount of canned product, we've got to come up with it. No excuses."

"Is that *it*?" Christine asked. "That's no worse than your standard everyday hassles there, is it? I had the idea there was something else."

Sara leaned forward and put her head in her hands. "Oh, Chris, there is. I'm just working up my nerve to say it."

"Good grief, it must be terrible. Better spill it. Do you think you'll cry? I'll get you a Kleenex."

"Well, maybe later. I just…" She paused, the words choking her. She knew with what depth and abiding passion her sister loved Ben.

"Chrissy," she began haltingly. "Do you remember when I told you about Evan's airplane-wing invention and asked you not to tell anyone… Well…did you? Tell anyone?"

"No. Of course not." Christine was off the couch and crouched on her knees before Sara. "Not a living soul. Only Ben, of course."

Sara sighed. "Did you warn him not to let it slip to anyone else?" she asked carefully.

"Of *course*. Sara, what *is* this?"

"Somehow or other, Chick Enderby got hold of the information. Now he's mentally got half the work force laid off."

"Oh, drat that man!" Christine said in exasperation. "Well, it didn't come from Ben. You can be sure of that, sis." Blue eyes looked into blue eyes with complete candor, and Sara had to look away first.

"Okay," she said in defeat. "That makes me feel better." But it didn't. Christine might be sure of it; she wasn't. Not that Ben had divulged information maliciously—she'd never think that. But he might have let it slip, just accidentally.

"I wish you'd believe me, Sara." Christine's voice was sober. She sat back looking hurt. "You don't know Ben the way I do."

Sara was saved from responding by the sound of the telephone ringing in the kitchen. Christine sprang up with an energy that suggested relief and went to answer it. Sara found herself straining to hear. She didn't know why.

"For you, sis," Christine said from the kitchen doorway, and Sara hurried into the kitchen. Who knew she was here? Oh, Grant, of course. She had told Grant. It must be something about the office.

She took the receiver of the yellow wall phone from her sister's hand.

"Hello? Grant?"

There was an odd pause with some voices in the background, and then a male voice responded. "Sara. Yes, Grant here." Then another pause, a tense interval when nothing came over the line. Then Grant spoke again.

"Sara. I'm sorry...but I thought I'd better call you right away... you and my father..."

Homer. Something was the matter with Homer. It hit her like a thunderbolt. That's what Grant had been upset about this afternoon. She was suddenly cold, with little ripples of shock running over her skin. She stared blankly at two layers of white cake cooling on a rack. Christine must have baked this afternoon.

"Grant? It's Homer isn't it?" *Nothing must happen to Homer.* She fought against the idea.

"Yes. I'm sorry. I wanted you to know. It's over. He's gone."

For a long moment she stood pressing the yellow phone receiver to her ear, unable to absorb the news. There was a fluffy pile of white coconut on a plate. The broken pieces of the hairy brown coconut hull lay neatly on a paper towel. Coconut cake. Ben's favorite.

"Sara? Are you there?" Grant's voice, not sounding like Grant at all, seemed very far away.

"Yes," she said remotely.

"What is it?" Christine whispered. "What's wrong?"

"When the end came, it was sudden," Grant went on. "I'm glad of that anyway. The . . . the service will be Tuesday. Sara . . . sometime, when this is over, let's talk about . . . things. You were his good friend . . . and I appreciate it." His voice dwindled off.

"Is there anything you want me to do?" she heard herself asking. *Oh no, not yet, not yet,* her mind was wailing. *Not just yet, Homer.* Why had she let so many weeks slip by without going to see him? Why had she allowed her own petty problems to become excuses for staying away?

"Sis?" Christine was looking at her, wide-eyed.

"No. Nothing right now, really." Grant sounded tired. "You know how it is here—I'm awash with Jarvis relatives. Maybe Monday, if you could telephone some of his business associates—I doubt I know them all. You know, his old cronies. . . ."

"Yes. Yes, of course. Monday," she repeated vacantly. *Homer was gone. There was no one else, now. She was absolutely alone.*

Grant's voice came again, sounding desperate. "It was easy, Sara. He just went to sleep and . . . slipped away. It was easy for him."

She was grateful for that. She sagged against the wall.

"Grant. I'll get in early Monday and start phoning. I'll make a list this weekend of everyone who will want to know. And Grant!"

"Yes?" His voice was unsteady.

"Hang in there. I'll...help all I can." What else was there to say? "I'm sorry," she added helplessly. "I'm so sorry."

She hung up the phone and turned to Christine.

"It's Homer Jarvis, Chrissy. He's gone," she said. "He passed away," she continued inanely. "Quietly, in his sleep."

"Oh, no," Christine cried. "Not that wonderful old man. Oh, sis. You and he used to have such times together." She turned and darted from the room.

Sara started to cry. She felt so silly. She was crying out loud, like a little girl, and she couldn't stop. Then Christine was back and pressing something into her hand.

"Have a hanky," Christine said. "A big one. It's Ben's." And Sara felt herself folded into her sister's arms.

"I MUST LOOK like the devil," Sara said later in the living room, where they sat over a fresh pot of tea.

"No. Not the devil," Christine said, close beside her. "I always think of the devil as red. You're pink. Pink eyes. Pink nose. But you'll fade back to your own color pretty soon."

Sara gave a shaky laugh. "I didn't realize Homer's death would hit me so hard. I've been expecting it for a year."

"Doesn't matter. Someone's dying is always a shock. It's always too soon. And in the next few weeks you'll think of a dozen things you have to tell him."

"Yes, I suppose so," Sara said dolefully. "Oh, Chrissy, I'll miss him."

"More to the point now," Christine said. "What about this weekend. You're not going to brood over it, are you?"

"How do you mean?"

"You'll be alone. Don't forget you sent your little chick off camping with Evan as caretaker. Do you really think you should be by yourself? Tell you what. You stay here with us this weekend."

"No," Sara said too quickly. She didn't want to stay with Christine, much as she loved her sister. She didn't want to watch Christine in her unflappable serenity in the middle of her family in her lovely, shabby, lived-in home.

She wanted . . . she wanted . . . what did she want?

"But, Sara, you've had a bad shock. He was one of the best friends you've ever had. You can't just sit over there all by yourself." Christine's voice seemed to come to her from a great distance.

There had sprung into her mind the image of Evan, and she had the sudden crazy conviction that Evan would understand how she felt at losing a friend, a dear friend. Evan would somehow *know*.

She rolled Ben's damp handkerchief between her palms and then handed it to Christine. "I think I've changed my mind about that camping trip. I should have gone anyhow. I'll drive on up. It'll do me good to be with Donna and . . . her friends. Nothing like five kids to take your mind off yourself."

Christine was looking at her thoughtfully. "Maybe that's not a bad idea," she said slowly. "Next week isn't going to be easy. A two-day break might help. Go ahead. Go on. I'll help you get ready."

Trust Christine to understand, Sara thought.

SARA WAS DRIVING across Lion's Gate Bridge when she could feel the tension begin to ease. She had known for a long time that Homer's death was imminent. She had been on her own, really, since Homer's retirement. It wasn't so much his guidance that she would miss now—it was his friendship. Even in the past months, when she'd rarely seen him, his telephone calls and the knowledge that she *could* go to him, had been a subtle reassurance. A tremulous smile curved her lips for a moment.

Heading northeast toward Mount Seymour, where the campsite was, she looked down into the Burrard Inlet. The sun was low now, and small boats were heading in across the dull gray satin of the wide water. The smell of pines came in, wrapping her in fragrance. The scent was so fresh, so clean. The deep peace of the towering forests and the ancient hills caressed her with its healing magic.

Darkness had rolled over the mountainside by the time she found the campsite. She drove within yards of it, slowly, crunching twigs and pine cones under the car's wheels. Donna saw her first.

"Mom! You came!" Light from the campfire showed the flash of pure joy that transformed the girl's face. She threw down an armload of firewood and came running to fling herself at Sara as she left the car.

"Well, hi." Evan's cheerful voice greeted her from the other side of the fire. He got up and strolled toward them. "Couldn't resist the call of the wilds after all? That's good. There's even enough food left to give you something to eat. You have terrific timing."

At the invitation, Sara felt a sudden gnawing hunger. For a moment she was embarrassed, not knowing what to say. But there was no need.

"Mom, guess what? *We* put up all the tents. The rest of the girls and me. Evan just stood there and told us what to do. This is really fun."

Sara had never seen Donna so animated. She looked admiringly at the four small pup tents arranged in a fairly even row.

"And, Mrs. Fletcher, guess what? Evan let us cook dinner," one of the other girls shouted from the campfire. "He even let us open the cans of beans. And that's hard with the little can opener."

"No electricity out here," Evan said with a grin as he came up to her. "Where's your stuff? I'll get it."

She handed him her keys. "In the trunk." Her throat tightened. She glanced down his lithe frame, immaculate in sweatshirt and jeans. "You look awfully clean for a woodsman," she managed to say.

"I made the kids do all the work. I figured if they got really tired, maybe I—" He smiled. "I mean we can sleep until dawn. No child labor laws out here, either." He got Sara's new sleeping bag from the trunk and the small case of her personal things. "I did promise to unroll the sleeping bags. That's my major contribution."

"Put Mom and me in the same tent," Donna ordered. "I'll get my sleeping bag. Mine's the red one." She rushed across the clearing to the pile of rolled-up bags.

Sara's, "Shush—shush, don't get so excited," was lost on the night air, fragrant with the smell of evergreens and the smoke from the campfire.

"Okay," Evan said easily. "Did you ladies decide which tent was whose, or whoms, or whatever?"

"Here," Donna said, staking her claim. "This is mine. Ours. Mom's and mine. Closest to the trees." She dumped down her roll.

"Right." Effortlessly Evan lifted the red bag and commenced undoing the ties. Then he stood up to his full height and let it unfold.

As it did, the half-open side zipper gaped, and money began to fall out. A wad of bills fell, then two wads of bills. Next a plastic bag, loosely closed with a twist at the top slid to the ground with the sound of clinking coins. The bag came open and the coins spilled out and rolled about.

"What the devil?" Evan stared at the money spread among the pine needles and dirt.

"Oh," Donna said, her voice sounding small in the vastness of the night. "It's my money. I forgot my money was in there." She gestured the other girls away. "I'll get it. I'll get it." And then she was on all fours among the pine needles, her small hands darting about, gathering up the money, bill by bill and coin by coin, muttering softly to herself as she did so; seeming to forget she was not alone.

"Just my money. I have some money. I put some money away sometimes."

CHAPTER TEN

"SARA—"

"I'm glad I came. It's so peaceful up here."

"Sara—"

"Listen to those girls giggle. You sure have a way with kids. They adore you. I wish you'd teach me your secret."

Evan reached for a handful of sticks and threw them, harder than he'd intended, into the fire. Sparks skittered in all directions. "*I* wish you'd stop avoiding the issue. I've been waiting hours for you to say something."

Sara hunched forward to grip her knees. "Sometimes it's best to wait awhile and let things simmer."

Simmer, Evan thought. *Go away, you mean.* "We can't put this off any longer. There wasn't a time for a discussion before the girls went to bed, but now we should have one. I care about Donna. If she's into something—"

"Donna?" Firelight darkened the hollows beneath Sara's cheekbones. In the dancing shadows, he saw her bemused expression. "What about Donna? I thought... No, of course not. How could you know?"

She wasn't making any sense. "Know what?"

"Nothing." She shivered and got closer to the fire. "Did Donna say something I ought to know about?"

Her hand hovered near her mouth. "Something about Prairie Crawford?"

"You've lost me, Sara." He pushed to his feet and stood over her. "The money. That's what's got me in a cold sweat. Where would a thirteen-year-old get that much cash?"

"Where? Oh, good Lord." She grabbed his hand, and he hauled her up. "I thought you looked a bit sick. It's hers. She hasn't spent her allowance in months—I'm sure of it. I never gave it a second thought."

Relief swept warmth into Evan's every vein. "Why didn't you say so?"

"I didn't think. You shoved it all back in her sleeping bag, and then there was so much going on. It never struck me you'd think . . . what *did* you think?"

"Forget it."

"No, Evan. Tell me. Did you think she stole it?"

He felt foolish and suspicious. "Yes. I never saw a kid have that much money before. And any who did would normally spend it, not stuff it in a sleeping bag."

Sara turned away and shoved her hands into her jean pockets. Her shoulders came up. She was shutting him out.

"I said something wrong again. What did I say this time?"

The dark head bent forward. She didn't reply.

"Oh, dammit all. There's so much running around in that brain of yours. I wish, just for once, you'd stop hiding your thoughts from me."

She turned swiftly and thrust her small body against him with enough force to make him take a step back-

ward. He crossed his arms slowly over her back and
held her tight. "Sara, Sara," he whispered. "What's
wrong? What is it I wouldn't know about? And who's
Prairie what ever her name is?"

"Just hold me."

"I will. I will." He wanted to hold her forever. "Sit
with me," he said.

They huddled together on a pile of blankets. Evan
rested his chin atop Sara's head and watched black
smoke laced with glinting embers spiral upward into
a circle of indigo sky between the inky outlines of
pines. If she wanted to tell him what troubled her, he'd
listen. But he wouldn't push.

"You think what they all think, don't you? And
you've been talking to Chris." A slight tremor vi-
brated in her voice.

He frowned. "Sara. You really aren't making a
whole lot of sense. Let's take all this slowly. If I'd been
talking to Chris—and I haven't—what would we be
likely to discuss that you wouldn't like? Tell me that
first, then go on and give me the dirt on what everyone's supposed to think."

A faint rocking motion of her body made him hold
on tighter. "You said a normal kid wouldn't hoard
money; she'd spend it."

"I said it seemed unusual that she hadn't spent it,"
Evan said patiently. "I didn't say Donna wasn't normal."

"You thought it, though. And you think I'm a bad
mother, the way Christine does."

He sighed. Somehow he'd got out of his depth here.
"I think you're a damn good mother. And *if* I ever

discussed the topic with Chris, I'm sure she'd think so, too."

She raised her face. Her nose was cold against the base of his throat. He felt as if he were going crazy.

"Christine thinks Donna's too quiet. She thinks she'll do something awful one day just to make sure I give her more attention."

"*Chris* said that?"

There was a short pause. "Not exactly. But I know what's in her mind."

"Or yours?"

Sara pushed away, putting several inches between them. "How did you get so wise, Evan McGrath? When did you learn to read people's minds? Is there a school for that, too?"

He touched her hair, but she jerked her head to one side. "I just know you're worried about a lot more than you're telling me. And since we're being open, I think you're giving Donna too much money. From what I saw, you have to be. Money doesn't do what love can, Sara, and all the money in the world won't take your place with her."

"Don't!" Swiftly she picked up one of the long forks they'd used for toasting marshmallows and poked the fire. "I'm not trying to buy her affection, if that's what you mean." Each word was punctuated with a prod from the fork. "I never had any money when I was a kid. I want Donna to have everything."

"What she wants most is you." He was hurting her. She might draw away from him, but that was a risk he must take. "Remember Laura Fenton—Laura Hunt?"

Sara shrugged.

"My friend in San Francisco. She used to be a professional clown."

"I remember. So what?"

He shuffled behind her on his knees. "She was orphaned as a baby. Her uncle, Mark's father's partner, and his wife, adopted her."

Sara looked at him and he held her face toward him, rubbing its contours lightly. "Laura's case was different from Donna's—totally different. It's up to us—to you, to make sure it stays different."

"Say what you're thinking." She covered his hand with hers, but made no attempt to remove it from her cheek.

"Laura was adopted out of family duty. She was tolerated, constantly reminded what a burden she was. She wasn't *loved*. She had all the material things a kid needs—but she never felt she belonged. And in the end she went overboard trying to be noticed. It was an accident, but she killed a man."

Sara took a deep breath. "Who? How?"

"William Hunt, Mark, her husband's, father. She ran with a wild bunch who did a lot of drinking. The morning after the high school prom, her date was too out of it to drive, and Laura had to take some papers by her uncle's law offices. She should have run the errand the night before, but she forgot. Anyway, in the morning, she was tired and it was raining. Bill Hunt stepped off the sidewalk in front of her car and died almost instantly."

A deep shuddering racked Sara's body. "Those poor people. Was she prosecuted?"

"Yes. By Mark—the man she's married to now. It was a tragic accident. The case against Laura was thrown out. Nothing could ever bring William Hunt back. Laura left San Francisco, she thought for good, but her inheritance of part of the law firm forced Mark to seek her out. I never saw two people more in love than they are now." He looked away, a little tightness at the back of his throat.

"And you think Donna could end up doing something dreadful to make me notice her? You thought she'd stolen money for that reason?"

"Not really. I overreacted. But I do think she adores you and wants you more than anything. Whatever happens, I don't want to see another person I care about suffer the way Laura did."

Sara didn't miss the wistfulness, or the pain in Evan's voice. This Laura Fenton Hunt had meant a great deal to him—probably still did. She had a feeling there was a lot he wasn't saying about his relationship with the other woman.

"I'm frightened, Evan." Goose bumps shot along her arms. Comments kept popping out of her mouth unbidden.

"It'll be okay." Evan put an arm around her and sat down again, nudging her down with him. "Donna's a different case from Laura. You constantly let her know how much she means to you."

"Not enough. I need to spend more time with her. Maybe it's time I…" Homer's death was loosening her tongue.

"Yes?" He swiveled sideways and propped her against his drawn up knees.

"Nothing. Time to take a long look at priorities, that's all." It wouldn't hurt her to leave Jarvis now. But the time wasn't quite right and Grant must be the first to know if she did decide to quit, not Evan. Anyway, before she went, she must make sure she'd done all she could for the people who depended on her.

"You've got a lot on your mind, Sara. What aren't you telling me?"

Suddenly she was achingly tired. The weight of all that concerned her was like lead in her bones. "I keep expecting to open my front door and find Prairie Crawford on the step."

He tilted her chin. "*Who* is this mysterious Prairie Crawford you keep mentioning?"

My nemesis, Sara thought, but said simply. "Donna's biological mother."

Unconsciously, Evan clasped her thigh. "You *know* the woman? I don't understand."

"It was a direct adoption. Donna had been in a series of foster homes. The court ruled Prairie unfit and incapable of raising a child, and released Donna for adoption. Prairie is allowed to visit Donna if I agree. She called a few weeks ago, just after the birthday, and said she'd be in town soon. She intends to see Donna."

Evan swallowed audibly. "If you agree, right?"

"If I don't, I'm afraid of alienating Donna. She loves the woman. That's natural."

"You are so special," Evan said, a break in his voice. "How could you think anyone wouldn't know what a good mother you are?"

She laced her fingers through his. "Thank you, Evan. I needed to hear that. But I am slipping up somewhere. Donna *is* too good, just the way Chris says. And she is too afraid of making waves. It's as if she thinks I'll get upset and stop loving her, or send her away."

He made circles on her palm with a forefinger. "She hasn't had time to be completely secure yet. Only a year. When you were sick, she was terrified. She asked me if you were going to die."

Her stomach dropped away. "Oh, Evan. I didn't know. I've got to give her what she needs. She means the world to me."

"You'll do it," Evan said quietly. "It's already starting to work if you think about it. Look how well she's doing with her friends. Maladjusted kids don't have a bevy of peers dying to be with them."

Sara laughed and squeezed his hand tighter. "That's partly because of you. How many kids have inventor-cum-clowns who are also a whiz at arranging camping trips for friends? I'll never be able to thank you enough, Evan."

He was staring directly into her eyes. He had such a gentle, sensitive face. A sudden thought jarred her. She hadn't even mentioned Homer. Tears smarted, but she blinked them away.

"Trying to think of ways to thank me makes you tearful?" Evan teased.

"Homer Jarvis died today," she said softly.

For a moment he remained motionless, an uncomprehending frown drawing his arched brows together. "Homer Jarvis?"

"Yes." Her throat felt clogged. "He went into a coma and just slipped away."

"I'm sorry." He pulled her hand away, patted her knee and stood. "I know how much he meant to you.

I guess you feel the whole world's out to get you about now."

She had to tip her head to see his profile. "A bit."

"So that's why you came up here."

Seconds unrolled. His voice sounded strained. "In a way... yes... yes, it's why. Grant obviously wanted to be alone. He loved his father more than any of us realized." She hesitated, unnerved by Evan's stillness. "And Homer always said he didn't want any fuss when he went. No flowers or people crying. The services are on Tuesday. Everything quick and clean."

"That's okay for the one who dies. It isn't so hot for the ones left behind. People need to mourn. Poor Grant."

"Grant's going to be okay. It's probably a good thing he's got the business to think about now."

"Yes." Evan sounded even more distant. "A good thing. Work will be good for you, too. You were smart to use the camping trip as a diversion."

Suddenly Sara knew that Evan was disappointed. He'd assumed she came to be with him and now he felt used. *Had* she only come so she wouldn't be alone?

"Evan." She grasped his elbow. "Evan, look at me." Sara stood up.

He turned his head, and she saw the tightly compressed lines of his face.

"I didn't even think why I was coming up here. I did know I didn't want to be alone. But the rest was instinct. It never crossed my mind to go to anyone but you." Her scalp contracted sharply. What she said was completely true. "I had to be with you, Evan."

He stared into her eyes, then at her mouth. "You mean that?"

A rush of emotion flared within her. "Yes." She gripped his shirt beneath each arm and stood on tiptoe to kiss his jaw. "Yes, Evan."

His lips parted as if he was going to speak, but he only drew in several short breaths. She felt him tremble, and he pushed his fingers into her hair. He was so near. And he felt so strong. Avoiding this moment, this closeness with another man, any man, had been her unspoken vow since she'd suffered the pain of Michael's loss. She touched Evan's cheekbone, then his brow, with a kind of wonder. The briefest letting go of self, giving, touching, might rekindle that desperate emptiness she'd promised never to feel again.

"That first day—the day we met in Grant's office—I knew I wanted to hold you like this." Evan pressed his cheek to hers.

The air seemed thinner. She smelled his cleanness, felt the flexing of his solid muscles against her. "Evan." She leaned away until he looked at her. An intense glitter lighted his eyes, and she saw the flash of his teeth as he smiled down at her. The instant before she kissed his mouth, she quelled the last vestige of doubt. All the minutes and hours since they'd met had been pulling them to this moment, down a one-way path.

She kissed him softly at first, her lips closed, tentative, then with building fierceness, reaching up, forcing him to plant his feet more firmly, to steady them both.

Then he was in command, bending her body with his, caressing her neck, resting one hand gently on her breast beneath her jacket while he rocked her head with the ardor of his mouth and lips and tongue.

Sara closed her eyes tightly and let him mold her against him. The stroking at her breast was careful, light, but an almost forgotten searing flowed downward to the heavy heat that throbbed in her womb.

Their breathing speeded. Coherent thought was gone. He had hardened against her belly. When she pulled his shirt and sweater free to run her fingers over his skin, he felt fevered.

"Sara," he murmured against her ear. "I want to make love to you."

She crossed her hands over his smooth back. "We can't." Her lips found one collarbone beneath his shirt. "The girls."

"I know," he sighed. "But when?"

"I can't tell you that now." She clung to him, waiting for her heart to slow. "We have to think. There's too much at stake—for both of us—to make mistakes."

"Sara. Stopping now is tough enough. Don't make me wait much longer." He kissed her again, and in his lips and body she felt raw desire and desperation.

"It's just as difficult for me," she whispered. "Please, help me."

He straightened and set her from him with shaky hands. "A week from Monday I have to go to San Francisco. Come with me."

He was going away. "Why? Oh, Evan, don't leave me now. I don't know what we can have together—if anything—but I want to find out."

He raked at his hair. "I'm not staying away. I'm just going down for the christening of Mark's and Laura's baby. I'll be there a few days."

Sara turned to stare into the fire. "I couldn't leave Donna, not now."

His hands slid around her waist, and he pulled her against him. "Bring her. We'll manage."

"No." She shook her head. "I'm not ... I've never crept around, pretending, hiding what I did in closets. I'd feel dirty."

He spun her to face him. "There's never going to be anything dirty about what's between us. Never. Do you understand?"

His fervor shook her. "I understand. But I can't go with you. Those people don't know me. I'd feel like an intruder."

"You're my friend. They'll love you. Please, say you'll come."

They heard rustling in the tent where Donna slept.

"If she wakes up and I'm not there, she'll be frightened," Sara said. "I'd better go."

"Sara?"

She edged around him. "Good night, Evan."

"I'm not giving up."

A sudden wind gusted through the clearing, carrying the freshened scent of pine and encroaching winter. Sara paused and Evan came up beside her. His arm went around her shoulders and they stood still, side by side, listening to their breathing.

"You mean so much to me," Sara whispered. She took his hand and kissed the palm, before ducking low and darting through the tent flap.

"DID YOU KNOW ABOUT this San Francisco thing?" Grant asked, staring out his office windows.

"Evan did mention it," Sara prayed he wouldn't probe too deeply. She wasn't about to tell him she and Evan had been camping over the weekend. The presence of five girls was unlikely to impress Grant with the innocence of the event. And rightly so. She blew thoughtfully into one fist.

Grant paced back to his desk and flopped into the chair. He appeared to have aged overnight, his skin sallow, purplish smudges beneath his eyes. The man was grieving, Sara thought, with a sudden rush of tenderness toward him. In his own way he'd loved his father very much.

"He's losing interest."

"I'm sorry, Grant." She sat up straighter. "I don't think I follow you."

"McGrath. He made up some excuse about needing to see to his business in the States, royalty statements or something. That kind of thing can be handled by mail. Then he went on about having to be a baby's godfather. I think he's cooling on the plant project." The brown eyes were dull, their whites bloodshot.

"I disagree." Sara spoke carefully, weighing each word. "He knows he's under contract. He also knows we're into this for too much money to draw back now." Saying the truth aloud hurt, but she kept her expression neutral. "And he is going to be a baby's godfather. I knew about that the day I met him."

Grant peered at her, then rubbed his jaw hard. "I'm not convinced."

"Evan wouldn't quit. He wouldn't just go away and leave...." She closed her mouth firmly. One slip and

Grant would know exactly what her major concern had become.

"What makes you so sure?" He cocked his head to one side. Sara didn't remember the strands of gray that showed at his temples.

She folded her hands in her lap. "Grant, how are you doing? It helps to talk about—"

"No," he almost shouted. "No. I'm sorry. I know you mean well and that you're suffering, too. But I can't talk about...I can't talk about it yet. After we get through tomorrow...the...funeral. Maybe then. I don't know."

This temptation to go to him, to hug him, was unbearable. Instead she studied her fingernails. "I understand."

"You haven't had a holiday for a long time."

His comment took her by surprise. "We've been too busy."

"I want you to take one now. Go down to San Francisco with Evan next week. I'm sure he wouldn't mind." Grant looked away. "Keep an eye on him. And while you're at it, take a look at some canneries down there. It never hurts to get an idea of the opposition's techniques."

He wanted her to be Evan's bodyguard and make sure he returned. *Good Lord.* "I'm not some sort of nursemaid to errant inventors, Grant. I couldn't make Evan McGrath return here if he didn't want to."

Grant stood and supported his weight on the desk with both hands. "Oh, I think you could. In fact, one word from you and I think he'd go just about anywhere."

This situation was getting sticky. Unfamiliar loyalty to Grant struggled against her negative attitude toward Evan's work. And, at the same time, the mere hint of losing him entirely turned her brain into mush.

"Sara. Will you do it?"

"I . . . what about Donna?"

"Take her. She'd love San Francisco."

She didn't know what to say anymore. "Evan," she started. What about him? "I can't sneak around like an undersize Remington Steele, hopping out of sight if I think Evan's looking."

"No need. We'll be open about it—almost." He pressed a buzzer on his intercom. "Margaret? Hi. Did Evan get here? Good. Ask him to come in."

Sara half rose. With the click of the door, she sank back and watched Evan enter the room. Every nerve in her body jumped.

"Hi, Grant—Sara." He smiled, keeping his eyes on hers a fraction too long. "Missed seeing you at the plant today."

"It's Monday," she mumbled. "There's a lot to get through. You know how it is." When he'd dropped her at the house the night before, after returning from Mount Seymour, she'd hurried inside, deliberately avoiding mention of when they'd meet again. He'd tried to call four times today. She'd been "out" on each occasion. Anne Parker could hardly contain her curiosity.

Evan sat easily in the chair opposite hers, his eyebrows raised expectantly.

"Well," Grant began as he pushed papers around his desk. "I was just telling Sara about your trip to San Francisco."

Evan made a politely innocuous noise.

"Yes," Grant went on. "It's a coincidence really. For months I've been talking about having her go to the Bay area to take a look at some of their fish-processing plants. She wasn't very keen on going alone."

"Really?" Evan smiled benignly.

Sara made a mental note to accidentally trip Grant when the opportunity arose.

"Yup," he said, studiously avoiding looking at her. "New cities can be a bit intimidating for a woman on her own."

Sara's blood started a slow boil.

"No sweat," Evan said lightly. "She can come on down with me." He turned the full force of one of his disarming smiles on her. "Don't worry about a thing. I'll keep an eye on you."

I'll bet. "How kind. But I think I can manage. Donna's going with me. We're pretty used to looking after each other."

"I insist." He closed his eyes and raised one palm. "Leave everything to me. I know the perfect hotel for you. I'll make the arrangements. Will you be able to leave on Monday morning?"

Sara smiled tightly. She felt like a bug on a pin. "Certainly we can be ready by then."

"Fine." He stood and closed the top button on his suit jacket. "I'll call you with the time of departure. We'll ride together to the airport, of course."

"Of course." A mixture of annoyance and excitement brought hot blood to her cheeks.

"Until next Monday, then." He'd reached the door.

"Next Monday."

CHAPTER ELEVEN

THE HOTEL IN SAN FRANCISCO looked out over the water, its terraced front rising in a series of balconies, each set farther back than the one below it. The effect was a beautiful blending with the city's hills. Ornamental plants, draped artfully over the balconies, added to the charm. Their perfection left Sara with the sneaking idea all the foliage had been put in just before dawn and would only be allowed to remain until tomorrow's dawn when new greenery would be installed for the tourists' pleasure.

In crossing the really splendid lobby, Sara had felt Donna's hand slide into hers. All the shining marble, hanging plants and polished brass in torturously twisted designs was somewhat overwhelming. Elevators like glass balloons soared upward many stories pausing, as if hanging here and there when stopping at various floors, then descending in the same graceful fashion. She and Donna had seemed surrounded by great, slowly bouncing bubbles.

She wished now, most fervently, that she was back at the hotel. Well, actually, she wished she was back in Vancouver. At home. At work. Going about her everyday business. She did *not* want to be here in the graceful living room of Laura and Mark Hunt's palatial Pacific Heights home. She shifted uneasily in her chair and took another tentative sip of the delicate white wine Laura had so eagerly served to her.

Sara begrudged the hours she must spend in Laura Hunt's company. She had carefully planned her time-table. Just so long for this get-acquainted brunch, or whatever it was. Then so much time tomorrow for the christening ceremony. After that she would attend to business. She had arranged to rent a car for this afternoon and most of tomorrow. Already, she'd set up appointments to visit a fish cannery here in San Francisco and one in Monterey. It would be difficult to adhere to her plans for a working holiday in the face of Laura's graciousness.

"You have a lovely child, Sara."

She started, almost spilling her wine, and looked up into Mark Hunt's startlingly tawny eyes, unexpected in a man with such blond hair.

"Thank you, Mark. I think she's pretty special, too. Funny how you don't know how much a child can mean before you have one of your own."

He smiled down at her. His was a genuine smile that made deep dimples beside his mouth. "Isn't that the truth? Little Evan's taken over the roost around here."

"He's sweet. And handsome, as well." One was supposed to say all the right things to the parents of newborns. "I suppose he gets that from you."

"Hah." Mark tilted his head and laughed. He had perfect teeth. "The baby's good-looking all right, but he takes after his mother in that respect."

She followed his gaze to Laura. Mark was clearly as desperately in love with his wife as Evan had re-marked.

Laura Hunt. This was the woman who had been the grand passion of Evan's life. Covertly Sara watched her while she tried to keep up her end of the conversation. The wide, piercing blue eyes, the cloud of soft dark hair, the classically chiseled features of her cameo face, the grace—the exquisite grace—with which she moved. A clown, Evan had said. But before Laura Hunt had been a clown, she must have been a dancer or a gymnast.

And there was something special between Laura and Evan—that much was clear, too. At some point after their paths had crossed, a bonding had taken place between them and it remained to this day, firm and strong.

Mark had asked her a question. Sara stared uncomprehendingly at him. "I'm sorry. I didn't hear what you said."

"I'm not surprised over all this chit-chat," he said, laughed. "I just asked if you'd excuse me. I'd better see if I can do something useful."

Sara nodded and smiled, registering his tall, well-built body as he moved away. Mark was an attractive man. She went back to watching Laura, watching her with Evan. She reached the reluctant conviction that it would always be the same with these two. There was a deep *understanding*. They had a shared awareness that must be precious to both of them. It made Laura's quick laugh commence before Evan finished his joke. It made Evan's eyes film over the moment he took Laura's baby into his arms.

"She's pretty, isn't she?" It was just the faintest whisper from Donna, who had come to wedge herself into a big chair beside Sara.

"Very," Sara murmured in return, smiling vacantly. Donna was feeling somewhat shy in the group of strangers and only ventured far enough to get more fruit punch or one of Laura's exquisite canapés.

This was just to be a "family brunch," Laura had said. Sara let her gaze roam over the group. She saw Laura and Evan, talking to each other over the baby's head. Then there was Mark, effortlessly being a perfect host. And Bruce Fenton, Laura's cousin; fairhaired, rangy, pleasant, humorous but a bit diffident in manner. The last member of the group was Irma, Mark's mother, too elegant in her calf-length suede skirt to be a grandmother, but enjoying it anyway.

"She's not as pretty as you, Mom."

"What?" Sara looked sharply at Donna, who frowned into her punch glass.

"Mrs. Hunt isn't as pretty as you, and Evan doesn't like her as much."

This *child* of hers was too wise. "It doesn't really matter very much anyway, Donna, does it?"

Donna's frown deepened. "If you say so, I guess."

"I do say so."

Irma Hunt got up now and came over to Sara, seating herself on the low ottoman by her knees.

"You should see those two doing their act. Evan and Laura, I mean. They were awfully good together—almost as if they had one mind. Do you like clowns?"

"Oh yes," Sara agreed. "Who in the world doesn't? Did Laura give it up when she married?"

"Oh, no. She does a lot of benefit performances. And she's taught classes in clowning, too. It's quite an art, you know. That is, if you're really good."

"I'm sure it is," Sara agreed politely. She was just barely listening to Irma's account of the plans for the christening tomorrow of little Evan. Sara wished with a burning intensity that Laura had chosen any name but "Evan." And this godfather business. Was it a way of more closely binding Evan to her? He was obviously besotted with the infant. Evan liked children and was good with them. Donna had been his devoted slave since her birthday party. The stint they'd served together as her own watchdog had only deepened their relationship.

Sara felt her confidence sink even lower. Whoever married Evan had better be prepared to give him children, probably several. And why in the world had Laura chosen Mark? True, he was handsome, but Evan was even better looking. And funnier. And nicer.

And was Laura regretting her choice now?

Unable to stop herself, Sara swung her gaze back to Laura.

"Laura and Evan are such good friends," Irma was saying. "They were both living in Seattle and each had been through a bad time, so they propped each other up—or so Laura says. She makes light of it, the way people do sometimes about important things."

Wise lady, this Irma Hunt. Just how far had Laura and Evan's "propping up," gone, Sara wondered.

She sank back in her chair and watched Evan get up and leave Laura, the baby in his arms. *Don't bring him to me,* she said silently and, with a plummeting heart, watched him approach.

"Isn't he terrific?" Evan asked her, his eyes shining. "If you're desperate to hold him, I'll let you. For five minutes. But he's *my* godson—we mustn't forget that.''

Dismayed, Sara held out her arms, able to do little else. She quelled a sudden wild panic. She wasn't used to babies. She had held each of her two nephews when they were small, but she enjoyed them now they were older. She could almost hear Christine's voice *Hold his head,* and she slid her hand beneath it.

He was a lovely baby. She knew she was making the correct comments as the four of them, Evan, Donna, Irma and herself all hung over his little face. Then suddenly, angrily, the tiny features crumpled and he started to cry. Rationally, she knew it had nothing to do with her, but she felt like a fool and hastily handed him back to Evan.

I'm jealous, she thought, with a feeling of shame. It was a sobering idea. *Jealous and angry.* How ridiculous and unreasonable. A few weeks ago she had not known that Evan McGrath existed and her life had been orderly and good. Now she was seated in Laura Hunt's lovely room, seething. Jealous that Evan had had a rich and varied life before he met her. Jealous of the bond between him and Laura. Angry at whatever malignant fate had made her path cross his and awakened in her again emotions she had thought long gone. And *now*—of all times—when she was in an embattled position, holding onto her career by her fingernails. *Now*, when she was thirty-seven and past the age she could start having a big family of children. Everything was all wrong. She was startled by Donna twisting around to give her a quick, feather-light kiss on the cheek. The child must be sensing her unhappiness.

Panic engulfed her. Had she revealed in her expression any of the turbulence in her mind? She lowered her face over her wine glass, hiding, and let the others' conversation eddy around her for a moment. Then, to her vast relief, Laura's housekeeper announced that brunch was ready.

It was Laura herself who came to Sara's side as they walked into the dining room. "I'm so glad you could come and be with Evan—and us, of course. He's always been a bit of a loner. I'm always happy when he makes a good friend."

Sara took the seat assigned to her. *A good friend.*

Thoroughly miserable, she pushed food around her plate at the beautifully appointed table.

"It'll probably get worse, you know," commented a low voice at her side, and she realized she was next to Laura's cousin, Bruce.

"What do you mean?" she asked, really looking at him for the first time. He was personable, almost elegant. Not exactly handsome but with the look of privilege, as if he had never had much trouble getting by in life. His eyes were dark gray with a glint of humor, his hair thick and fair, and faintly tousled looking. He had an air of casualness, possibly because he had arranged his very tall body loosely and comfortably at the dining room table, something not easy to accomplish.

"It's the OPB syndrome. There's a limit to the amount of it I can take. I can see it's beginning to wear your edges down too." There was a languid quality in his voice that made her want to smile.

"OPB—what's that? I'm Canadian, you know. Maybe you'd better translate."

"Other People's Babies. Before we sat down to dinner, the total conversation of six adults and one child, for the last ninety minutes, concentrated exclusively on The Infant. If they can't control it better I'm going to suggest a game or something—although I usually despise games. Would you like a little more wine?"

"No, thanks. And I'm not much for games myself. If you're thinking of a card game, I'm afraid I'm a dud."

"Actually, I was thinking more of something like let's-throw-the-baby-out-the-window."

Sara gave a little yelp of laughter in spite of herself. "Evan's making a real fool of himself," she agreed, and could have bitten her tongue. Then she felt a sudden warmth in the flash of understanding in Bruce's eyes. Somehow she had revealed her feelings and he had seen. She had the odd comforting feeling that she'd found a friend in an unlikely place.

"Be waspish going home," Bruce advised. "Really stick it to him. He's got it coming."

"I intend to, but I have to be careful. My daughter's crazy about him. Although she may change her mind if he continues being so besotted with The Infant."

This wasn't the case, however, as Donna had become at ease by now and seemed to hang on every word pertaining to The Infant and tomorrow's ceremony. Did she miss not having any brothers or sisters? Sara wondered.

Forget it, Sara admonished herself. This was no time to start worrying about whether or not Donna should be an only child forever. She had enough on her mind.

As hurriedly as politeness allowed after brunch, Sara prepared to leave. Now, at last, she could break up the cozy Laura and Evan twosome, she thought, as in decency he'd have to offer to take her back to the hotel so she could pick up her rental car. A moment later, however, she swallowed her exasperation. This was not to be. Somehow, it was necessary for Evan to stay here for some business matter with Mark Hunt.

"I'll drop you," Bruce offered, and she felt a rush of gratitude. Maybe it was better this way. Evan was so intuitive that he would know immediately she was upset and want to know the reason. She couldn't very well say, *I'm jealous as sin of Laura Hunt, and I'm so sick of your crummy little godson, I could scream*. She could only thank Laura as warmly as could be managed for a lovely time and agree blandly to Donna's anxious request that she be allowed to stay with Evan and the baby. Sara was thoroughly ashamed of herself. She had always felt that jealousy was a contemptible emotion yet here she was, helplessly burning with it.

Three hours later, after a visit to the San Francisco fish cannery, Sara was actually humming in the shower. She felt a lot better. There was nothing like the smell of ten tons of fish cooking to make a person feel at home, she thought, and Evan was hers for the evening. That had a lot to do with it, she knew.

"We're driving across Golden Gate Bridge in the nighttime," Donna was shouting from the bedroom.

Evan was *theirs*, that is, hers and Donna's.

"That's nice," she called back.

"He said those funny gooseneck lamps shine yellow and wavery, did you know that? Can I wear my jeans?"

"No, I didn't know it, and no to jeans." Sara turned off the water and stepped out onto the bath mat. "You wear a dress."

"And then we're going to eat at a real posh place in Belvedere," Donna shouted, "right on the edge of the water."

"Shh. You don't have to shout now. I'm out of the shower."

Big deal, she thought. What was so great about eating right on the edge of the water down here when she could do it any day of the week in Vancouver? Donna didn't think it was such a big deal there.

"What'd you say, Mom? I can't hear you when you mumble." Donna's voice, speaking in a hoarse whisper, sounded as if she were just on the other side of the door, leaning against it.

"Nothing, dear. You can have the bathroom now. I'm through." Drying off she made a mental vow to put jealousy behind her. It was juvenile, immature and totally unworthy of her.

The next morning, Sara tried to recall what fun the three of them had had but it was cold comfort now. In exactly thirty-three minutes she would be standing in Grace Cathedral at a christening. She hoped Bruce Fenton would be there. Evan, changed now from the charming escort of last night back into a tiresome godfather of today, was pacing downstairs in the lobby. Heaven forbid that they be late for the christening of Laura bloody Hunt's baby. And *of course* the glass bubble elevator would be slow in coming.

When it finally did, she closed her eyes going down. Looking into the marble-floored lobby miles below made her even queasier.

Driving up the hill of California Street with Evan, in one of Mark Hunt's cars, she duly took note of the Cathedral as soon as its austere soaring towers came into view. Everyone back at the office would want to hear all about what she had seen in San Francisco. Okay, she was seeing a gray stone cathedral that seemed to spread over a city block and was about a mile high. That would be impressive.

When they entered into the nave proper from the outer hallway, she was a little stunned at its size. No service was in progress, but there was a scattering of people, some kneeling, some just sitting apparently in meditation, possibly waiting for the next service to begin.

"We're around here," said Evan as he took her arm and led her to the left side of the main altar. There, tucked in toward the back and scarcely visible from any of the pews, was a small jewel of a chapel. "We're in St. Vincent's Chapel for this," he added, as they walked under a row of tall, narrow stained-glass windows. Sara had an impulse to pause and look up at the figures depicted in gem-colored tones, but Evan hurried her along. The windows had seemed odd, but it was probably just the angle.

They were all there. The Hunt family and a dozen or so of their friends. Sara pasted a wide smile on her face and went in, knowing Evan would immediately disappear from her side to take his place by the parents around the font. She let go of Donna's hand and watched her child also go directly to the front row.

Then, with a small sigh of relief she saw Bruce Fenton in the next to last row and went to stand beside him.

They had got to the part of the rite in which Evan was saying, "I present Evan William to receive the sacrament of baptism..." when she gave a small gasp of surprise, as she realized suddenly why the stained-glass windows seemed unusual. They didn't depict saints at all. Or if they did, the saints were in modern dress.

"What's up?" Bruce whispered almost inaudibly.

"The windows," she whispered, "the saints are—"

Bruce was shaking his head. "Not saints," he mouthed. "People. Earthly overachievers. Henry Ford. Thurgood Marshall and other American folk heroes."

"Really?" she breathed, fascinated. "Imagine that." Then the woman next to her said, "Ssh," and both she and Bruce meekly subsided.

Immediately after the service she went to Evan.

"Evan, did you know that the windows..." Her voice trailed off. He didn't even hear her. He wasn't even listening. He was handing Laura Fenton Hunt her baby, and their eyes met in a long look. Sara went cold. She was filled with a sense of dull gray depression, as cold as the dull gray walls of the stone cathedral.

Did he wish this child were his?

Or was he simply back in another time of his life, when he was in love with Laura Fenton and they were clowns together, laughing?

CHAPTER TWELVE

BRUCE GLANCED DOWN at the straight-backed little figure beside him. The kid looked scared to death. Maybe bringing Donna to Chinatown hadn't been such a hot idea.

"Wild, huh?" He fixed a grin in place and stopped walking. "Did you ever see so many people or so much stuff?"

The small, perfect face turned slowly up. "No."

He saw more than heard Donna's reply. Her eyes slid away briefly, then returned to his. Their dark, unblinking quality suggested an inner calm belied by the set of her mouth.

"Hey—" Jeez, he must have been nuts to get into this. What did he know about miniteenagers, or what they liked? "Ah...is this place a bit crowded for you? Would you rather go somewhere else...Ghirardelli Square, Fisherman's Wharf, Union Square. Anywhere?"

She shook her head and smiled. Beautiful girl. No wonder Sara Fletcher adored her, and Evan McGrath already behaved like a doting uncle. Bruce returned the smile and shoved his hands in his pockets.

"There's a bunch of trendy little boutiques in the Ghirardelli Square and clowns and mimes—"

Again, the black braids wiggled back and forth over her shoulders. Did thirteen-year-olds usually still wear braids? He didn't know, but the hairstyle made her look even younger.

"Okay." He wished she weren't quite so silent. "We'll push on, then. This end of Grant Avenue's pretty touristy, but farther down you get to the shops the local people use. You'll probably enjoy that more."

He'd volunteered for this duty, and it was in a good cause, he reminded himself. The tension between Evan and Sara had been palpable. Without being certain, he had a pretty good idea what was wrong. He'd watched Sara sizing up Evan's behavior around Laura. She probably felt threatened by Evan and Laura's old ties.

"It's so loud," Donna said, leaning toward him, and he started.

Words formed quickly behind his lips. Adult words. Sure, most city streets were loud, and San Francisco was particularly densely populated in its central areas, but nervous thirteen-year-olds needed something other than facts when they were unsure.

Hesitantly he held out a hand. "It sure *is* loud—and pushy. How about holding on to each other? That way we won't get lost—at least not without someone to get lost with."

Donna didn't hesitate. She curled her fingers around his palm and clung tight. "I'd like to see the stores where the people who live here shop."

Her jaw tilted determinedly, and Bruce felt his throat tighten. Apart from casual contacts with the children of some of his clients—and baby Evan—he'd had no exposure to young people. He'd always thought he had no affinity for them, no real interest. Maybe he was missing something.

He let Donna set the pace. She half ran, and he had to lengthen his stride. Gradually a little color returned to her pale cheeks, but the viselike grip on his hand told him she remained tense.

"This street goes on and on," she called breathlessly over her shoulder. "Is it always so busy?"

"Yes," Bruce said. "Slow down. We've got all afternoon."

She pulled back to a trot. They were among the neighborhood shops now. Before they had left the christening party, he'd told Evan and Sara the sightseeing tour would take some hours—and that he'd call before he brought Donna back to the hotel. He liked those two. From what he'd heard about Evan, the guy deserved some happiness. Maybe if he and Sara could spend some time alone, they'd find a way around whatever was troubling them.

Donna yanked his arm. "What's that smell?" She wrinkled her nose. "Like cinnamon mixed with dust."

He leaned to see across her. "The vegetables, I guess." Heaps of produce spilled from baskets on a sloping display. "I come here a lot—for business. I used to notice all kinds of things I don't anymore."

She picked up a head of Chinese cabbage. "Mom got this once. Tastes okay."

"Yeah. Bok choy." Surely she was used to all these things. "What do you call those?" He pointed to some large, white lumpy vegetables that resembled clumps of bleached carrots.

"How should I know?" She quickly withdrew her hand from his. "Is this some kind of test?"

"Of course not." He frowned, surprised, and crossed his arms. "I just thought you'd know—"

"Beacuse I'm...I'm half-Chinese? A half-Chinese kid should know about Chinese vegetables, right?" She blushed furiously and bowed her head. "You brought me here to let me see a bunch of people like me, too, didn't you?"

Bruce clasped the back of her neck and shook gently. "Donna, I didn't consciously bring you here because of your background. I thought you'd like this part of the city. *I* do. It's fascinating to me."

"Because it's full of people who look different from you?"

"Good grief. Where are you coming from, young lady? That's *not* why I come here, or what I find interesting about the place. I like the feeling of life here. I..." *Hell.* He looked at the sky. He was really making a huge success of his little rescue mission. "Look. I don't know about you, but those fancy bits and pieces at the party didn't fill me up. I'm hungry. Let's eat. We'll get away from here and find a restaurant."

Donna lifted her head. "I'm sorry I was rude," she said in a small voice.

"You weren't—just honest."

She blinked rapidly, and he saw her swallow. "I am a bit hungry, but I don't want to go somewhere else."

Now she was trying to make amends. He wanted to put her at her ease. "We can easily hop on a cable car—"

"There's a hot-dog stand over there. You like hot dogs? They're my favorite food."

Bruce laughed. She was delightful. "You bet I do. Lead on."

In a few minutes, they sat on a wall to eat their paper-wrapped food and drink bilious green punch touted as the limeiest fruit concoction in town. Donna took a sip and set her cup aside without comment. Bruce drank some of his and grimaced. "This stuff is poisonous. Careful where you dump it, it'll rot the concrete."

Donna tipped back her head and laughed, squeezing her eyes tightly shut and showing perfect white teeth. She snorted and covered her mouth with the back of one hand. "You're so *funny*."

He gave her what he hoped was a modest smile. One thing about kids, they were easily pleased, or this one was.

"So," he said when they began retracing their steps on the other side of Grant Avenue. "What do you think of this place now?"

Donna's shoulders came up to her ears and flopped back.

"You aren't comfortable with it, are you?" he persisted. "But you think you ought to be."

The depthless eyes found his again and he thought he detected sadness, and perhaps confusion, there. "I don't know," she said. "Kind of, maybe."

"I should have thought of that. You can't be part of this. I couldn't, except as an outsider, and your world's the same as mine. Grown-ups can be a bit dumb sometimes, huh?"

She touched his arm. "You're not dumb. You're neat, and I'm glad we came. I should be able to cope with my whole self."

His stomach pulled in. "So little and so old."

"I'm not little." An exasperated frown puckered her smooth brow. "I'm thirteen."

Not thinking, he pulled one of her braids. "I forgot for a moment."

"Stupid braids. I'm the only one in my grade who still wears a kid's hairstyle."

He wasn't about to respond to that comment. A silver-and-purple fish kite billowed above a nearby shop doorway. "I've been in here before." He poked at shiny scales, and the kite twirled. "Come on. We'll see what they've got."

The interior of the shop was dark and crowded with merchandise. Embroidered satin slippers vied with brilliant tassled lanterns. Jars of pickled peppers and little string bags of dried radish and fruit were tucked between lacquered boxes.

Bruce had picked up a doll with a beautiful porcelain face when he noticed the proprietor talking quietly to Donna. The diminutive body was stiff again. She seemed rooted to the rough board floor.

"What is it?" He approached quickly, keeping a smile on his face. Then he knew the answer. The lady was bowing and talking to Donna in Chinese.

"She, uh..." Bruce cleared his throat. "Donna doesn't speak Chinese. She only knows English."

"Ah, I see." The woman grinned broadly. "Sorry. But she is very beautiful. Wait, I have something for you—something very lucky for a beautiful girl."

Donna stayed quite still, her eyes downcast, until the shop owner returned. "Here. A thousand tigers—very lucky." Her black eyes were warm.

"A thousand?" Wonderingly, Donna turned the tiny ivory tiger in her palm.

"Yes, a thousand," the woman insisted. "The rest are all inside—too small to be seen."

"Thank you." Donna stroked the little effigy repeatedly.

Bruce bought the doll and left the shop with Donna. For moments they walked in silence.

"I've never let myself think about my father," Donna said suddenly. "I don't think I want to. I've got my family now—I've got Sara and Evan."

Bruce noticed how naturally she'd included Evan but made no comment. "That's the way it should be. We can only handle so much before our minds and hearts go on overload."

She stuffed the tiger into her pocket and patted it. "I'll always keep this, though." She looked at him quickly. "Just as a memento."

"Right," he said. "Keep this, too." He shoved the doll in its tissue wrapping into the crook of her arm. "Don't worry, it's not a kid's doll. You can put it on a shelf."

Her smile was impish and trusting now. "You know a lot about people, don't you?"

"Do I?" Trust was a wonderful thing. Made a man feel ten feet tall.

Donna nodded sagely. "I love Mom and Evan, but I can't talk to them the way I can you."

Bruce squeezed her shoulder. "And I didn't think I'd exactly batted a thousand this afternoon."

"I wish you didn't live so far away," Donna said wistfully, then blushed. She made much of rewrapping the doll in its tissue paper.

"Donna—" Bruce put a hand over hers "—do you feel you need another ear sometimes? Someone else to bounce things off?"

She nodded, keeping her head bowed.

"You could..." He looked at the sky. Fenton was rushing in again, but he would never learn to ignore his dumb heart and he liked this kid. "If you ever feel like it, give me a call."

"On the phone?" She stared at him now, her eyes round.

He grinned. "Might be a bit difficult without a phone unless you've got a bigger voice than I think you do."

"Oh, you." She was the lovliest thing when her face turned pink. "I wish I could call you sometimes only Mom might have something to say about long-distance calls to San Francisco."

"Reverse the charges." Drat, he was really going overboard.

"I could? Really?" Her small fingers were surprisingly strong where she gripped his forearm. "Oh, I will then. But not too often, I promise. You really do understand a lot about people."

Wordlessly, he started forward again. When she slid her hand into his once more, he chafed the backs of her cold fingers and kept moving. There was a lot he *didn't* know about people—and about himself.

"THIS IS SOMETHING, isn't it?" Evan angled forward in the bubble-glass elevator to look at the hanging plants they passed.

Sara peered at the tops of heads in the lobby below. "Uh huh. Something."

"It was good of Bruce to take Donna out. He's a great guy—a bit serious—but solid."

She checked the illuminated panel overhead. *Twelve, thirteen*— "Bruce is a nice young man. Very bright, too. Mark was telling me how hard he works."

"Mmm." Evan followed her glance to the lighted numbers. Fifteen now. Two more floors.

The giltwork around the elevator windows gave off little prisms of light. She was glad Evan had chosen the Hyatt Regency for her and made the bookings. It had been a good choice.

"Almost there," Evan said brightly. "I don't know about you, but I've about had it. I'd give anything to get out of this suit and lie down—" His lips remained parted, a horrified expression in his eyes.

Sara fiddled with a blouse button. The atmosphere between them was charged. Evan's nerves must be as tight as hers but she couldn't help him. Sexual tension was supposed to be history in her life. Now she found she remembered it only too well, but not how to diffuse it.

The elevator bumped to a stop on the seventeenth floor and the doors opened. She passed Evan, then felt him close behind her in the corridor.

At her door, she started fumbling in her purse. *Cool Sara—the lady always in control.* Why didn't her fingers want to work?

"Sara," Evan said gently. "The key's in your hand."

She stared at him, then at the big square tag trailing from her palm—the palm of the same hand in which she held her bag. "Yes," she said, "of course. How stupid of me."

He laughed. "You don't have the corner on that. Remember, I always lose my keys?" No humor reached his eyes.

She opened the door and closed it again when they were both inside. "Here we are. Can I order you a drink, or something?"

Evan crossed to the window, taking off his jacket as he went. "Not for me, thanks. You've got a great view of McArthur Park from here, and East Bay. I've seen this place from the other side. It always reminds me of a terraced mountain."

He tossed the jacket aside, and his tie, and begun rolling up his shirt-sleeves.

"You suggested we talk." Everything that came out of her mouth sounded contrived. They both knew what was probably going to happen in this room.

He faced her. "You were uptight at the christening party."

"Not really."

"Let's not play games, Sara."

She was unbearably hot. "I don't play games. I don't even like them. If my memory serves me, you're the one with all the tricks."

"Damn." He raked at his hair with both hands. "We don't have that long before Donna comes back. Do we have to waste what time we do have arguing?"

"Instead of having sex!"

She threw her purse on the chest of drawers and shrugged out of her suit jacket. The hammering in her chest was suffocating.

"I don't believe you said that."

"We aren't coy teenagers." She turned her back and began unbuttoning her blouse. "On Mount Seymour you said you wanted to make love to me and couldn't wait very long.''

Evan's hands, firmly gripping her shoulders, spun her around. His face was a rigid mask. "What's the matter with you? What are you doing?" He took in the length of her, deliberately, pausing to stare at her breasts beneath her lacy camisole before concentrating the power in his eyes on her face. "I said I wanted to make love to you, yes. Not that I wanted to *have sex*. That's always available.''

She would not tremble. And she *would not* cry. "You loved Laura Hunt once, didn't you?"

"I..." Evan closed his eyes, and his fingers bit more deeply into her arms. "Yes, I probably did. Just as you once loved Michael Winston. Both over. Right?" His lashes flickered.

"Michael's dead. Laura's very much alive.'' Even as she finished speaking, she hated the words. She sounded jealous.

Evan grasped her jaw, ran his fingers through her hair to clamp her head. "And I have to prove I don't love Laura anymore. You don't have to do a damn thing to make me believe you're emotionally unattached. How convenient..." He was hurting her scalp. The hard little kiss he planted on the side of her neck sent a shaft of heat into her loins. He pressed his lips into the hollow above her collarbone, then swiftly, more gently, against the top of her breast. "You think I'm still pining for Laura, is that it?''

"No, I mean ... I'm not being fair. Evan—"

He shook her, pulled her to her toes. "How do I prove I love you? How do I make you believe I think of you every damn minute of my life? I want you. What does it take to make you believe that?''

She opened her mouth but no sound came. He'd said . . .

"Don't you want to be with me? Am I repulsive to you? Say it, Sara—say you want me to go away and I will.''

Her blouse slipped from her shoulders and caught at her wrists. "I love you, Evan. I love you. Stay with me.''

"*Say* it!''

"Evan," she whispered. "I love you.''

Slowly the wild light left his eyes. The bright gleam of passion settled over his features. "You love me?''

"Please take me to bed." She tried to put her arms around his neck but her sleeves pulled. "I've been so afraid . . . so very afraid. I only cared about one man before you, Evan. He said he'd never leave me. I couldn't take it . . .''

"God willing, you won't have to." His fingers shook as he released her cuffs and waited for her to pull her hands free. "Don't you think maybe some-one up there knows we both need a one-only friend for keeps?" He stroked her hair, kissed her jaw again, her throat. "I know I do." His voice turned gruff.

Little shards of disbelief drove relentlessly into every nerve. "Evan. Don't get mad. I saw the way you looked at Laura—and little Evan. You wished they were yours, didn't you?''

He sighed, his lips in the hollow between her breasts. "I was glad they are mine—the way they are— as special parts of my life.''

Her throat ached. "You make me feel so small and so petty."

"Does that mean I have you in my power?" He raised his head and stared at her narrowly. "Getting to this point hasn't been easy, you know. I'd like to be sure exactly where I stand."

For an instant she wavered, then laughed. "Evan McGrath, you *are* a clown. How does anyone recover that fast? A minute ago I thought you'd never forgive me for being suspicious."

"I'd forgive you anything, lady," he murmured. "Anything. Don't you know that, yet?"

Sara watched his mouth. "Kiss me."

His lips, wide, firm, covered hers gently. He did kiss her, again and again, his hands ranging over her back, her sides and waist and finally, her bottom, drawing her tight against him.

"Let me..." Sara began, only to succumb again, breathlessly, to his stroking mouth, his carefully probing tongue.

She forced her hand between them to unbutton his shirt and push it from his shoulders. He *was* an athlete, beautifully toned and muscled, his long sinews smooth beneath her exploring touch.

"It's still daylight, Evan..."

She heard his laugh, felt the warmth of his breath on her ear, before her actions and reactions, her emotion and senses swept into unison with his.

Their clothes became a tangle on the floor, and they clung to together on Sara's narrow bed. Their limbs, their mouths—the words that came from body and heart and two minds—bound as one.

Evan coaxed, "Relax, my love," and smoothed her face and hair. He kissed her lips. His broad hands massaged soft skin yearning for his touch, surrounded breasts too long denied a man's adoring touch.

She heard her own whispered request come from far, far away, "Close the blinds." Rather than severe, she sounded husky, sexy, even to herself. "*Evan*, it's daylight."

He laughed and said, "Such decadence, my sweet," against her ear, blowing, kissing the sensitive spot below. "Love in the afternoon."

She pulled away to look at his face. "Isn't that the name of a book or a movie or something?"

"If it isn't it should be," Evan said against her neck. "Maybe we'll write one anyway—later."

He aroused her until her flesh throbbed. He covered her body, used his own, every part of it, until she felt her defenses destroyed, laid raw and longing to be forever vulnerable.

With his mouth and hands he made her pulsate, beg, demand that he come to her. When he did, their union dragged a cry from her soul, but Evan's yell eclipsed the voicing of her passion.

"YOU'RE SURE Donna's spending the night with Irma?" Sara asked.

Evan massaged her neck. "Mmm. For the fourth or fifth time. That's what Irma said on the phone just now. Relax."

She lay back against him in the bathtub. On either side of her body, a flexed thigh hemmed her in. "I didn't talk to her. So I wondered . . ." The muscles in those thighs were so solid. She trailed the backs of her fingers from his knee to his groin and smiled when he jumped. "Evan, you have the sexiest legs." Bending, she nipped her way along the path her fingers had taken.

"Stop, fiend!" He clasped her forehead and tilted her head back until he could kiss her lips. "Stop for a second anyway, and concentrate—" His other hand scooped water over her shoulder before he stroked, then covered her breast, rotated a palm over her nipple. "Would I want Donna to walk in on us like this?"

"No." She squirmed and rolled her head from side to side.

"Look at me."

"That's not possible."

"Anything's possible."

"Evan—stop—"

Under the powerful tutelage of his hands she was turned to kneel astride him in the huge tub.

"Possible?" he demanded, grinning.

"Possible, you depraved—"

"Yes?"

She spread her hands wide over his chest. "You wonderful, depraved, incredibly sexy man. Anything's possible."

Water dripped from her hair onto his upturned face and, curling slowly lower, she kissed the drops from his lips, his chin, his chest, down over his flat stomach until he grabbed her shoulders and held her fast. Yet again, the voluptuous longing thrummed in her belly. "Donna." She turned her face, rubbing him with her cheek. "Donna's spending the night with Irma because Irma wants her to." Evan kneaded her back, moaning quietly. Sara pressed her face against him once more. Every inch of this man was precious and he had the power to disconnect her brain. She looked up into his face, her blood pumping harder and harder. "Mark and Laura don't wonder where you are because they think you're with Bruce. And Bruce...?"

"Is a terrific, understanding guy. Don't concentrate anymore, except on me." His hands beneath her arms, pulling, dragged her breasts slowly over the length of him until she felt his breath on her face.

"Yes." Her legs slid and her mouth met Evan's. "Terrific," she managed to say, feeling him enter her again. "You're terrific."

His hips lifted against her. "Only with you, my sweet one. And never before. I adore you." He closed his eyes, and his lips parted in a lover's warm smile.

Sara looped her arms around his neck and gave herself to the ancient rhythm that was human love. She couldn't lose him—ever. Somehow she'd make this work for all time.

CHAPTER THIRTEEN

EVAN PULLED THE MERCEDES to a quiet stop in front of her house and Sara sighed gently. It had been such a perfect evening.

After a hassle-filled two days back at work for both of them, trying to catch up, they had decided on a leisurely Friday night dinner to unwind. They had gone to the Granville Hotel on Granville Island for a late and delicious meal. Afterward they had lingered over an after-dinner drink in the crowded, noisy bar. Taped music throbbed around them, precluding all conversation, so they had simply sat close together, hands clasped loosely between them on the banquette, and sipped their drinks. They had kept looking at each other and smiling—it seemed impossible not to smile. Sara felt she would remember the evening for the rest of her life. It was a small and perfect gem in her memory already. Evan had had Drambuie and she a liqueur flavored with roses that she had never tasted before. There had been a hint of bitterness in the aftertaste, as there is a faint bitterness in the heady scent of roses breathed too deeply.

Now, she leaned her head back against the seat and the lights of a passing car shone clearly on Evan's face for a moment.

"You're almost smiling," she said. "Why?"

"Because you leaned your head back. That's a good sign."

She laughed softly.

"I'm taking it for a sign that you're a girl who makes love on the first date."

"Evan!" She sat up. "First date! What *are* you talking about?" She felt warmth rise in her face at the sudden remembrance of their time together in San Francisco. Without volition. she moved fractionally closer to him.

"This is our first official date," he said. "Don't you realize that? We've never really had a date before, Sara. Tonight was it." He sounded wistful, half turning in the seat, placing his strong hand at her waist. Another moment and he would draw her into his arms.

She felt a rush of yearning mingled with dismay. He was right. Their relationship had been backward and awry from the very beginning. First she had been intent on getting rid of him. Then, a short time later, she had lain in his arms in a hotel in San Francisco. It had gone too fast. Thinking that logic had little to do with love, Sara rested her hand on his, holding it for a moment against her and then moving it away.

"Even so, we're a bit past the stage of making love in the back seat, aren't we?" She wanted to laugh and at the same time felt a sting of tears in her eyes.

He did laugh. "I wasn't thinking of the back seat, my love. I was thinking of your lovely round bed. The first time I saw that bed it nearly undid me."

They were both laughing now. "Oh sure," Sara choked. "And we'll just tell Donna to run along and play."

He groaned. "Oh hell. I love that kid to death, but..."

"Yes, but..." She slid her hand under the door handle and gave it a push. "That says it all for the moment, I'm afraid."

"For the moment, you said? That sounds hopeful. Well, I'll see you to the door anyhow. I presume I'm stopping at the door. Are you positive on that point? Think a minute."

"Positive. And believe me, I'm sorry," she added.

"My place then," he persisted. "Look, we've both had a tough couple of days at work. We're entitled—"

"Evan," she interrupted him, laughing. "Mrs. Beamis is here baby-sitting. She probably wants to go home. Okay?"

He sighed. "Okay. But I had to try. You must understand that," he insisted, getting out and coming to her side of the car.

They mounted the porch steps, and Sara was groping in her purse for her door key when Mrs. Beamis flung the door open wide. For a moment, with the hall lights behind her, they could not see her face.

"Oh, Mrs. Fletcher. At last. Come in please." The housekeeper's voice was thick.

Sudden panic flared in Sara and she hurried inside, Evan close behind. "What is it? What's the matter?" Her voice trailed away as she saw Mrs. Beamis's swollen eyes and reddened face. "Oh, Mrs. Beamis, you've been crying," she said in dismay. "Come in here. Tell me what's wrong." Displaying more confidence than she felt, Sara put an arm around the other's waist and led her toward the living room.

"It's that Crawford woman. Donna's...you know...mother. She came. And I tried to get you at your office, but you'd gone. And they didn't know where. And I didn't know what to do. I tried..." Suddenly the woman was crying again and embarrassed that she was. "I'm sorry," she muttered. "I'm really sorry."

Sara had gone suddenly sick at the mention of Donna's biological mother, but she pretended calmness.

"Sit down here." She eased Mrs. Beamis into a big chair and pulled the ottoman up close to it, for herself. "Evan, can you get Mrs. Beamis some water, or something? Please, Mrs. Beamis. Don't cry. Just tell me what happened. Where's Donna now?" She was patting the woman's arm, trying to quiet her.

This brought a fresh deluge of tears.

"Oh, *damn*," Mrs. Beamis said, coughing. "I never cry. I *never* cry," she added in a kind of outrage. "It's just that she's so sweet...Donna, I mean. She's such a kind little person. You know that, don't you? Did you know she fetches and carries for me a dozen times a day because I have arthritis? You didn't know that, did you?" She buried her blotched face in her large capable hands.

"Here, drink this." Evan went down on one knee beside the chair, one broad hand on Mrs. Beamis's heavy back, rubbing back and forth. "Come on, now. We're here. Everything will be fine. Drink this. Just take a sip."

Mrs. Beamis raised her streaming face toward him blindly and took the glass in shaking hands, obediently swallowing some of the amber liquid.

"I said water," Sara commented faintly.

"Well, obviously she's upset. I thought this might be better. It's just a weak bourbon and water. It will help calm her down a bit."

Mrs. Beamis took a second swallow and shuddered slightly.

"Thanks. Thank you, Mr. McGrath. I'm sorry." She breathed deeply. "That woman—girl—whatever. Prairie Crawford came this evening. Walked right up to the door as large as life and rang the bell. Come to see Donna, she said. So what could I do. After all, she *is* Donna's real mother. I . . ." Her voice got quavery again, and Evan patted her shoulder.

"Hey, hey," he said softly. "Hang on now, give us the whole story. You're doing fine."

"Well, they talked a while, see. I couldn't very well stay in the room and watch them like a jailer, but I stayed close. I want you to know that, Mrs. Fletcher. And pretty soon they went upstairs and then they came downstairs. I was at the bottom of the stairs, waiting. I had wanted to follow them up but didn't feel it was right, somehow, you see what I mean?"

"Yes, of course," Sara said, her voice tight. "Go on."

"This Prairie person—and that's a stupid name for a woman, I must say—this Prairie person had Donna's suitcase. Her *suitcase* Mrs. Fletcher. And Donna had on her backpack." She was twisting her hands together in her lap. "And they said they were going away for a few days. And I said, 'a few days, what do you mean?' and 'does your mother know about this' and they were going out the door. Mrs. Fletcher, it happened that fast. Then Donna, that darling Donna, turned around and said, 'Don't you worry, Mrs.

Beamis. It's only for a few days. Just for a visit. And I left Mom a note upstairs in her bedroom.'"

"Donna left a note!" Sara said, her throat constricting.

Evan was on his feet. He took the stairs two at a time.

"I tried not to worry," Mrs. Beamis continued, "but I couldn't help it. She seems to...that Crawford woman...seems so vague, so addled. I can't help but worry. And then I called your office..." Her voice trailed away as Evan came leaping down the staircase.

"Here it is." He handed the note to Sara.

She took it, a lump the size of a boulder in her throat. Donna had used her prettiest letter paper and had secured the envelope with her special blue sealing wax. The big *D* was stamped clearly in the middle of it. She had taken great care with her handwriting.

Dear Mom:
Prairie came to see me today. I hope you don't mind. She had a lot to talk about. I was very polite even when she repeated herself. She looked pretty nice today. She wants me to go and visit with her for a little while. I told her I couldn't miss school anymore. She didn't say where we were going because she didn't know yet. I'll be back soon, Mom.

Love,
Donna

PS Will you feed the fish in my aquarium? Please don't forget. Tell Evan hello.

"That doesn't sound too bad," Sara said, when she could finally speak. "She says she'd be back soon, you see?" She handed the note to Evan, who had been reading it over her shoulder.

"Has she done this before?" he asked soberly.

"No," Sara admitted. "But she spent the first years of her life with Prairie, and certainly she loves her. She couldn't help but love her. It wasn't her idea to be put up for adoption. It's just that Prairie couldn't care for her and . . . and . . ." She stopped, biting her lips.

"I'm sorry. What should I have done?" Mrs. Beamis spoke from the chair, sounding exhausted.

"Nothing. You tried to get me and couldn't. I should have called home and told you where I'd be. I didn't. If there is any fault, it's mine." Sara paused a moment, thinking sickly of Donna. Where was she now? At this moment, where was her daughter? In some bright neon-lit arcade with vacant-faced, aimless Prairie, putting coins in slots? In some cheap motel eating greasy fried chicken from a paper bag? She felt her hands clenching into fists. She wanted to scream. Instead she forced herself to speak calmly.

"Evan, could you take Mrs. Beamis home? I should stay here in case there's a call."

"Sure," he said quickly. Then, at the door, he added, "I'll be back, Sara."

Sara shut the door behind him, returned to the living room and stood in the center. *How odd,* she mused realizing she still had her coat on. Even so, she sat down on the hassock again without taking it off. It didn't matter. She felt cold in the perfectly warm room. She huddled there, bracing herself for the guilt-laden if onlys. If only she hadn't wanted a career so badly. If only she had been content to stay at home and have her family like Christine.

Husband. Home. Children. Maybe Christine had the right idea after all. For years she had secretly resented Christine wasting her college years. Now, somehow or other, it seemed Christine might be right and she might be wrong. At least Christine had her own children. No pale, vague, little child-woman could wander in and take any of them away. *She didn't say where we were going because she didn't know yet.* Christine didn't have to build herself a counterfeit family by borrowing the child some other woman had borne. *I'll be back soon, Mom.* She would, too. Donna would come back. She must. Because she wanted to, needed to. Because this was her home, and Sara was her real mother regardless of who had borne her. Or because Prairie would get tired of her again and return. *Please,* she prayed. *Oh, please let it be because Donna wants to come home,* she pleaded silently in her mind.

Was she really any better a mother than Prairie had been? The ugly idea startled her. She sat upright on the hassock, looking vacantly into space. Bitter as it was, she must admit that her efforts at mothering so far had been mediocre at best. She would have to do better—oh, much better. She had committed herself to raising Donna to adulthood. Seeing that she got a fair start in life. She had promised herself, and Donna and Prairie, and the provincial government, that she would do this. The adoption had been, in its way, as sacred as a wedding vow. "I, Sara, take thee, Donna, to be my child, and from this day forward..."

Yet, what of the vow when Prairie came wandering in again? Where had she been? She had been sitting beside Evan in a noisy bar. *Oh, Sara, for shame, for shame. Christine would have handled it better.*

Christine had Ben, and he was truly hers. She wasn't stealing precious hours with him, knowing it wouldn't last, couldn't last. *I'm too greedy,* she thought. She had wanted the home, the family, the love, the career—but *all* of it together and without paying the toll the way Christine had been willing to do. And had Christine really "wasted" her education? Wasn't she able to simply build a richer, fuller life because of it? How then could it have been wasted?

Greedy, greedy Sara who now had to make do with a borrowed child and a borrowed lover. Because Evan was borrowed. Sara closed her eyes remembering Laura Hunt's baby and Evan's rapt expression as he looked at him.

Yes, he was borrowed. Sara would have him for a little while—*for as long as she could*—but the time would come when he would leave. He would have to. The "right" woman would come along for Evan.

Someone like Christine.

Sara was still sitting on the hassock in her coat when Evan came back. He entered quietly and stood before her, touching her hair gently.

"You okay?"

"Yes." The word sounded hollow. "I've been sitting here brooding, I guess. How's Mrs. Beamis?" Sara got up, feeling old and stiff.

"She's all right. She wasn't crying, anyhow. I kept talking all the way, just to keep things going. I think I convinced her she didn't commit any sort of crime. She didn't, did she? This will come out all right, won't it?"

"Yes. I think so. Donna's a levelheaded kid. And she said she'll be back." Her voice shook slightly. Without any thought at all, she moved toward Evan and felt his arms slide around her beneath her coat. He held her close, resting his chin on her head. It felt so good, so safe.

"I don't mean to be a pessimist," Evan said after a time, "but should we speak to the police? *Should* some authority be alerted?"

"No." She withdrew from his embrace. "I couldn't do that to Prairie—to Donna, really. Donna loves the woman. I had a chance to observe them a couple of times after the adoption. Donna...it's hard to explain. Donna kind of takes care of Prairie. It's a strange little reversal of roles. It's only with me that Donna can be a child, relax, have fun, leave the worrying to someone else. I wanted to give her that, Evan. Childhood can be such a magic time. I wanted to give her a childhood."

Evan picked up Donna's note again and read it. "Well, she seems straightforward enough. She wasn't—kidnapped—or anything. It all seems rather matter-of-fact—the business about feeding the fish and so on. You say you observed them, when? When was that?"

"Oh, early. Not long after the adoption. I know some hold the theory that there should be a complete break with the original parent. I don't—I didn't. Not when the child is so old. It seemed unfair, unnecessarily harsh. Prairie came around, I think, three times. She stayed an hour or two, just visiting with Donna. I left them alone, of course, but I couldn't help now and then getting the drift of the conversation. It was like two girl friends talking, not like mother and daughter at all.'' She was finally getting warm now and let the coat fall to the couch.

"You said that was early in the adoption. She hasn't come around lately at all?" Evan asked, still holding the note.

"No," Sara said tiredly. "Not for a long time, months and months. I had given permission to Prairie from the very first to visit if she wanted to. I thought—with Prairie being the kind of person she is—that she would visit a few times and that would be all. I thought I had been right when she stopped coming. Now..." Her voice shook.

"How long do you think Donna will be gone?" Evan asked after a moment.

Sara shook her head. "Maybe she'll be back tomorrow. Or Sunday. Sunday night at the latest. She has to be in school Monday, and her note said that she told Prairie she can't miss school now." Sara's voice was desperate with hope. "I trust Donna. If she says she'll be back then, she'll be back. It's just a matter of waiting a little while."

Evan dropped the note and went to her. She clung to him, tremors going through her body. "Evan...Evan...Evan..." she whispered against his shoulder. "All of a sudden, I'm so tired I can hardly move." She tried to laugh, but it didn't sound right.

"How would you like a lift up to your big round bed? I can do my Florence Nightingale act again. I should get a badge of some kind, I think."

"You should," Sara agreed, "I'll see to it myself first thing Monday morning. One badge for Evan Nightingale." She felt herself lifted up into his arms and carried across the room to the foot of the staircase. She could feel herself drifting away, withdrawing from all her problems. It had been such a hellish week of too much work, done too fast, with too many unanswered questions hanging over her head. And then to come home and find her "Dear Mom" letter.... A thin wisp of hysteria made her want to laugh but she was too tired. Sleep was smoothing and caressing the ragged edges of her mind, enticing her, enfolding her, covering her up with her silky white down comforter on her round bed. Everything was warmth and softness. And it wasn't even necessary to undress because she was only wearing her slip now.

The turning off of the bedside lamp roused her slightly. Evan stood in the bedroom doorway, clearly outlined by the hall light. "Where are you going?" she asked distinctly.

"Downstairs. Go back to sleep, my love. You need it."

She tried to say thank-you, but it was too much effort.

When she awoke again, she could see gray sky outside the window. It was almost dawn. She had been dreaming of Donna, but couldn't remember the exact content of her dream. She struggled to remember it for a moment and then gave up. Where was Donna now? If only she would call. If only... if, if if...

Sara turned over and watched the familiar shadow of the giant chestnut tree outside her room. Its swaying branches stroked the walls and door. The door. It was partly open and the hall lights were still on. She pushed aside the comforter and went, barefoot, to turn them off. She should have made herself stay awake to at least thank Evan, at least tell him good-night. She snapped off the hall light, only to see the reflected glow of lights downstairs. Then Sara came to the quiet conviction that she wasn't alone. She padded to the head of the stairs."

"Evan?"

"Yeah." He came to the foot of the stairs. He had taken off his jacket and turned up his shirt sleeves. A rolled-up magazine was in one hand. He twisted it into a tighter roll, making the muscles of his forearm move. The light from the living room shadowed half his face.

"Can I get you something? You okay?" His voice was strained.

A steady warmth rose in her body. Evan's skin was gleaming. His shoulders were so broad. She became aware of her bare legs, the clinging lines of the thin cream-colored slip.

"You've been sitting down there all night? Oh, Evan..." She saw his suntanned throat move as he swallowed.

"Better down here than up there, lady." He tried to laugh. "And I wasn't about to leave you all alone."

"Oh, Evan," she whispered. "It's all right. I mean..." Suddenly Sara felt almost overcome by loneliness and need.

"No. It's *not* all right. You're upset, vulnerable. I'm not about to take advantage of an upset, vulnerable lady. I'll wait until you're in fighting form again."

"Oh, you idiot." Her voice caught in her throat. "You don't have to be such a white knight. Come up here." As she said the words, her body felt too hot beneath the silky slip. Holding the banister, she watched him desperately, willing him to come up the stairs.

He stopped when he was two steps below, looking up at her. "You realize, of course, they'd kick me out? You wouldn't want that."

"What? Who'd do what?" She reached out and touched the side of his face.

"The White Knighthood group. They wouldn't stand for this sort of thing." He turned his head so that his lips were moving against her palm.

She caught her breath. "I'm lonely," she whispered. "I need you... with me."

"Sara, Sara." Her name escaped his lips on a long breath. "I need you, too. But is now the time, when you're reaching out for someone, anyone?"

She turned her head away sharply. "You know that's not what I'm doing." There was no question of anger at his words. He was only trying to be sure she knew what she was doing. "It's you I want—need. Oh, Evan." She wrapped her arms tightly around her ribs and sat on a stair.

A slithering, flapping noise made her glance up. Evan's magazine, twisting, sliding, step by step. He'd dropped it, and they both watched until the shiny pages opened flat and fell beneath the railing to the living room floor below.

"You're going to get cold," Evan said quietly. He sat beside her feet. "Go back to bed. Maybe Donna will call."

He'd been waiting for the call, too. "I thought about that when I woke up." Sara entwined her fingers tightly to stop herself from touching him. "She'll come back, Evan. Tomorrow. Sunday. In time to get ready for school. You'll see."

"If we believe hard enough, she will," he agreed vehemently. "And I do believe she will, Sara. She loves you."

"Thank you for saying that."

"It's true."

Sara crossed her arms on her knees and rested her head. Peaceful certainty stole over her. Donna would be back.

Undermining her peacefulness was a tight little ache. It climbed the nerves and tendons in her thighs, wound between her legs, higher, into her belly. Her breasts, so warm inside the bra and slip, swelled. She desired Evan and felt no shame at her wanting.

"Evan," she whispered. "Will you come to bed with me?" Seconds passed, and Sara kept her head on her arms. Each breath thundered in her ears.

Finally a finger passed across her toes. "Yes, sweetheart." Evan encircled each ankle in a strong hand. "You know I will, if you'll let me."

Sara heard him move and looked up, directly into his shadowed face. He knelt before her. "Do you have any idea how you make me feel?" His hands swept upward over her shins, her knees, upward across bare thighs, thin silk panties, until he clasped her waist beneath the slip. "All the time I'm not with you, I think of being with you, like this. I spend time when I should be doing other things imagining what I'd do if we were together. I feel like a star-struck kid. And I love feeling that way. My love...my love... I..." His voice broke and he leaned forward between her knees, buried his face against her breasts, pushing her back on the steps.

The rug burned her skin, but Sara only cared that she held his wide shoulders in her willing hands and urged him closer.

"Sweet, sweet Sara. How I love you." He stood, sweeping her into his arms. "I'm never going to get enough of you."

He kissed her there, standing on the stairs, bracing his weight against the wall to keep them both from falling. Sara parted her lips beneath his, gripped his neck tightly, pulling at his shirt to feel as much of his skin as she could reach.

When Evan carried her up the staircase, he stumbled, step after step, regained his balance each time, kissed her again and again; her lips, her jaw and chin, the hollow at the base of her neck. And all the while her need mounted.

In the bedroom he set her down and moved a few paces away. Tiredness still lingered about his features, but now his eyes burned with an intensity she remembered very well. This man would take her body, and she'd revel in the giving.

Pink light had molded with gray, giving the room a mother-of-pearl sheen. The soft glow painted Evan, the deep white rug and the rumpled quilt on the round bed he coveted.

Sara held out her arms. He circled the room slowly, always facing her, and she walked, too, matching his pace, step for step. He unbuttoned his shirt, pulled it free of his pants, tossed it aside.

"Come here, Sara."

His voice scarcely more than a whisper, broke the rhythm of their slow, silent dance.

She went to him.

"Will you finish this for me?" He touched his belt, then dropped his hands to his sides.

For one instant she watched his eyes, then his mouth. Wordlessly, she undid the buckle, pulled the strip of leather from its loops and dropped it in a soft coil on the rug. Again, she met his eyes.

Muscles in his jaw flexed. "Do the rest for me, Sara. I want you to."

She nodded. The button just below his navel slid free, and the zipper with its sibilant swish. And she hugged him quickly, wrapping her arms around his body, pressing her lips to his chest. "Evan," she murmured. "There are things I've never..."

"I know," he said, "I could tell before." He held her away. "And I like it that you haven't done it all. I like your gentleness. You're my Sara..."

In a single motion he pulled the slip over her head and let it trail from his fingers. The look in his eyes made her feel beautiful. Although no man had ever mentioned her size, before she'd always held the suspicion she was too small, too immaturely built to be a truly desirable woman. Feminine yes, but never voluptuous. With Evan, Sara felt totally alive, totally female.

She breathed deeply and saw him watch the hard rise and fall of her breasts. Swiftly she tugged his pants downward, sinking to her knees, following the path of fabric with her mouth and tongue. What she was doing seemed so natural.

Evan muttered something and she glanced up, folding his hips in a tight embrace. His face was tilted, the tendons in his neck distended. She could fulfill him. "Evan," she said distinctly. "Lift your feet." *Take command,* she ordered herself silently, and reveled in her power to please the man she loved.

Obediently, he let her finish undressing him. He stood still while she kissed his rock-hard thighs, his tensed abdomen. Her splayed fingers on his waist, the small of his back, his buttocks, brought violent trembling. Then he moved, and she knew once more who was the stronger.

"My turn," came his hoarse whisper while he pulled her onto the bed. "Oh, my turn, lady."

He swept her down, falling over her, supporting his weight on his elbows while he stared into her face. Moments passed while he studied her expression. "I'm going to love you and love you, Sara. I'm going to make you forget everything but me."

In seconds he'd stripped away her bra and panties and covered her writhing body with kisses. He clamped a knee on each side of her, spanned her narrow rib cage and lifted her breasts until he could seize first one and then the other nipple between careful teeth and lips.

Sara cried out, but didn't know her own words. Evan's mouth was marvelous torture. "Make love to me," she gasped, trying to still his head, his hands.

He laughed low in his throat. "Soon. Be patient, little one." His mouth moved on over her sides, his tongue and lips wetting her waist and belly, gently pulling and nipping downward to the center of her.

"Evan!" She stilled, clutching his hair. "Evan . . ."

She closed her eyes, squeezed tight the lids. Her skin was afire. The ache became a searing torment straining toward release. She knew this release would be precious, the start of knowing him as she'd known no man, of becoming as close as they could be, as intimate as any man and woman could ever be.

Evan rubbed her hips harder, reached up to cover each breast and she felt in one fraction of a second, first a letting go, then increased desire. "Come to me, my love." Her voice was so soft, she wondered if she'd spoken aloud.

"Gladly." And he was over her, parting her thighs, pressing inside her, filling her. "Gladly, gladly."

They made love in the morning light, rising sun dappling their sweat-slick bodies. Their next cries were wild, yet beautiful in Sara's ears. At this moment, they loved, truly loved, and there could be nothing to surpass the taking—and the giving.

Whatever happened, she would always love Evan McGrath.

THE ROOM WAS in full daylight now. He watched through half-closed eyes as Sara slid silently, inch by inch, to the edge of the bed, trying not to wake him. She shivered slightly, reached his shirt from the chair beside the bed and slid her arms into it, pulling it close about her slim body. Soundless on the carpet, she left the room.

He had to follow her. He just had to. For the rest of his life it would be like this. And he was glad. He pulled on his shorts and went into the hall. He wondered if she had gone downstairs before he noticed that the door to Donna's bedroom was open. He went to stand there. The thin autumn sunlight was brighter now, coming in the window to shine on Donna's fish tank, and on Sara's black silken curtain of hair on his shirt hanging off her shoulders, and on her slim, bare legs.

Very carefully, she was feeding Donna's fish. His throat ached at the sight of her, so small, so vulnerable, so faithful to what she perceived to be her commitments. She was trying to be sure her child would come back to her. For a few hours he'd managed to dull her concern about Donna but only for a few hours.

She glanced over and saw him, and he wanted to withdraw. Her gaze was distant and thoughtful. There was a remoteness in her blue-gray eyes that made him suddenly embarrassed because he had followed her. It seemed as if she had drawn apart not only from him, but also from the whole world, as if she was preparing herself for something.

What would happen if Donna didn't come back, but said she wanted to return to her original mother? Evan knew he had to help prepare her for the worst.

"Sara, are you thinking about Donna?"

"Yes. I see she's taken that doll Bruce Fenton bought her. She really loves that doll." Her eyes roved over the room. She rubbed fish food between her fingers and let it fall onto the water. "There is the possibility," she added cleary, "that Donna may want to return to live with Prairie. Her going off like this is way out of character."

"Well, you could put a stop to that in a hurry. You've legally adopted her, Sara."

"No," she said slowly. "I couldn't stop her. It would have to be what Donna wants and needs." Something like pain came and went in the clear eyes, and a steady trembling moved the slim figure in the big shirt. "She will have to decide between us. I'll do whatever Donna wants."

CHAPTER FOURTEEN

THEY'D BEEN TALKING upstairs for hours. Evan stopped pacing to check his watch. Well, it had been an hour anyway, but it seemed like forever.

He crossed the basement once more and yanked the curtain aside from a high window. Rain pelted from a moonless night sky, splattering the panes. He couldn't remember a more cheerless Sunday evening.

Just as Sara had foretold, Donna and Prairie had showed up in time for Donna to get ready to start the new school week. Now the three of them were upstairs making those decisions Sara had spoken of so calmly for the past two days. He prayed she was still calm and that Donna would decide she wanted to remain with her adoptive mother. He'd insisted on leaving them alone. Perhaps it would have been better if he'd stayed. In her anxiety to preserve everyone else's rights and feelings, Sara could end up being the one hurt. Lord, let him know what to do and say if that happened.

He heard footsteps and turned to see Donna, her freshly chopped-off hair bobbing as she leaped downstairs. "I just talked to Bruce on the phone," she announced breathlessly.

Evan's mind went on overload. "Bruce?" he asked blankly. "Bruce Fenton?"

"Yep." She landed with a thud on the basement rug. "He told me to call him if I ever needed someone to listen. So I did."

This wasn't the time to get irritated. Patience was essential if they were all going to make it through this crisis. He walked slowly to the rattan couch and sat on its edge. "I see." He must sound reasonable. "And what did Bruce have to say?"

"He said to talk to you."

"Talk to me?" Evan repeated. "Good idea. Come and sit here." He smoothed the seat beside him. He was going to need all the help he could get, and he prayed Bruce had calmed Donna down.

She sat as far away as possible. "I made a mess of my hair, didn't I?"

He smothered a grin and ruffled the ragged ends around her face. "We'll get that taken care of." Donna's massacred hair had been one more shock for Sara to absorb since the girl's return.

"When I was in San Francisco, Bruce thought my braids made me look like a kid."

Thanks, Bruce. "You're going to look wonderful when it's trimmed." He punched her shoulder lightly. "So what did he say about everything else?"

"A lot of stuff."

Getting anything coherent out of her was going to take a crowbar. "Feel like talking about any of it?"

"Sure." Her fingers worked a hole in the bottom of her grubby sweater. "Bruce said he bet I'd look cute with short hair."

"Well, he's right. Bruce is a pretty good judge of these things." It took effort not to add that why Bruce should have the magic touch with any kid was a mystery to Evan.

Donna scooted down and rested her head against the sofa back. "Bruce said it's awful tough to make a choice between two people you love."

Bruce was a veritable guru—original to boot. Evan waited silently.

"He said . . ." She looked sideways at him, pausing as if for dramatic import. "He said I have to make sure no one thinks I'm going to stop loving them, only that I'm trying to decide what's best for everyone. He said you'd agree with that being the best way."

"Yes," Evan said slowly, sickness growing in his stomach. "I can't argue with that." But he couldn't bear to watch what would happen to Sara if this daughter she loved so much went away.

"That's what Mom was saying, too, wasn't it?" Donna leaned to hug her knees and rock back and forth. "That's why she told me to choose where I want to be—with her or with Prairie."

Suddenly, Evan wished, almost violently, that Bruce was here, for it was clear Donna thought more of Bruce's opinion than anyone's. The fact rankled. Donna had only spent one afternoon with Laura's cousin, and now it was Bruce this, and Bruce that.

"Evan?" Donna's voice had risen.

"Oh, yes. I'm sure your mother meant for you to think things through that way." He stood abruptly and went to bang discordant notes on an old piano in the corner. "So, what do you think?"

"I want you to talk to Prairie."

He stopped, his hand suspended inches from the keys. "Talk to Prairie?"

"Yeah. Bruce said you'd know what to say."

Bruce said. Evan turned slowly. "What am I supposed to be talking to her about?"

Donna got up and came close. She pushed a blunt clump of hair behind one ear and looked into his face. "I can't go with her, can I?"

He closed his eyes for an instant. Relief made him almost weak. "No," he said quietly. "Of course you can't. But I have to know why you decided that before I can help Prairie."

"Prairie doesn't need me as much."

Evan opened his mouth but no words would come.

Donna sniffed and leaned against him. "Prairie has lots of people. They come and go like she does, but they all love each other in a way. She's happy most of the time. Bruce said maybe she just thinks she *ought* to want me and try to look after me."

"I see." He put an arm across her thin shoulders and stroked the side of her face. "Bruce may be in the wrong business. He sure sees people clearly. He'd make one hell of a psychologist. And I think he's right on this one, too."

"He's wonderful. Bruce is the best friend I ever had." Quickly she raised troubled eyes to him. "Except for you and Mom, of course."

Evan pressed her face against him once more and tucked in the corners of his mouth. "Thanks, sweetie. You're sure this is what you want? To stay with Sara— with your mom?" He needed to hear her say the words. She hadn't said she loved Sara.

"I'm sure. Mom needs me more than Prairie does. She needs love."

Evan squeezed his eyes shut. His skin felt tight and cold. This thirteen-year-old had worked it all out. She understood Sara Fletcher better than Sara understood herself. God, he hoped Sara would begin to understand what she had in this girl, truly had, and to give the lion's share of herself where it mattered most—to Donna.

"Hey." He let out a long breath and held her away. "What say you go up and tell your mother what you just told me? She and Prairie are probably staring at each other wondering what to say by now. Ask Prairie if she'd mind going for a drive with me so we can talk."

"I DO LOVE DONNA, you know."

Evan looked sideways at Prairie Crawford, at her long straw-colored hair streaming across the top of the open car window. "I know you do. And she loves you. But it's going to be best this way, Prairie."

"We had a good time these past two days." She clasped a worn, red leather purse closer to her chest. "We were going to do the country. *On the Road*, kind of... like Kerouac wrote about. We'd have gotten an old van and just up and gone when we wanted. Stayed a few days when we liked a spot." Her pale eyes flickered, seeing sights he could only guess at. "She's my kid."

"And you love her.?"

"I already said that."

"What would you buy the van with, Prairie?"

Bitten fingernails rolled an edge of her old black coat. "We'd have used up Donna's money first. Then I'd have thought of a way."

How many people were there like this? Evan asked himself. Forgotten children of a troubled age, still hanging on to hopeless dreams and unreality?

"It would take quite a bit of money to get a van. Then you'd need more to eat and pay for places to sleep."

"We'd have slept in the van." Moisture welled along the rims of her eyes now. "And we could have worked."

Evan squinted at the road. He'd agreed to take Prairie to the bus station, and they were almost there. "Donna's only thirteen years old. She's a schoolgirl. Would it be fair to take away her chance for a good home and a good education?"

Prairie sighed, long and shakily. "I guess you think what they all think."

He glanced at her.

"That I'm no good. Irresponsible."

"I didn't say that." But he'd thought it. "Just that you're a dreamer. The world needs dreamers, too."

He pulled in to a loading zone by the bus station.

Prairie reached behind the seat for her backpack, then hesitated, holding her bundle in both arms. "I want what's best for Donna. And I like Sara." She looked at him, her gaze oddly sharp. "You like her, too, don't you?"

He nodded, a heaviness in his heart. "I like her very much. And I like Donna, too."

"That's all right, then." She grasped the door handle. "Are you and Sara going to get married?"

She wanted him to say yes. This little scarecrow of a woman longed for her child to have the security of the complete family she could never provide. He cradled the steering wheel and stared into the lighted entrance to the building. Rain speckled the windshield.

"Mr. McGrath?" A fleeting touch brushed his shoulder.

"Yes," he said distinctly. "I think so. If everything turns out the way it ought to."

"You can make it," she said, pushing the door wide. "You're strong and she loves you—I could feel it. You make sure she marries you and then make my daughter yours. Girls need fathers."

He considered and discarded the idea of calling out to offer Prairie money. Her figure, inside its flapping garb, disappeared, head down, into the terminal.

A horn blaring behind him brought Evan to sharp attention. He'd rested his head and folded arms atop the steering wheel. His mouth was dry. Automatically he changed the idling car's gears and pulled out into traffic. God watch over Prairie Crawford, he prayed silently. Watch over all the Prairie Crawfords.

The front door of Sara's house opened as he pulled to a stop at the foot of the steps. Two silhouettes, both small, stood close together against the light from inside. Evan slid from the car and climbed wearily toward Sara and Donna.

"Is she all right?" Sara reached for his hand.

Evan smiled and knew she'd see in his eyes all the love he had for her. She was special, and she must be his. Even now, when she'd come so close to losing her only child, she could worry about another woman's pain.

"She's fine," he said quietly, and held out his free hand to Donna. "She's a lovely person. How could she be anything else and have had a girl like ours?" He kissed Donna's fingers. "Let's get in out of the rain."

CHAPTER FIFTEEN

SARA STOOD IN her bathroom, gripping the edges of the basin to keep from falling. *Was she or wasn't she going to be sick?* This was the third time since she had got dressed she had rushed back to the bathroom, only to have the nausea recede. She picked up a fresh facecloth and blotted her face carefully, trying not to mar her makeup. She had caught some rotten virus again, and it would just have to run its course. Shakily she went back to her bedroom and sat down. She was already late for work, and there was so much to do. How could she manage to catch the flu twice in two months?

One thing Christine had going for her, she didn't have to go out to work when she was sick. She could stay at home, doing only what was absolutely necessary. None of this careful dressing for the office, careful application of impeccable makeup. Sara leaned her aching head against the back of the chair and felt sleep about to claim her. She would have to ease up a bit on her work load but not now. She was scheduled to see Grant in forty minutes. Then she was going over to the plant to see Evan's new mechanical wonder, which he was to install during the noon hour. It was, he had assured her, the simplest and least expensive type of robot assembly—a "pick and place." The robot picked something up here and placed it there. And since there would be three such robots, three stacking jobs would be eliminated. And she had had to cope with that problem.

Outside, the crisp autumn air, already hinting at winter's bite, revived her, and she felt much better by the time she reached the Daon Building. The sickness had gone and so had the headache. It might not be too bad a day after all.

"I'm sorry I'm late," she said as she entered Grant's office. "I'm a bit under the weather. I picked up another bug, I think."

"Oh, I'm sorry to hear that. Forget about being on time these days. I don't even have the stuff out I was going to talk to you about. I've been hung up on the phone with the plant."

Something in his voice, so tired, so harassed, touched her. "What's up? More trouble?" She could have bitten her tongue. She shouldn't have said "more," but he appeared not to notice.

"Yes. The workers are making such a production out of those three stacking robots Evan's putting in. You'd think we were laying off half the force. Did you find other places for those three guys, by the way?"

"Yes, I did, but . . ."

"Well, what are they griping about? I can't see that stacking trays of canned fish is a career job, but the way those guys are complaining you'd think it was a cherished vocation."

"I didn't finish. They had to take a slight pay cut. Two of them are running the small forklifts, and I put Danny Ferguson out on the loading dock on the warehouse payroll."

"Oh, I didn't mean they should take a pay cut, Sara. After all, they didn't ask to be moved," Grant said, frowning.

"I know, Grant, but you can't pay them more than others doing the same jobs. Not unless you want to give their co-workers a raise right across the board."

He gave a dry laugh. "Not exactly. Money's too tight these days to play Santa Claus. But I am sorry they had to take a cut. Did you explain... Oh, hell, Sara, never mind. I know you did." His voice broke. He pushed aside a folder that lay before him and lowered his head to his hands. He kept his head down, and Sara got up and quietly crossed the room to look out the window.

Grant was having these—what should she call them? Small breakdowns? He would be fine, all business, for days, and then suddenly it was as if he came to an invisible cracking point. It had taken her a while to figure out. Now she understood. He was grieving for Homer, deeply, and now and then the loss seemed to sweep over him, leaving him distracted and oddly uncaring, defenseless for a moment.

She gave him a couple more minutes to compose himself, and then went back to his desk. He had taken some more folders out of a desk drawer and spread them on the desktop. She saw, with aching sympathy, the unsteadiness of his hand, the deeper lines on his face and the heaviness of eyes that didn't get enough sleep. He was grieving and worrying. Things weren't going too well with the business, and they both knew as much.

"I wanted to alert you, Sara, that by the end of next month we'll have packed enough to fill all our existing contracts for the fall." He spoke carefully as if he hated saying this aloud.

"That's good. Things do go faster now that Evan has started tinkering and rearranging." She tried to make her voice light. She'd been in this business too long not to know what was coming.

"I managed to get two new contracts for very small packs and the fish to fill them, but I haven't been able to get enough to avoid some layoffs if things don't pick up."

At the dreaded word "layoffs," Sara's heart sank.

"It's too close to Christmas, Grant. Homer always—"

"I know," he said wearily. "Dad always managed to keep the plant running year-round. No layoffs. Especially no layoffs at a time like Christmas when everybody needs the pay packet. Well, I'm not my father, but I dare say you've noticed that."

"I'm sorry, Grant," she murmured miserably. "That comment just slipped out. Maybe you can pick up another order or two. Don't give up yet. If you just got a couple of medium-size contracts, we could carry the full payroll through until the first of the year." Even as she spoke, she felt a sense of desperation. She rubbed her temples. Her headache was coming back, as well as the queasy feeling in the pit of her stomach.

"I'll do my best. You can count on that." He sounded humble, and it shamed her. Grant had lost all the high confidence he had started out with. Seeing him this way broke her heart. If only he hadn't hired Evan? A small quiver went through her body. Grant's failure wasn't Evan's fault. He had counted on the company business increasing while he streamlined the workplace for faster production. He was doing his job. They weren't doing theirs.

"I've been thinking about it," Sara began tentatively. "A couple of ideas have surfaced, but I haven't really pursued them."

"Well, pursue them, my dear." Grant laughed bitterly. "At this point I'll listen to anything—anything at all. Well, we'd better get over to the plant and see what Evan's got." There was dread in his voice now.

Events were unfolding exactly as she had said they would, and he had refused to listen to her. She should feel victorious, but she didn't. Hers was an empty little victory, and she could only feel sorry for Grant.

When they got to the plant, the noon whistle had just blown and workers were streaming out of the loading-dock entrance, lunch pails in hand. There was a chill in the air, but it was sunny enough for some men and women to sit along the wharves, legs dangling over the edge, and toss crusts to the gulls. Less hardy souls would be in the cannery lunchroom, a great barn of a place with trestle tables and benches and several battered coffee urns. The plant itself was nearly empty as they crossed the wet cement floor to where Evan was standing.

As always, Sara felt her pulse jump at the sight of him. Grant knew how she and Evan felt about each other, now. Their growing love was one more thing causing him pain, and Sara was sorry for this, too.

"They're not stacking anything," she said when they stopped in front of Evan and the first stacking device, which appeared to be several pieces of unrelated machinery spread on the floor. She meant the comment as an attempt at lightness, but her humor fell flat.

"No, and it won't for a while, either," Evan said, his voice grim. He was squatting down, peering at the parts, his hands black with grease.

"Why not?" Grant asked sharply.

"Because it's not all here," Evan answered, standing up and wiping his hands with a stained cloth.

"I thought the shipment came in yesterday," Sara said. She knew very well it had. She had heard the news from several different sources in the company grapevine. Evan McGrath's first stacking robots had arrived, and next week all three human stackers were to be demoted to other jobs.

"Oh, it came," Evan said tonelessly. "I checked it all over myself. But overnight a piece of each assembly has simply got up and walked away. And unless I can find them, I'll have to have new parts made. That will take a couple of weeks at least."

Grant looked vacant-eyed at the useless hardware.

"You're really saying this is another bit of deliberate mischief, aren't you?"

"No, not mischief, Grant," Evan said carefully. "Sabotage. When it gets this expensive, call it by its real name."

Grant winced. "Hell. Were any more of your blueprints missing?"

"No."

"How'd they know what to take?"

"They didn't. They just took a single piece from each assembly. They didn't know what they were taking. I know that. Because they also took a half-dozen other things—bolts, grommets—all standard-size items I could replace in half an hour at any hardware store. No big brain did this. It could have been anybody."

Grant gave a harsh little laugh. "That narrows it down to a couple of hundred suspects, then, doesn't it?"

They stood by and watched as Evan began gathering up the pieces of machinery.

"Why don't you folks go up to my office," Evan said, his head down, not looking at them. "There's something I want to discuss with you. I'll be up in a minute."

Sara and Grant waited for him wordlessly in his office. Sara staring unseeingly at the corkboard with the girls' thank-you cards still pinned to it. So much had happened since that wild, happy kids' party. She was concentrating on not feeling sick and looked up eagerly when Evan entered. He was pushing a hand truck with the crate of equipment on it. Evan could take her mind off trouble, if anyone could.

He placed the crate next to the other open crates against the wall and stood a moment looking at them. For the first time since she'd known him he looked defeated.

Oh, not you, too, Sara thought. They were all being vanquished by this.

Evan sighed gustily. "Look, I'm sorry, but I heard something unpleasant today. And not by accident. I think I was meant to hear. I might as well let you have it. There's a lot of talk about a strike here."

Grant's head came up with a snap, and Sara stared at him, stunned. They spoke at one time.

"That's all I need," moaned Grant.

"There's never been a strike at Jarvis," Sara said firmly. Then she added. "I'll check it out, Grant. They'll talk to me. I'll get to the bottom of this. You go on back to the office. Evan can run me over later, can't you, Evan?"

"Of course," he answered, but he was looking at Grant. "I'm sorry as hell about this, Grant. I feel . . . responsible."

"Forget it," Grant said with an effort. "I'm responsible. I put you under contract to do a job. You're doing it. It's up to me to take care of the rest, and I haven't."

"Don't talk like that," Sara said sharply. "This isn't over yet. I'll find out who's at the bottom of everything and put a stop to it. I'll call you at home tonight. Now, please go back downtown. I'll handle things here."

Somber and silent, she and Evan watched him go.

Then Sara turned to Evan, "Oh, Evan, he makes me want to cry. Hold me." She slid her arms around his neck and clung to him.

"Careful, love. My hands are filthy." He held them out to his sides to avoid touching her clothes.

"Never mind. I've got work to do." She reached up and kissed him lightly on the mouth. "I'll try not to take too long."

"Hey, wait. I'll wash my hands. I'll shower. I'll scrub down completely." He tried to lighten her mood but failed. They were both too worried.

The questioning took Sara three hours. She talked kindly, firmly or in whatever manner she needed to, to all those people she knew best, the old hands and some of the newer people. By four o'clock she knew what she needed to and went slowly upstairs again.

Sara went into Evan's office and leaned against the door, looking wilted. Evan glanced up from his drawing board and put down his pencil.

"I see you got the bad news."

"Yes. So far it's just talk, but it's definite. This time next week a committee led by Ben will call on Grant at the Doan Building. They feel they have a grievance. It's slow going for them because Jarvis workers have never been involved in union activity before—they're having a hard time getting their act together."

"Let's hope Grant can come up with something positive before they do get their act together," Evan muttered.

"I don't hold out much hope for that at the moment," Sara said dolefully. "Are you about ready to go?"

"Yes. I have one thing to check, and then we're off. It's on my way out. Let's go. I just want to stop at the weighing tower and ask the scale man a question. Some of that weighing machinery is pretty old. The guy who operates it seems to have it strung together with rubber bands and paper clips. He's always having to improvise to make it work properly—or so I'm told, anyhow."

Outside on the wharf the wind was blowing, rippling the greenish, thick-looking water into angry little waves. They slapped against the hull of the *Western Star* as she unloaded her catch. The boat was sitting high in the water, so the unloading was almost finished. Sara jammed her hands into her jacket pockets and watched Evan mount the ladder to the weighing tower. She had an impulse to go with him, regardless of the clothes she wore now for working in the Daon building. She started up, the roar of the machinery a blast against her eardrums.

Inside the open doorway of the tower she watched Evan talking to the weighmaster. She couldn't hear

what either man said. The weighmaster nodded and
replied, gesturing as he did. Everything here was so
familiar—Sara had a moment of nostalgia, wishing
they hadn't moved the offices. She could see the conveyor belt extending from the deck of the boat far below, into the open side of the tower. As fast as
possible, the men below loaded their catch onto the
belt and it came rolling upward, the setting sun
gleaming on the bouncing jiggling fish that were carried along.

High overhead hung two gigantic square metal
buckets with collapsible bottoms, moving back and
forth over the conveyor belt. At the touch of the
weighmaster's hand on a switch, either could drop two
tons of wet fish. The noise was deafening, and the air
was rank. Hundreds of tiny fish scales danced, silver
glitter, in the thin sunlight from a slit window.

She turned her attention back to Evan, who had just
raised his arm in farewell. The man at the controls
gave him a brief unsmiling wave of the hand. Evan
turned to go. At that moment, the bottom panels of a
just-emptied bucket slammed shut and the bucket
veered aside, the other, full bucket, swung forward.
But just before it was in place, another scream of
metal tore Sara's eardrums and the bottom opened,
the huge panels coming downward and the tons of released fish poured out. Evan leaped aside just in time.
Only the yawning bottom panel of the bucket caught
him a sharp blow on the shoulder as a river of fish
missed the belt and fell. The whole load came tum-
bling and sliding onto the floor of the shed, almost to
the doorway where Sara stood, transfixed.

"Evan!"

"It's okay. It's okay," he gasped, his body twisting in pain.

Gray-faced, the weighmaster slammed gears and levers, shutting off the giant machinery, stopping both the belts. He came scrambling down from his seat and waded through fish to Evan.

"Jeez, I'm *sorry*. I'm *sorry*. I don't know what happened. It was an accident! It was an accident!"

"Of course it was an accident," Evan said jerkily. "I'm fine. It's okay. But, buddy, I can think of better ways to go than under two tons of dead fish. I..." He paused, and a shudder ripped through his body. "Hey, give me a hand. Oh hell, I think I'm going to pass out...."

CHAPTER SIXTEEN

THE CLINK OF ICE against glass in Grant's whiskey tumbler jarred Sara's nerves. She, Grant and Evan were waiting for Ben to arrive from the plant. Dear, kind Ben—Christine's husband—a good man, not Sara thought, a saboteur.

"I can't take this," she muttered.

Evan stopped pacing. "Neither can I. Let's call the whole investigation off. I got hit with a damn bucket. I had a raging headache for a few hours, and I've got a bruise that looks a whole lot worse than it feels. Big deal. I should have been more careful. Accidents happen."

Grant shoved his half-empty glass away. They all watched the golden liquid inside slosh wildly, then slow to a gentle sway.

"Don't you think this situation bothers me as much as it does you?" Grant's voice was unnaturally tight. "I like Ben Murphy. My...my father liked him, too. But if we don't do something about what's been happening, a bruised shoulder from a falling bucket may look like a hangnail. At this point, I'm nervous." He stared at Evan. "I have a feeling that anything can happen."

"No!" Sara shook her head. "No, Grant. Who-ever's responsible—if anyone is—didn't think that far ahead. And Ben would never..." She bowed her head and buried her fingers in her hair.

"Sara, listen." Evan came close, stroked her neck, knelt to pull her forehead onto his good shoulder. "There's an explanation we're missing somewhere. I feel it as strongly as you do. But Grant needs to be sure for all of our sakes and for the rest of the people at the plant."

"He isn't questioning any of them."

"Shh. Shh. Ben's going to be able to clear himself. I'm sure of it."

Grant coughed, and Sara lifted her face. He was staring at them, no malice in his expression, only a mirror image of the same trapped look that had been on her face from the moment she knew this interview was coming.

The intercom buzzed. "Margaret?" Grant said. "Yes. Thanks. Send him in."

The door opened and Grant's secretary, her face slightly flushed, urged Ben into the room.

Evan saw the woman's hand at the man's elbow, discreetly squeezing, reassuring. *Damn all this,* he cursed silently. He needed some quiet time now, to finish his task and, above all, to smooth the path for a future with Sara. If he couldn't find a way to control what was unfolding here, all his plans might collapse.

"Come on in," Grant said, standing and extending a hand.

Ben moved with jerky formality, shoving out his own big, reddened hand to grasp Grant's. Evan studied Grant's face, and he suppressed a wry grin. It must have cost Grant something not to flinch under that bear grip.

"Sit down." Grant waved Ben into a chair dead-center between Sara's and the one Evan had been using. *The guy looks like he's on a witness stand,* Evan thought, then made himself walk nonchalantly to sit down again.

Ben had said nothing.

"How are you?" Evan leaned forward, pressing his forearms hard against his thighs. "How're Chris and the boys?"

Ben's color deepened. "Fine, thank you, Mr. McGrath."

Evan winced and shot a helpless look from Grant to Sara. Both of their faces were pained. They were good people. Since his return to Canada, so many good people had become a part of his life, and he wasn't about to watch such relationships crumble.

"Ben, you don't have to say a thing," Sara insisted. She scooted to the edge of her chair and reached out to lay a hand on Ben's arm. Her slender fingers smoothed the rough plaid wool of Ben's jacket, and Evan closed his eyes fractionally. He loved everything about this sensitive woman.

Ben gave her a closed-lipped smile. "It's not every day I get called up here." His eyes jumped nervously around the plush office, touched Sara, Grant and came to rest on Evan. "I'm real sorry about what happened to you, Mr. McGrath, real sorry. But I think I know what happened...."

That's smart, Evan thought, surprised. *Attack first.* Immediately he let his eyes find Sara's. She pleaded silently for him to remain open.

"I'd be glad to hear about it, Ben," he said evenly.

Ben smoothed the knees of his carefully pressed jeans. He was a big, bluff, but roughly handsome man. Evan suddenly recognized what Chris must see in him. Ben was direct and reliable. He flexed the muscles in his jaw. The best of men had made mistakes while under pressure.

"First, I think I can guarantee it was an accident. Without pointing a finger or anything, I think Louie blew it. He's been weighmaster here for seventeen years, and he's pretty set in his ways. Every time Mr. Jarvis...old Mr. Jarvis, that is...suggested new equipment out there in the tower, Louie talked him out of it. He always makes a big deal of being the only one who knows Letty's habits."

"Letty?" Grant asked.

Ben reddened. "That's what he calls that bucket. The other one is Rita. Rita never plays up. It's just a dumb game he plays. Mr. Jarvis told him, and I told him, maybe a hundred times, that we need complete new bucket assemblies out there. But it's like any old piece of equipment, the person who works it has to know when to kick here and push there. Letty's fell—fallen—open before."

"And he just happened not to kick it or push it at the right time when it fell open on me?" Evan asked. He couldn't help but sound skeptical.

"I'm sure that's the way it was," Ben said earnestly. "Louie's a good guy. He made a mistake, that's all. I'd trust him with my life."

Grant cleared his throat lightly. "In point of fact, Ben, we rather trusted him with Evan's life, didn't we?"

"I'm sorry about that," Ben said humbly, and Sara reached over and patted his arm again. "Maybe he was upset or something?"

"He could have been," Evan said slowly. "I had just asked him how old the equipment was."

There was a heavy silence. Finally Grant lifted his glass and swallowed noisily. "Ben, other things have happened. Rumors have been spread. Evan's wing-assembly device, the talk about labor-efficiency studies, I...damn, this is tough...Ben, Sara talks to Chris and Chris talks to you. You're the only one at the work-force level who has easy access to the kind of information that's caused all the trouble. That information has been bent and embellished, and now it's working against every one of us...including you. Why'd you do it?"

Ben shook his head. "I didn't mean any harm. I only said what I'd heard, and I never did that unless I was asked questions. I've never been any good at pretending."

"You're saying you gave privileged information to the other workers?" Grant laced his fingers tightly.

"I...no...yes. That is I mentioned the wing business."

"And you decided to whip up some opposition to the changes we propose? You decided to stop Evan from doing any more work at Jarvis?"

"No, sir!"

Sara bolted from her chair and stood beside Ben. "You don't have to say another word. This isn't a trial. You wouldn't do anything to hurt Jarvis, we know that. Your word's good enough for us."

In that moment, Evan knew pure frustration. She was sweet and decent, and he understood her point of view, but he didn't blame Grant for needing more reassurances. "Sara," he said soothingly. "Relax and let Ben talk to us."

"Relax!" she half shouted, and inhaled sharply. "You are so damn good at telling other people to relax." She met his eyes and blushed. He felt his own color rise. "I'm sorry," she went on. "That was uncalled for. We're all pretty uptight. You're right, Evan. We need to hash this out."

"Mr. McGrath..." Ben's gaze was earnest. "Mr. McGrath, I can't talk to you. I don't know anything."

"Evan, please. We got past that Mr. McGrath stuff a long time ago. Listen, Ben. The evidence against you is pretty damning, but we don't have one iota of proof. Can you give us anything that will either help convince us you had nothing to do with any of the mishaps we've had in the past few weeks or tell us who *is* responsible?"

He hated the role of devil's advocate. If he made a wrong move, he could alienate the woman he loved. She was loyal. She'd stand by her brother-in-law, Evan was certain of it. A sidelong glance at Grant proved the other man had temporarily abdicated responsibilty.

"I didn't do anything wrong, I swear," Ben said distinctly. He continued to stare levelly at Evan. "I've never done anything dishonest in my life, let alone tried to hurt a man. And I wouldn't even if I did think my job was about to go up in smoke. I like you, Evan. Chris likes you. And Sara...well...enough said."

"Facts, Ben," Grant said thinly. "We need facts, or it will be out of our hands."

Evan winced. "Grant—"

"No, Evan. I know you don't like making waves. You're a peaceful sort. But I've got a business to run here and if I don't bring things back into line, who knows where all this will end? I can't let my employees decide what course I ought to take."

"Grant, don't." Sara gripped the edge of the desk.

He kept his eyes on his glass, turning it this way and that between flattened palms. "I'm sorry, Sara. I'd do anything I could for you, as you well know. But right now I'm fighting for this company. You, of all people, should understand that. Unless Ben can convince me I shouldn't, I'll probably have to take official action."

Evan's stomach turned over. If he didn't get a grip on the situation, they wouldn't simply be on the edge of a disaster, they'd be too far involved to draw back. "Grant," he barked, trying not to flinch at the quality of his own voice. "Listen to me. Listen to me, all of you." Immediately he had their full attention. "I've got some ideas about what's been happening. No proof—but some ideas. Ben, do you still insist you had nothing to do with what happened yesterday, or any of the other times?"

Slowly Ben nodded.

"Right. Then we're going to carry on as usual for a while and see what happens."

"In other words," Sara said softly. "Keep your nose clean, Ben, and we'll forget anything that's gone before. You've judged him, Evan—without a real trial."

"Wrong," he snapped back. "I'm asking for some breathing space. I admit that if absolutely nothing else goes wrong after today, Ben's going to look pretty guilty, but something else may happen. Would you rather Grant call in the cops right now and break up a happy family?" *Nice going, McGrath,* he congratulated himself bleakly. *You make one hell of a diplo-mat.*

Sara's features were a cold wall. "Well put, Evan. No choice right? McGrath's rules or the end. What do you say Grant, Ben? Do we go with McGrath's rules?"

Ben gripped the arms of his chair. "He's only trying to make things better, Sara. This is rough. What he says makes sense to me."

Evan breathed easier until Sara spoke. "Oh, Evan always makes perfect sense, Ben. Of course, we'll do as he says. What choice do we have?"

"None." Grant was on his feet. "Thanks for coming, Ben. Time will tell, right? Call me if there's anything you want to talk about."

The three of them watched Ben's tall figure walk resolutely from the office. The door closed, and Sara spun around to face Evan. "Do you know what you've done?"

He shook his head. Nothing he said would be right.

"Sara," Grant said. "We can't let this get any further out of hand."

She ignored him. "You've put Ben in a no-win situation. If something else goes wrong, he'll still be under suspicion, and if nothing happens, you and Grant will nod and smile and convict him. Damn you both." She planted her hands on her hips and turned away.

Evan felt Grant's stare but wouldn't meet it. He had to work his way out of a corner fast. "I don't believe Ben Murphy's guilty—okay?" He waited, but Sara didn't move or speak.

"I don't, either," Grant added.

"Sara," Evan said persuasively. "*Think*. What choice do we have but to wait . . . unless we *do* choose to call in the authorities?"

"None, I guess. Oh, Evan, it'll destroy Chris if it turns out Ben's involved."

He went behind her and held her shoulders. Gently he turned her to face him. "I know that. This isn't very original, but life's a gamble. We're all gamblers most of the time. Now we're gambling on Ben. Trust, Sara. And pray. If this goes wrong there's no winner to take all...everyone's a loser. Trust, sweetheart, I'm going to." He stroked back her hair and pulled her against his chest. "Shall we call a truce and start hoping?"

She nodded against him and this time, Evan looked at Grant Jarvis. The man was watching Sara, and his heart was in his eyes. The bond between Sara and himself as a couple was obvious now, Evan thought, and Grant, although it hurt, was gracefully accepting the fact.

"We're caught in this, aren't we?" Grant pinched the bridge of his nose. "Maybe I should never have tried to take over here. It seemed like the right thing to do, and it was what my father wanted. Sara . . ." He waited until she turned to look at him. "You'd have made a better job of this than I have. I thought I was finally making the business work, and with...since my father died it's seemed even more important. I didn't want to fail."

Sara stiffened in Evan's arms. "Grant, stop it!" She pulled away and backed her weight on the desk, glaring at Grant. "If one or two little setbacks are all it takes to make you fold, you're right, you shouldn't have tried to take over. But you aren't going to fold, do you hear me? You aren't going to give in. You started out to accomplish something, and you better damn well pull it off. There are a lot of people counting on you.''

"I know," Grant mumbled. "But sometimes everything seems so impossible.''

"Only if you decide to give in. Homer would never have given in.''

Evan stopped breathing. This lady didn't pull her punches. Either Grant would come out fighting or creep into a corner.

Grant stood up slowly until he towered over Sara. Carefully he leaned on the other side of the desk, leveling his gaze with hers so that she was forced to tilt her chin. "I know my father wouldn't have given in. I'm sick and tired of hearing what my father would or wouldn't have done. Evan's solution is the right one. We wait and see. And don't judge my reactions, Sara. Just because nothing else happens—and I hope to God it doesn't—I won't condemn Ben out of hand. It's perfectly possible whoever's responsible will be scared off and figure this is the perfect way to make Ben a patsy. I'm not a complete fool.''

"No," Sara said. "You aren't, Grant. You're a very smart man. Your father knew that and so do I.''

Grant pulled his briefcase from beside his credenza and began piling in papers. "I'm a lucky guy. I've had the love and respect of some special people...." He let his words hang in the air for a while before going on. "It's going to take time to get over my father's death, but I'm getting there. I've lost more than him—in a way." His eyes flickered past Sara to Evan. "But we have to accept losses. Then we get on, hope for the best and try to mend our fences. I must get home.

I promised a lady I'd show her what a good cook I am tonight. I never cooked anything in my life. Wish me luck.''

"Good luck," Sara said, smiling. "You'll have a wonderful evening." He'd cancel his plans in a panic, she thought, if he knew she planned to spend *hers* in the deserted cannery. But nobody else in the company knew that cavernous old building as well as she did. She'd been formulating a plan since Ben's interrogation. If she could just have some time at the plant—alone—to prowl around maybe, just maybe, she could find some answers. And they did need answers.

SHE'D NEVER BEEN to the cannery at night before. The building loomed, a black hulk against the moonless sky. In the distance, the lights of North Vancouver spread out like a spangled carpet. She pulled into an alley and switched off the car's ignition. To the west, she saw bright ribbons of color shivering across the waters of Burrard Inlet, reflections from the illuminated facades of a dozen hotels.

Her hands were frozen. Fear had contracted her veins. Fear of what? Sara asked herself. With a grim smile, Sara spread her fingers on the steering wheel. Creeping around deserted processing plants at midnight wasn't her forte. Only a fool *wouldn't* be scared. She climbed from the car, closed the door carefully and skirted forklifts and stacks of wooden trays to get to the entrance. There was probably nothing to be found here, nothing that would help Ben or provide the clues she needed, but she must try.

Cautiously she passed the entrance and checked the lane on the other side of the cannery. Only equipment lined the walkway—there were no private vehicles to be seen. She'd found out which security guard was on duty tonight and called to tell him his shift had been switched. Later she'd have some explaining to do. But she wanted to do her investigating in private, and not start any wild rumors. Now it was time to get inside.

The lock on the walk-in door was stiff. People usually came in during the day when the great doors on the loading dock were open. Sara had to use both hands to turn the key. Once inside, she locked the door again and fumbled along the wall until she felt the bank of power switches. She threw on every one in the top row, splashing garish yellow light over the silent machinery. The only windows in the building were in the offices upstairs, so no illumination would be visible from outside.

Investigating the employee locker room for starters was her best bet, Sara decided swiftly. Her tennis shoes squeaking on the concrete floors, she darted between the paralyzed belts, the empty racks and dry spigots, to reach the area where workers stored personal possessions during the day. At night there should be only rubber aprons and boots in the metal cabinets lining two walls, so she wouldn't be meddling with anyone's personal belongings.

Most doors stood ajar. One or two were wide open. Sara attacked these first, dumping boots upside down, running her hands over the high shelves, kneeling to poke into back corners. Finding anything could help: a communication from another cannery, documentation on the Jarvis operation that could be intended for a competing firm, something from Evan's drawings, one of the many tools steadily disappearing—anything. Best luck of all would be finding a part from the stacking robots.

She searched every locker and found nothing unusual. Discouraged, she sat on an old armchair and began poking back clumps of discolored stuffing that escaped through worn fabric.

Evan had been at the Daon Building all afternoon. When she turned down his invitation for dinner, he'd been clearly disappointed and said he'd call it a day and go back to English Bay. That meant his office had been empty most of the day—and all night. Deciding to go there next, she returned to the production floor and crossed to the stairs.

Halfway up she stopped. *This is useless,* she thought. Ben had told the others he'd been sent for by Grant. If one of his co-workers was guilty of underhand activities and deliberately letting Ben take the rap, the culprit was unlikely to make a move while his scapegoat was downtown with a perfect alibi. Anyway, Evan locked his office door and forcing it would be too obvious.

Sara leaned against the railing, trying to decide what to do next. She was about to give up and go home, when she heard the sound of multiple clicks ricocheting through the silence. Instant darkness walled her in. Slowly, gripping the rail with both hands, trying to adjust her eyes to the darkness, Sara peered over her shoulder.

A breath made it as far as her throat before she swallowed painfully. An oblong of dusty gray leaped out of the gloom. The door she'd closed was open. She opened her mouth to shout, then closed it again. Whoever had come in must have seen her. He knew where *she* was.

A shadow moved in the distant doorway, then was gone. Seconds later she heard the shattering crack of the metal door smashed into its jamb, and the indistinct opening was obliterated.

Sara tried to take a step down, but found her legs wouldn't support her. She sank slowly to sit on a stair. Was he inside or outside? Where was he waiting? She must go up, quickly, not down. There was an emergency phone in the hall, or, if she dared take time with the keys, she could get into Evan's office and barricade herself inside while she called for help.

The sound of her own hoarse breathing roared in her ears. Bending to feel the stairs with her left hand before moving each foot, she made slow progress toward the top. Her skin crawled. Tension knotted every muscle in her back. Just a few more steps and she'd be in the loft. But the intruder could be upon her at any moment.

Her fingers touched the wall leading into the corridor, and Sara almost cried out with relief. She let go of the wall and ran—into something solid.

He was here, in the dark, pressing her down, falling on her. A wrist came down across her throat. *Oh, God,* she thought, *I'm going to die in this black place.*

"Please...I..." Her voice was a croak. He was strangling her. "Please..." Finally she fought back with nails and knees. Wildly, she clawed at where she thought his face must be and grabbed a handful of hair. "Get off me," she screamed, horrified at feeling something human, at hearing his breathing. She punched lower, toward his neck and shoulders and heard him gasp. "Get off me!"

"What the hell? Sara? Oh, good Lord, woman."

Only one man had that voice. The pressure rolled away, and she was gathered into familiar arms. "Evan! How could you? Why?"

She was half dragged, half carried the last few feet to Evan's office, and he switched on the light. "Are you all right?" he demanded. "What have I done to you? Where do you hurt?"

"Where...? I don't believe this. I hurt all over. You just knocked me down and lay on top of me. Why did you sneak in and turn off the lights? How did you get past me on the stairs?"

He stiffened, still gripping her arms. Slowly he pushed her farther into the room. "Shh." His face was close to hers. "I thought you were an intruder. I've been up here for hours trying to work things out. Then I heard the door slam downstairs, and the next thing I knew I was being attacked."

"Attacked?" she mouthed incredulously.

"You know what I mean. Now, stay here while I see who our visitor is."

"No!" Sara yelled, then covered her mouth. "No, Evan. He might have a gun. We've got to call the police."

He backed her behind the door. "We can't call the police, can we, Sara? Just in case—"

Her heart thudded. "In case it's Ben? Oh, Evan, you're wrong about Ben. You and Grant. If I ever had a doubt about Ben's innocence, I don't now."

Evan gave her a thoughtful glance. "You're probably right, but I've got to get out there. Please, Sara, do as I ask."

She nodded wordlessly. He left, moving with the grace she never failed to notice.

Sara checked her watch again and again. Seconds crept by, then minutes and she heard nothing. At last, muted light from the plant floor seeped upward and Evan returned, his dark hair tousled, strain imprinted on every feature. He rubbed absently at his shoulder. The bruise had taken more punishment, and his injury from the accident wasn't as painless as he implied in Grant's office.

"Well?" She extended her hands, and he held them.

"Gone," he muttered, heading for his chair and pulling her with him. "There's nobody down there. At least I don't think so. If there is, he's well hidden and he'll be sneaking away by now. Let me hold you." He eased her onto his lap and cradled her tightly. "You scared the hell out of me."

She laughed nervously. "You didn't do a whole lot for my stress level, but Evan—look at me." His head came up and she brushed back his hair. "Evan. I came here tonight looking for a lead—something to help us clear Ben. I didn't expect what happened out there. I probably wouldn't have come if I'd had any idea what was waiting for me, but I got my proof. Whoever's messing around with your work, it isn't Ben."

He exhaled raggedly. "He could have decided to come back here and pull some stunt just to deflect suspicion."

Sara shook her head violently. "No. Why don't I call his home? I bet he'll be there." She reached for the phone but Evan stopped her.

"No point in getting them upset if we don't have to. And you may be right in your deductions, sweetheart, but someone tried to scare you to death. That was a warning. *Keep your nose out of this, lady.* And that's what I want you to do. Understand."

She opened her mouth, but he tapped it with two fingers. "No. No arguments. Let me do this my way. Any idea where the guard was tonight, by the way?

"I told him he wasn't on until tomorrow."

Evan arched a brow. "How resourceful of you."

"Right," she sighed. "Now I'll have to explain my way out of it with the guy who's on tomorrow. Maybe I'll just tell Chick some story and let him sort it out. He loves an excuse to be important."

"Will you promise me not to do anything like this again?" Evan spanned her waist with both hands. "If you don't, I may just have to stay at your side twenty-four hours a day."

Sara bowed her forehead to his. "Watch it, I may already be planning another nocturnal escapade."

"Promise?"

"Evan, this is serious. Where did you park your car? I didn't see it."

"I didn't bring my car. I took a bus."

She squinted at him. "How were you going to get home? The buses must stop running by now?"

"I've got feet. And I intended to take up the whole night one way or another. It gets pretty lonely in that condo."

She tried to stand but he held her fast. "This isn't the place for this. And it certainly isn't the time," she said.

"When will it be the place and time again, Sara?" One wonderful afternoon and evening with you in San Francisco—months ago—and a few stolen hours at your house. Twice won't last me a lifetime. Come home with me now."

"I can't, Evan. Donna's at one of her endless slumber parties, but she's coming home early in the morning."

"When, then?" His lips, pressed repeatedly to hers stopped any answer. "Just tell me how long I have to wait." He rested his chin on top of her head and held her in arms that trembled slightly.

Didn't he know she was suffering, too? "I don't know how long, Evan. We've both got a lot to sort out. You know sex isn't casual for me."

"And you think it is for me?" He stood with enough force to slam her hip into the desk.

She couldn't help wincing. "No, of course not. I'm sorry. I'm always saying sorry to you, or to someone. And I'm sick of that, Evan, so very sick." And as if to underscore her words, a wave of nausea wove into her belly.

"Try to understand my point of view. I can't let go and enjoy myself with you the way I want to when my sister's future is hanging in the balance. And I'm still worried about Donna. I don't know—" She pushed her arms around his rigid body and lay her face on his chest. "I'm not sure everything's okay with her. She isn't going to forget Prairie, ever. Sometimes I think I'd be better off giving up my job and making a normal home for Donna. Don't you see..." Her eyes sought his. "I'm too unsure about every aspect of my life to know what I want for us."

Evan was silent for a long time, his lips set in an unyielding line. "Sara," he said at last. "I told you I loved you. And you said you loved me. Has something changed?"

"Can we let this go for now?" The pain in his eyes hurt Sara, but she wasn't convinced either of them was totally rational. "Like you said this afternoon. Let's wait and see."

He stepped away from her arms. "Yes. We'll do that. It's a very logical approach. Particularly to a situation that might get sticky. Right?" No reply was expected. He grabbed his corduroy jacket and pulled it on over the dark turtleneck he wore. "I'll see you to your car."

Her breathing quickened. "Thanks. I can run you home—"

"No." He bluntly cut her off. "No, thank you. I'd rather walk."

NOT CHICK ENDERBY, Sara thought frantically. Not this morning of all mornings when she already felt awful. She pressed the intercom button again and hesitated before speaking. "Can't you put him off, Anne? You know what a mad schedule I've got today."

"I don't think it's a good idea. He sounded like the sky was about to fall. You know how he gets."

"Yes," she sighed. "I know how he gets. But buy me an hour will you? Tell him to come in at eleven. At least I can make a dent on my in-basket."

"Will do," Anne said brightly. "Okay if I go to the mail room?"

"Sure." She flipped off the speaker and reached wearily for a sheaf of papers. Work pressure was definitely getting to her. Every day she went through these spells of weakness when all she wanted was to crawl away somewhere and go to sleep.

Urgent. Grant's familiar red flag slashed the top of the first page. Everything was urgent these days. She started to read, then tossed the document on the desk. It listed more complaints about late deliveries. And it detailed plans for expansion. *What a laugh,* Sara thought. They might be about to have the most streamlined fish-packing plant known to man, but they couldn't manage to keep up with the business they already had. The only bright spot at Jarvis—and it was little consolation—was the workers' failure to organize a strike. They were still too confused to act.

Sara pushed back her chair and stood. Suddenly the floor seemed to be a long way away and she sat again, abruptly. If she didn't start feeling more human, and soon, she'd have to see her doctor. She wrinkled her nose at the prospect. Giving in to illness always rankled.

While she stared at the papers on her desk, they blurred together. How could she work when she felt like death and her world was steadily closing in around her? Sara's thoughts continued to wander, this time to her child.

Donna alternately moped or had wildly happy moods. She continued to call Bruce Fenton in San Francisco with a frequency that embarrassed Sara, yet she didn't want to say anything that might upset the girl more. As if he must have guessed her discomfort, Bruce had called Sara at the office once and reassured her that he liked talking to Donna. He suggested it might be nice if he returned a call once in a while since she obviously needed a lot of reassurance at the moment. Sara rubbed her eyes. Bruce was a nice man, intuitive, but a stranger and too closely entwined with Laura Hunt.

Laura and Evan . . . was there still something there? She shook her head and picked up the papers again. If Evan wanted anything but friendship from Laura now, it was almost certainly only support. She visualized Evan's face and felt the familiar stricture of her heart. Yes, she loved him, but she didn't want to replace Laura Fenton Hunt as his prop. Irma Hunt had said that of his and Laura's relationship. They'd both

gone through some bad times and taken turns at
propping each other up. Some men—and women—
looked unwittingly for nothing more than a caretaker
in a partner, and that wasn't the kind of relationship
that Sara wanted. Not that any kind of relationship
had been a question in the two weeks since their en-
counter at the cannery. She'd seen him a few times,
but he hadn't called, or asked her out. In his eyes she
saw a clear message: *it's up to you now, lady*.

The sound of a knock on the door startled her.
Anne always ran interference with visitors. It couldn't
be Grant; he made it a rule to call before coming to her
office. "Come in." She gripped the edge of her desk
and pulled closer.

Chick Enderby came into the room, puffing, his
face slightly purplish. "Got here a bit early, Sara.
Can't afford a car, y'know, so I had to get a bus and
they don't run regular."

She sighed. "That's okay," she said, although he
hadn't exactly apologized for barging in. "Come and
sit down, Chick. What's on your mind?"

He sat with a huff and balanced his cap on one
plump knee. "I decided it was time to come and get it
from the horse's mouth, so to speak."

Conversations with Chick always required patience. "What's *it*, Chick?"

"You know." He thrust out his bottom lip and
sniffed. "All this business at the plant. The layoffs.
Work cutbacks...you know."

"I don't know, Chick. As far as I'm aware, not one
employee has been laid off and no one's working less
than a forty-hour week. I admit there hasn't been
much overtime lately, but this isn't the first time that's
happened and the reason is the loss of the *Nancy*

Belle's catch. Once we get a steady replacement for her load, we'll be full strength again.''

"How much longer is that Evan McGrath going to be around?''

His blunt approach shocked Sara. She looked at her hands, gathering strength. "When did the executive decisions of Jarvis Foods become your business?'' Under her hard stare, his head shrank into his collar. "Answer me, Chick. What gives you the right to come in her asking policy questions?''

"My position,'' he blustered after a few seconds. "The guys have made me their spokesman. They want you people to know they're not happy, and if they're not happy they may not be able to work so good...if you understand me.''

Acid burned her throat. *A go-slow.* She swallowed but still felt sickened. "You're threatening us, Chick. Why did you come to me instead of Mr. Jarvis?''

"I...um.'' His eyes slid away. "You're personnel and anyway, I figured he, ah...he might listen to you.''

Now her head ached. "I'll ignore the last innuendo, except to say that Mr. Jarvis is no more likely to be swayed by a woman than a man.'' This was not quite true, but Chick didn't have to know. "And you are threatening a strike again, aren't you, Chick. Or at least a go-slow. It was rumored before. But this is a frontal attack. You want a bunch of assurances from us, including the stoppage of Evan—Mr. McGrath's—work. You aren't going to get those assurances, Chick. So what do you intend to do?''

"Well. Don't you think we could talk about this a bit?'' He fidgeted with the braid on his cap. "If you could just give me a few pointers on how to handle the rest of the workers, some promises of good stuff . . . something . . . I could go back and see what I can do to settle them down.''

Sara leaped to her feet. ''*You'll* see what you can do to settle them down? Since when did you become so important?'' The faint buzzing started in her head once more. She had to get Chick out of her office. ''Look—'' she lowered her voice ''—this isn't a matter I can deal with on my own. I don't have the authority. And it's going to need a lot of discussion. So let's do this. You go back and tell the others everything's in hand—we're aware of their concerns and intend to work them out. Can you do that?''

He nodded, his jowls wobbling. At her uncharacteristic outburst, the fight had seeped out of him.

''That's good, Chick. I'll be talking to you.''

''Yes, ma'am.'' He shot to his feet and crossed to the door with remarkable speed.

''Oh, and Chick.'' She waited until he turned around. ''You might make a few enquiries about the things that have been happening—you know what I mean. Do it just for me and don't tell anyone else what you find out—if anything. Okay?''

''Right.'' He opened the door. ''I'll do that.'' Sara caught the sound of his gusty breath as he went.

For several minutes she stood still, leaning on the desk, then she placed a short telephone call, put on her coat and left.

TWO HOURS LATER she sat in her doctor's small consulting room, buttoning the cuffs of her blouse. He'd examined her, run some tests and told her to wait.

She closed her eyes and let her mind drift. Exhaustion had been Dr. Cambie's immediate diagnosis. He was probably right. Maybe it was time to get out of the rat race. Donna needed her, and with Homer gone, she no longer felt as drawn to her job.

"Taking a snooze, Sara?"

John Cambie's voice brought her back to reality. "I guess," she replied, smiling. "I seem to need a lot of them lately."

"Well. I'm not too worried about you. You may have to cut back on your work for a bit, but you'll be fine."

His reassurances made her feel instantly better. "Good. I was worried for a while."

He sat in a chair beside her and flipped through her records. She noted that his sandy hair had thinned in the ten years she'd known him and his features were sharper, but she still liked his kind, professional manner. He'd been a friend of Michael's and at one time, a frequent dinner guest. All that seemed so long ago.

"You did say you weren't sure when your last period was, didn't you, Sara?"

She frowned. "Yes. I've never had a regular cycle. Must have been in July or August, I think. I don't keep track."

"Hmm. That's what makes this more difficult. You were never pregnant, were you?"

"No." She blinked. She'd wanted to undergo tests to find out why they never conceived, but Michael had insisted there was plenty of time for that. "I...Michael and I would have liked children, but I think there was always something wrong with me because nothing happened." An unexpected thought sprang to her mind. "This is the start of the menopause, isn't it? How stupid of me. Lots of women begin early. Dizziness, nausea—tiredness. Oh, John, I'm sorry to take up your time for nothing."

"Sara." He closed the file and tapped it rhythmically on his knee. "The reason your irregular periods are a problem to me is because they make my calculations more difficult. You're pregnant."

CHAPTER SEVENTEEN

"YOU'RE KIDDING!"

John Cambie grinned faintly. "A lot of women say that, Sara. And I really don't know why. There is such a thing, you know, as cause and effect."

"This isn't funny, John," she said weakly. "There are... I already have a child," she said with a gasp. And what would Donna think?

"I know. Donna, your little adopted daughter." He tossed the file onto the desk. "Children aren't rationed, you know. People can have more than one."

She wasn't listening, and her eyes widened as another idea surfaced amid the wild confusion in her mind. "But I'm so *old*, John. I'm *thirty-seven*."

"Yep. That's what your records say. And you are a lovely, healthy woman. True, thirty-seven is a bit old for a first child, but I foresee no real difficulty. I'm going to refer you to a good OB man—or would you prefer a woman?"

"Anybody," she answered. "Gender doesn't matter. I just... I just have to think it over...."

"Well, since I'm your friend as well as your doctor, I won't mention that the time for thinking it over has passed. What you'd better think about now is rearranging your life somewhat about six months from now—if my calculations are right."

"But I'm thirty-seven years old and..."

"You mentioned that, my dear." He picked up a pen and a pad of paper. "If I'm not worried about it, you shouldn't be."

She felt a sense of outrage at her stupidity. "But I should have known better."

"Well, I can't argue with that," he said, writing busily. "This is the name of the OB man. I want you to call and make an appointment, and within the next week or so, Sara. Don't put it off. We have to get things moving."

Get things moving? Fear engulfed her. Things were moving already, and she was no longer in control. She had to get away from here, be alone for a while, *think*. She did some mental arithmetic. The only time it could have happened was when she and Evan had made love in San Francisco.

As she left the building she identified the feeling in her stomach. It was a lump of raw dread. *What am I dreading?* she thought. *I can deal with this, dammit. I just have to sort it out. I'll take it one thing at a time.*

She pushed her hands deep into her raincoat pockets. It had looked like rain this morning, and the day was still gray and overcast. Would it rain, or wouldn't it? She walked slowly down the street, past shop windows already decorated for Christmas. The air smelled wet. A gust of unruly wind plucked at her clothing and flung her hair across her eyes. It was getting very cold. She shivered.

Sara thought about Donna. It seemed as if she'd been just stumbling along in the motherhood business, knowing she wasn't doing too great a job. Donna, bless her, wasn't used to too much in the way of motherhood and apparently didn't know the difference. Sara felt her eyes sting. She hadn't coped well with one child—what in the world would she do with two? And one an *infant*. The idea was staggering.

She dreaded Donna's reaction. Would the girl feel threatened? Her world until a little while ago had been insecure; would this add to that insecurity? *Oh, Sara, your timing is really lousy.* She swallowed hard.

And there was something else she was dreading, something she wanted to avoid. *Come on, Sara. Face up,* she ordered herself.

"Evan!" She spoke his name aloud and stopped in her tracks, her eyes wide. A woman shopper walking behind bumped into her and muttered a hurried apology. A businessman coming toward her, briefcase in hand, looked startled.

She averted her face and walked quickly on. How in the world was she going to tell Evan? And she'd have to tell him. It was embarrassing. For both of them. They'd behaved like a couple of teenagers in the back seat of a car. How could she even say it? "Look, Evan, I know you're busy, but there's this matter that's come up..." No, that would sound idiotic. "Evan, I hate to mention it but I'm pregnant...." Now that would be too blunt. "Evan, sometimes when two people make love..."

She realized that she wanted to laugh, and that this wasn't a laughing matter—but she wanted to laugh anyway. And the awful feeling of dread was gone. There was in its place the sweet piercing of pure joy. She *wanted* this baby more than anything she had ever wanted in her life before.

The first drops of rain finally began to fall. Big splashing drops came down singly, hitting her cheek, her shoulder, the pavement before her, in big, coin-size spots. Beautiful rain, really beautiful rain.

She entered the Daon Building with a sense of urgency. There was so much to do. She gave the doorman a brilliant smile and looked appreciatively at the bank of elevators. It was an impressive building. Maybe Grant had been right to move from the old offices down on the waterfront. Everything here was so smooth and bright and clean. Clean surroundings probably made much better working conditions for pregnant women.

And she wasn't going to tell anyone yet. She would keep the secret to herself, hold it, savor it, cherish it, until she was ready for the rest of the world to know.

Once in her office even the stack of work and all the memos marked "urgent" didn't deter her. She was humming as she sat down, undaunted. She had to get on the phone and locate some more fish to pack because she was sure now—the *Nancy Belle*'s skipper had found another permanent market.

No, she wouldn't accept that. She called every place the boat's skipper might visit and left messages; and finally located him at home.

"Sure, miss," his gravelly voice explained. "I'll tell you why I took my catch over to Fentriss. It's because I got to have a steady market. I got my living to make. I got two boys in college. That doesn't come cheap."

"What makes you think Jarvis isn't a steady market, Sven? Jarvis has been a steady market for you for more than ten years. You were here before I came along."

"Well, with the rumors of strike and all, it seemed a good idea to move along."

"Sven, where did you hear those rumors? There isn't going to be any strike, you know." She made her tone very positive.

"Well, I got the information from a pretty good source, miss. I don't know where he got it. I will do you one favor, though. The skipper of the *My Lady II* was in talking to the boss at Fentriss last week. I think he's looking for a new market."

"Oh, Sven, the *My Lady II* has always been a Jarvis boat. They can't desert us, too. And listen to me, we've done business together for a long time. I think you owe me. I think you'd better tell me where you heard the strike nonsense."

"Well, okay. From one of your own people, miss. I got it from Chick Enderby. Now, I don't know where he got it, but you know Chick is all over that place. He's in a position to hear everything."

"He's also a worrier. If there isn't anything to worry about, he'll look until he's found something. I think you need a better source." Sara talked for another half an hour, until she convinced the *Nancy Belle*'s skipper to bring his loads back to Jarvis. When she hung up the phone again, she could feel the beginning of a tension headache and deliberately tried to relax.

Suddenly she wanted fervently to learn how to crochet and how to knit. *Christine will teach me,* she thought with an upsurge of excitement. *Oh, Chrissy, maybe you had the right idea all along.* She envisioned stacks of hand-crocheted bootees and cuddly little knitted clothes—what did Chris call those things with a drawstring at the bottom? She'd have to ask.

Sara was reaching for the phone when she remembered what Sven had said about the *My Lady II*. Grimly she dialed the first numbers, where she thought the *My Lady II* skipper might get a message. She actually found him at home. It took her longer than half an hour to convince him that there wouldn't be a strike, and when she hung up the phone there was the faint feeling of nausea again. *What am I doing here,* she asked herself. *I don't want to be here. I want to be home. I want to think about my baby.*

And did she really know there would be absolutely no strike at Jarvis? It was the livelihood of two skippers and their crews she was dealing with. She well knew the dead loss it was to a fisherman who brought his boat in with no place to off-load the catch. If the fish stayed too long in the hold, they were good only for fertilizer and much less money.

Grant had to get more business. He had to!

"Hi, gorgeous." Evan stuck his head in the door. At the sight of him, Sara felt a great upsurging of love. How wonderful he looked in his work clothes, jeans, sweatshirt and tennis shoes. He must be just passing through as he seldom came into the main offices in anything but his impeccably tailored business suits. And he was his old relaxed self again. Oh, she loved him.

"Well," he said, coming in. "You look like the cat that swallowed a whole fish cannery. What's up?"

Boy, have I got a surprise for you, she thought, and couldn't hold back a quick, delighted laugh.

"Okay, what's the secret?" Evan bent over to peer at her closely. "You're glowing. Why are you glowing? It isn't fair to glow and not say why."

"I just made a nice coup for Grant," she said, looking away. "I talked the *Nancy Belle* skipper into coming back to Jarvis. So we're not going to run out of product."

"Hey, good for you!" He leaned closer and kissed her forehead.

She laughed again, unable not to.

"I know. I'm not usually a forehead kisser. I'm a more direct type, but in the middle of a business day I thought I'd better restrain myself. Do you mind?"

"I'll try to manage," she said, grateful he'd decided to come to her. "Incidentally, the *Nancy Belle* captain got his rumor of trouble at Jarvis from guess who? Chick Enderby. I wonder where he got it?"

Evan looked thoughtful. "I wonder," he said slowly. "This gives me an idea..." He paused and didn't finish the sentence. Sara was so wrapped up in her own thoughts that she didn't notice.

Sara returned Evan's sound parting kiss—not delivered to her forehead—and returned happily to her papers.

After only an hour's overtime, Sara felt she couldn't stay in the office another minute. She placated her conscience by snatching up some trade journals. Homer had always relied on her to keep up on the latest food-processing news. Since Grant had arrived, she'd gotten behind in her reading.

Once she arrived home, Sara had the feeling that she was finishing, or completing some internal process, a sense that some time—soon now—this segment of her life would be over and she would be embarked on another, far richer stage. *Oh, Chrissy, you were right, you were right,* Sara told herself over and over. The career had been good and stimulating, but she had had that experience. She didn't discount her accomplishments—Homer couldn't have run his business as well without her—that she knew, even if no one else did. But whatever it was she had needed from being a successful businesswoman, she needed no longer. Now she longed for her home, her children and—if possible—Evan. He was desperately, totally vital to her. If she was wrong about him, and the idea of responsibility of a child cooled his caring—then what? Then she would go on, of course, but never feel wholly complete as a woman again.

Oh, Evan, Sara pleaded silently, *please don't let me down.*

But he mustn't feel entrapped. She tried to remember all the things he had said about his work. His calling had been that of a nomad in a way. A few years here solving this problem, then a few years—or months—there, solving that problem. She cared too much for him to want him if it meant he was giving up too much of what he needed, not if he would feel hemmed in and stifled. Not ever that.

Oh, Evan, please want the baby.

THE HEIGHTENED AWARENESS of all the lovely things in her life remained for the next two weeks. Now that the company was in trouble, they had—she and Evan and Grant—come together in a sort of team operation, all striving for the same thing, the survival of Homer's company. And as part of her job, she was faithfully going through all the unread trade journals, reading the sections on new products.

Close to midnight one evening, she put aside a magazine and stared thoughtfully at the wall. Wasn't there some old wise saying about looking in one's own backyard first? she asked herself, an idea taking shape in her mind.

She thought about her idea all the next week. Grant and Evan might need persuading, but she thought she could manage that. On Friday morning she invited them both to lunch in Grant's office. She had made sure in advance that Grant had no lunch engagement simply by having Margaret postpone the one he did have.

She went home at eleven o'clock and came back promptly at noon with her large picnic basket and thermoses of steaming coffee. She bustled around, laying bright paper place mats on Grant's conference table and setting out a platter of sandwiches covered in plastic.

Grant leaned back in his big chair and watched her through half-closed eyes. He looked incredibly tired.

"What's all this in aid of, my dear?" he inquired through the open door to the conference room. "I never knew you to waste motion or spin your wheels before. You've got a reason for doing this."

"You bet I have," she said briskly. "I finally came up with an idea I think you can use for Jarvis Foods."

"What is it? I'll use it."

"Not so fast—a demonstration's included."

He got up from his desk and came to look down at the beautifully prepared lunch.

"And it includes a big green salad and croissant sandwiches? Looks good. What's the stuffing, cream cheese and what?"

"You like crab, don't you?"

"Sure do. All shellfish. And those little green flecks—what's that?"

"Chopped parsley. And there's a hint of onion, and the whole mishmash is softened with mayonnaise. I've tried it and it's delicious."

"I believe you. It looks terrific. You said Evan's coming too?"

"Any minute."

Grant picked a crouton from the salad and popped it in his mouth. "You know, this is great." He laughed delightedly. "Even if you didn't have a great idea to salvage the company, an office picnic is a good idea. It'll ease the tension if nothing else."

Evan came at quarter past twelve. He had stopped to change his clothes and looked so handsome that Sara felt her legs go weak. She quelled the urge to reach over and touch him. She glanced quickly at Grant, afraid her reaction to Evan must be visible. Grant registerd no reaction. Like the innate gentleman he was, he'd withdrawn into himself tactfully as soon as he had seen the attraction between herself and Evan. Since then, there had never been even a hint of his own desire for her. Trust Grant to do the decent thing.

"What is this terrific-looking stuff? And what's the occasion? Somebody's birthday?" Evan strode over to the laden conference table.

"Crabmeat and cream cheese," Grant said. "Looks great, doesn't it? Sara's got something she wants to spring on us, and she's guaranteed us privacy by staging it here in my office. And she's breaking down our defenses in advance by feeding us. Watch yourself, man, she's up to something."

"Okay, it's all ready," Sara announced. "Come and get it."

It seemed as if instantly they were having a party. As one, they put aside the pressure under which they had been working and decided to enjoy themselves. Only once during the festive lunch was their problem mentioned.

"Have you heard the latest rumor at the plant?" Grant asked, taking his third croissant. "It's that you're putting in a whole new and faster cooking system, Evan. Importing the machinery from France at enormous cost. It was invented by a man called Flambé.'' He couldn't finish what he was saying without laughing. "Surely some guy named Flambé didn't invent a cooker, did he?''

Evan put down his sandwich and looked thoughtful. "Not to my knowledge," he said. "Flambé, huh? Interesting, I must say.''

They were topping off the meal with sliced pears, dripping sweetness, when Sara cleared her throat and tapped lightly on the table.

Both men, replete and good-humored, laughed.

"I guess she's calling the meeting to order," Grant observed, sitting forward.

"Okay, we're all attention. Let's have it," Evan said, looking at her with such patent love in his expressive eyes that she couldn't speak for a moment.

"Did you like the sandwiches?" she asked.

"That's a great beginning," he said. "Yes, I think I can speak for both of us. Now, what's next on the agenda?''

"What was it?" Sara pointed to the one remaining croissant. "The filling, I mean?''

Grant answered. "Why, cream cheese and crab, you said.''

"No, I didn't. You just assumed it was crab.''

Evan reached for the last croissant. "I can't let this go to waste," he murmured. "There are people starving in the world. My mother always said that was why we mustn't waste anything." He took a large mouthful.

"No," Grant said. "Just before lunch. I asked what it was, and you said crabmeat.''

"Not exactly." Sara leaned back and crossed her arms. "What you said was, 'What's the stuffing, cream cheese and what?'"

"And you said crab," he said triumphantly.

"No. I said, 'Do you like crab?'"

"Oh, foul. Foul!" Evan said, swallowing the last bite of his sandwich. "Trust a woman to be devious. What was it—now that I've eaten ten pounds of it?"

"Surimi. Imitation crab. A product of Japan made mostly of bottom fish."

Both men started to speak at once.

"Western people don't eat bottom fish," Grant said flatly.

"*Imitation* crab—are you joking?" Evan demanded. "That tasted great."

"Western people *will*—and do—eat bottom fish," Sara said. "If it doesn't *taste* like bottom fish. The substance is there. The nutrients are there. And if it tastes familiar, we'll eat it and like it." She paused, watching their reactions carefully.

"How do they do it?" Evan asked after a moment, a faraway look in his fine eyes.

"Mainly by a long washing process—I won't go into detail now. Why should the supermarket chains have to import this frozen? Why can't it be available in cans—or maybe even fresh—here? I've made a set of notes on the process for both of you. I was thinking it would be great for the fisherman to be able to sell some bottom fish to *us* instead of the Soviet and Japanese factory ships, the way they do now. There's plenty of the product up in the Bering Sea. Then shortages and controls on the regular fish don't apply. And it might just bail out Jarvis if we . . . if Evan could come up with a method of washing, or whatever it takes to..."

"Yes. Yes," Evan said slowly. "Why not? Of course."

"And we needn't stop at imitation crab, either," Grant said animatedly. "What about other things—fish cakes ready to fry or whatever—what do you think, Evan?"

Evan reached to take Sara's hand. "I think the lady's come up with a winner."

CHAPTER EIGHTEEN

SARA GOT a plastic trash bag from Margaret and started clearing away the remains of lunch, feeling satisfied with herself. Both men were elated. They sat hunched over Grant's desk, talking in excited, half-finished sentences.

"No need to stop at mock crab," Grant was saying. "If that goes and it certainly will, the sky's the limit. We could—"

Evan interrupted. "The main thing is the washing procedure. There's an excellent water supply already, and I could install the sluicing mechanisms as soon as—"

Grant broke in excitedly, waving a pencil. "With an unlimited supply of bottom fish made attractive to Canadian tastes, we—"

"Hand me that pencil so I can jot down a few figures. We've got to think costs," Evan muttered.

"I've always had the idea we should get into the frozen food market as well as canning."

"Now, as for the Canadian market . . . Sara, you want to get in on this." Evan glanced up. "You know more about the markets—"

"Not only Canadian," Grant interjected. "We could export to the States. We do a lot of that already with the canned goods. It's simply a matter of . . . Sara, what do you think?"

After they had exhausted all the possibilities of her idea, Sara tidied up, stopping every few minutes to get articles from trade magazines for Grant and Evan to ponder.

"Oh, leave that for Margaret," Grant said at one point, but Sara calmly continued with her self-imposed task. She was *not* going to leave this mess for a Margaret. This was—in an odd little way—the beginning of her homemaking career, although the men didn't know it. The thought pleased her.

Margaret buzzed on the intercom, reminding Grant of a meeting appointment across town and putting a stop to what remained of the planning session.

"Damn," he said. "Oh, all right. I'm on my way. Look, Evan, can we get together first thing tomorrow on this?"

"You bet," Evan said eagerly, looking up with hands full of scribbled notes.

When Grant was gone, Sara put the last of the picnic remains in a plastic garbage bag and tied the top securely. She was suddenly aware of a heavy silence and glanced up at Evan. He was sitting motionless, at the end of Grant's desk, the notes still in his hands.

"What are you doing?" she asked, smiling. It was impossible not to smile.

"Watching you. The thing I enjoy doing most—well, almost most."

She let the bag fall to the carpet and walked toward him, as if magnetized. Looking into each other's eyes, the silence lengthened and then, as if embarrassed, both spoke at once.

"I've got a surprise for you," they said simultaneously, then broke into laughter.

"All right," Sara said. "You mentioned surprise half a second ahead of me so you tell me your surprise first." She didn't add that she thought her surprise was so stupendous that his could only pale by comparison.

"Okay. It's this. I've been doing my pink-panther act. I've always wanted to be a detective...." He gripped the back of his neck and eyed her narrowly. "Except for once when I was set upon by a huge and extremely dangerous suspect in the dark one night. That almost nipped my sleuthing aspirations in the bud."

Sara poked his side and his arm shot down. He held her hand tightly, grinning, his attempt at dourness ruined.

"Anyway," he continued. "I've finally detected something." He tossed down the notes and stood, placing his hands lightly at her waist. She drew back just enough to stop anything more.

"What have you detected?"

"Something you'll be glad to know. Ben's in the clear as the company troublemaker."

She felt an upsurge of mingled relief and gratitude and slid her arms around his neck. "Oh, Evan, you darling. You did it! How can I ever thank you?" She urged him close, pressing against him.

"Well, you're doing fine—just keep it up." His arms tightened around her back.

"No, you idiot. Just tell me how you found out— what you found out." She stiffened, gazing intently up into his face.

"From darling to idiot in two seconds. What'd I do wrong? Lady, you're a puzzle. I never know where I stand with you." His dark eyes were laughing and his mouth was enticingly close, but Sara made herself resist kissing him. She pushed him a fraction further away.

"All right," he said. "I get your message. I'll tell you everything. First, I was extremely clever about it—"

"Be serious, Evan."

"I am. I was seriously clever. I've done a lot of asking and probing and all that. And I got the rumor sources down to two people—Ben and Chick Enderby." He paused dramatically.

"And? And?"

"And then I made my master stroke. I told them both my future plans for Jarvis Foods. Invited them to share a couple of tuna sandwiches in my office. Then today—" He broke off before adding, "I felt it appropriate to have tuna sandwiches considering this is a fish cannery. . . ."

"Evan!"

"Anyhow," he resumed quickly. "Today, when Grant came out with that latest oddball rumor about new cooking equipment by Flambé of France—which, so far as I know doesn't exist—I knew the rumor monger was our friend Chick."

She looked blank. "I don't . . ."

"Oh. I guess I skipped a little. There were two tuna sandwich sessions. On two different days. I had one with Chick on Monday and one with Ben on Tuesday. Now Friday we learn of the Flambé rumor. I gave them each a different story, you see? Chick got Flambé. I told Ben about my foolproof system for cutting the number of packers down. Not one word of that conversation has surfaced. Chick's dropping the strike business to the *Nancy Belle*'s skipper could have been an isolated incident . . . accidental even. But this confirms my suspicions. Get it? I told Ben and Chick different stories, and Chick's took less than four days to reach Grant.''

"I get it," she said, grinning. "You're right. You were clever. Stunningly clever. Have you told Grant?''

"No." He turned away, looking slightly embarrassed. "I was going to ask you to do that. You're personnel, after all. I've already discovered some other, pretty damning clues, Sara. For days I've been fairly sure our problem was Chick. Remember the night at the cannery? When we got shut in?''

She frowned, her skin turning cold. "Of course I do.''

"Did you hear anyone drive away?''

"No," she said slowly, and closed her eyes, remembering the darkness, the silence, the waiting. She looked at Evan sharply. "But the person could have walked. You did.''

"The culprit did walk. But there shouldn't have been any need if he'd planned to get away. It would have made more sense to have a vehicle—probably with the motor running—if he thought he might have to make a dash for it. And he must have known that was a possibility. He obviously expected to find someone there.''

"So?''

"Whoever that was must have had a key, too, right?''

"Well, yes. I locked the door behind me, so he must have.''

"Who has keys to the plant and doesn't own a car?''

Sara thought for a moment. "Oh, good grief. He even made a point of complaining about catching buses because he couldn't afford a car. Chick, that is. He came to see me and said that."

Evan grimaced. "The old guy isn't too smart, but he's not all bad. He's just one of nature's malcontents, and he hasn't had enough excitement in his life—so he sort of invents it. The rumors, swiping notes and tools and parts. He's just a mischief maker. He'll break down the minute he's confronted with it all—I know he will. I didn't want...I hoped he wouldn't get fired or anything. What do you think? Sometimes Grant can be pretty tough."

"I know," she said thoughtfully. "Grant's first thought will be to let him go—or even prosecute. But..." She bit her lip and was silent a moment. "Chick's only a year from retirement. I think what I'll do is finagle it so that Grant offers him early retirement. He's got quite a bit of profit sharing...maybe he could get a small boat or something to keep him busy. That's what he's always wanted. I'll fix it. We really can't keep him on after this," she added decisively. She thought for a second, then kissed him lightly on the cheek. "I'll thank you properly later," she said, her voice husky.

"That's nice, but I was rather hoping for now," Evan murmured.

"Now about *my* surprise," she said, resting her hands firmly against his chest. "I'm not quite sure how to tell you this. Maybe I'd better just plunge in. Sit down, Evan."

"Sit down?" he said, laughing. "It must be some surprise. Why should I sit down? I like it like this." He moved a fraction of an inch closer.

She lifted her hands and framed his face, wanting desperately simply to say "I love you," but pushed the impulse aside. She mustn't entrap him, or give that impression. She must be calm and collected and give him the simple truth. Then let him do whatever he decided he wanted to do. She could make it alone—if she had to.

"Evan," she began, and in spite of her best effort her voice trembled. "I'm pregnant."

He kept looking at her for endless seconds, not really grasping what she'd told him. "I'll sit down," he finally said, his voice oddly rasping, and he sat with a thud in Grant's chair. Sara went down on her knees in front of him. Her instinct was to place her hands on his thighs. Instead she clasped her fingers together. She mustn't touch him yet, or entice him in any way.

"Do you mean you...you...you...you're going to have a baby?" His words came out in a hoarse whisper.

"That's the usual result of pregnancy," she said gently.

"But *us*...I mean *we*...I...you...how could this...?"

"The same way it's been happening for millions of years, Evan."

"But to *us*...." His voice cracked and rose in pitch. "Holy Moses, we're two adults—two reasonably—"

"I know, Evan. It embarrasses me a little, too." She could feel color mounting into her neck and face. "It must have happened in San Francisco." Her cheeks were on fire now. "I always laughed at those stories about people who got pregnant the first time they made love. We behaved thoughtlessly, like a couple of teenagers on the beach, but..."

But he wasn't hearing her. "I thought . . . you see I just assumed . . . I mean . . ."

"I know. You just assumed I was on the pill, and justifiably so. I should have . . ."

"No, no!" he almost shouted. "*I* should have. I should have taken precautions . . . or . . . or . . . at least *asked*, for Pete's sake."

She sat back on her heels, grinning faintly. "That would rather have ruined the mood. If I remember correctly, in San Francisco we were pretty much . . . caught up in the moment. I just can't imagine you having pulled back to ask, 'Excuse me, madam, are you on the pill?'"

"Well, no, I wouldn't have . . . I'm more tactful than that . . . *Sara, just think* . . ." He was staring at her, eyes wide, trembling slightly.

"I have been thinking a little of late, I admit. But I had to tell you. I thought you should—"

"Of course you had to tell me." He brushed her hair with his fingertips, then pulled her against his chest. "Of course I want to know."

She threaded her hands beneath his arms and clung tightly. Every word counted now. "This isn't something you have to worry about, Evan. Nothing will change for you, unless . . ." No, she mustn't suggest, hint. "I've already decided how to manage things. Everything will stay the same for you."

"The same?" He put her away sharply. "My dear, Sara, that's where you're wrong. Things will *never* be the same."

She bowed her head. "No, I suppose not." He was thinking about all the ramifications, about his work. There was still a lot for him to do at Jarvis before . . . She couldn't pretend, but it hurt to face that he must have plans for the future. She would do nothing to interfere with whatever he hoped to do with his life.

"What is it, Sara?" He chafed her arms from shoulder to elbow and back. "Is everything all right with the baby? Sara, are *you* okay?" His fingers dug into her flesh. "Sara?"

"I'm fine, Evan, fine." She was tired. What had she expected? Was he supposed to be delighted at the prospect of a child he didn't want?

"Have you seen a doctor?" he demanded. A hawklike watchfulness entered his expression. "You should see one immediately."

"Yes, I've seen a doctor. That's who I found out from, a doctor."

"Is he good? Is he the best?"

"Yes, I'm sure of it." She smiled weakly up at him. "Next time I go I'll ask, okay?"

He tipped his head to one side. "You do that, funny lady. Sara, we have to think about this and talk about it."

"Not now," she said softly. "I should get back to my office, and I know you've got a thousand things to get going on. Later will do."

"No it won't. This has to be now. We're two adults. Okay, we...what's the phrase?...we made a mistake. This isn't exactly according to any plan we had...not exactly planned parenthood. In fact, we hadn't ever made any definite plans that I remember."

"No, of course we didn't." She would cling to her pride. He was trying to let her down gently. "But I know I have to make some now and I've already started."

"What do *you* want, Sara...*really* want?"

The gentleness she felt in him almost swayed her. She almost said, *I want to marry you, Evan. I want to live with you always and bring up Donna and our baby wherever you and I can be together.*

He leaned closer and cupped the side of her face. "Tell me, sweetheart. I need to know."

"I want this baby." Her hand automatically covered her belly. "And I want to be the best mother to him—or her—and to Donna. I want to be there for them whenever they want me. I don't want to juggle my life between a family and a job anymore. I want a *real* family, Evan."

"Right." He was out of the chair, pulling her with him, a determined smile on his lips. "There's nothing more to think about, then. That's what you should do."

CHAPTER NINETEEN

"You're up to something, Evan."

"Why do you say that?"

"I can tell. You are going to take me back to the office, aren't you?" Despite the urging pressure of his hand at her elbow, Sara approached the parked Mercedes reluctantly.

"You'll be back at the office when you have to be."

"Meaning?"

His chin was lifted. "Smell that air. I love the feel of winter coming. This is a fantastic day." A broad smile deepened laugh lines around his eyes and mouth.

"Where are we going?"

"You'll see when we get there, sweetheart."

"Evan." Sara planted her feet firmly on the pavement of the parking lot. "I'm not getting into this car until you tell me where you're taking me."

"Women. Why must you always be so difficult?"

His eyes shone with that wonderful, deep humor that was so much a part of him. Could he be happy, or was he reacting to her news in some sort of hysterical way? She touched his cheek hesitantly and he clasped her hand to his mouth, kissing her palm softly, keeping his gaze on her face.

"Is that coat warm enough?" he asked, and felt the sleeve of her down parka. "It's pretty cold by the Bay."

"Ah." She removed his fingers from her arm. "You gave our destination away. English Bay. And what are we supposed to do there?"

"Pregnant woman need exercise and fresh air. We're going for a walk. And then we'll get you a good meal. Then you'll have to rest..."

"McGrath. Knock it off. Pregnant women aren't invalids. I've got work to do and so do you. I can't go wandering around Vancouver like a tourist. Besides, I've got my own car here."

"We'll pick it up later. You put in a good morning's work and then went through all that stuff with lunch." He stepped closer and she retreated. "You're something, lady. What's the proper name for that stuff again? The stuff I'm going to spend months of my life with?"

"Surimi. And I've got to get on, Evan. I can't shelve my responsibilities."

"No, you can't. We already discussed that, remember? I want you inside this car. Now." He opened the door. We'll talk as we drive. We've got a lot to talk about."

Resigned, Sara dropped to the seat and swung her legs in. Evan shut the door and stood, staring down at her for an instant, before he walked around to get in beside her. She loved to watch him move. How well she remembered him without clothes, the lithe play of muscle and sinew while they made love. She looked away from him. Only a naive kid would ignore the possible ramifications of sleeping with a man without taking precautions. Yet she'd truly believed herself unable to conceive.

The Mercedes glided smoothly onto the street and Evan headed east.

"I don't suppose there's any hope of changing your mind about English Bay?" Sara rested her head back. "I will have to get some stuff cleared up today, and I also need to be home in time for Donna."

"You're very beautiful. Have I told you that lately?"

She let out an exasperated sigh. "I..." *Dammit all, he was irresistible... and she was crazy about him.* "No, you haven't told me lately. Have I told you how beautiful you are?"

He laughed delightedly, showing strong teeth, driving a deep dimple into his cheek. "Tell me. Tell me."

"You clown."

"That's me. A beautiful clown. Boy, not every man gets compliments like that."

They passed brilliantly decorated stores. Overhead, glittering Christmas garlands were suspended between buildings. Evan maneuvered skillfully through the heavy holiday traffic on the downtown streets and eventually threaded his way onto Pacific Boulevard. Just being with him, feeling his strength and the life that emanated from him, filled her with reflected power. And inside her, a part of them both was growing, right now, as they sat side by side. Instinctively she held his thigh, felt it tense, not just from the motion of driving, but with the effect she intended to produce, desire.

"Is your seat belt fastened?"

She glanced at his face. "Yes. Why?"

"If you intend to make a habit of touching me without warning, I'm likely to run off the road, that's all."

"You mean all I have to do to get you excited is stroke your leg? Doesn't take much." Her bent head hid a smile.

He pulled the steering wheel abruptly to the right and parked. "I know you aren't a tease, my love. So obviously you're as frustrated as I am. I'm going to kiss you, and then we'll walk and decide together how to cope with all this frustration." The button on the cuff of his raincoat caught her earing and she yelped. Evan looked horrified and grasped her head, peering closely at her lobe. "God. I think it's bleeding."

It certainly hurt. "Oh, preserve me from these smooth operators." She winced, then slowly began to smile. "You should see your face. You'd think you'd knocked me up or something."

His lips parted, then came together. Blushes suited him. "You say the darndest things. Not suitable at all for a mother-to-be."

"Let's walk." She opened the door and scooted out rapidly to stand on the sidewalk, waiting for Evan to lock up and join her. He'd been right when he said they had a lot to talk about. She must make it clear that she had no intention of making him suffer because she'd been a fool.

"Is that ear okay?" He put a hand at her waist. "Should it be cleaned or something?"

Sara shook her head. "It's nothing. Look, Evan, they're still wind-surfing." She took his hand and led him across the broad street and down a flight of steps to stand in the lee of a concrete building close to the sea. "I want to learn to do that."

"Not for a while, you don't." Evan hugged her to him, crossing his arms around her back. "I'm so. . .

God, Sara, I don't know how to put what I feel into words. Confused does it, I guess, and scared as hell.''

"Me, too.'' She rested her cheek on his raincoat lapel and stared toward the ocean.

Blustery wind filled brilliant, triangular sails above the finned boards ridden by several hardy souls in wet suits. They tacked into the surf, bare feet skittering on slick fiberglass; they clung, using arms and legs and innate balance to wrestle each air current and twisting wave that tried to claw them down into swirling water.

"It excites me to watch them, Evan. I've never felt so alive, or filled . . . filled with life.''

"I'll always love you.'' He gripped her face, spread his fingers wide and kissed her long and deeply. "It's cold out here. Too cold, I think.'' He tugged up her collar and started walking, one arm around her shoulders. "We can leave the car where it is for now. We're almost home.''

They were only a few hundred yards from his condo. "Your home, Evan.''

"Yes. My home. Yours, too, now. People who start out on a life together and want it to last, usually throw everything they have into the venture.'' Several cars passed before he could guide her across the street. "We won't be able to live here, of course. Donna needs her friends, and the baby will need a yard. We have all kinds of things to figure out and not much time to work with.''

He strode on, pulling her with him as if unaware her steps had started to drag. Nothing had been decided, yet Evan behaved like a man with a mission to be accomplished—immediately. "Evan, don't rush, please. No commitments have been made. It's too soon for that. Give yourself enough time to decide what you really want."

He didn't reply. Instead he steered her purposefully into his building and up to the condo. Once inside, he walked her to the center of the room, unzipped her parka and slid it from her arms. Every action was capably executed while a spark of irritation flickered to life in Sara. She didn't need or want to be taken care of.

"Finished?" While he went to hang their coats, she folded her arms tightly and suppressed a shiver. The wind had chilled her.

He turned quickly, brows raised. "You sound cross. What'd I do this time?"

She looked at the ceiling, exasperated. "I'm not cross. Not really. It's just that I can't always read you. I've waited two weeks trying to decide whether to tell you about the baby...and how. I don't want you to feel trapped into...into...being with me. But I knew you had a right to know what's happened and how *I* feel."

"You bet your life I have a right. And you also told me you want to be a full-time mother and home-maker, didn't you?"

Shuddery sensations seized her body. "I didn't say I expected you to fall in with what I want...not all of it. I am going to quit work as soon as I can get things squared away there and make a proper home for Donna and..." The words were still so hard to believe, let alone say aloud: *our baby*.

"Oh, my darling. You're going to need lots of loving to show you how much I want all the things you want. A home, children—and above all, you as my wife. You will marry me, won't you?"

The downward curve of her lips was involuntary. Too bad she'd promised herself not to cry. "You feel trapped."

"Good God," Evan exclaimed and walked her backward to a couch. He set her down carefully but firmly and sat beside her. "If this is how bondage feels, may I never be set free. Ms Fletcher, will you do me the honor of giving me your hand in marriage?" He stared solemnly into her eyes.

Sara bowed her head. When he looked at her like that—even in jest—she couldn't think. "Can't you ever be serious?"

"I have never been more serious in my life."

"You're rushing things. You must give yourself time to think."

"Does that mean you won't marry me?"

"No!"

"Great." He reached across her for the phone and dialed, taking the opportunity to plant a sound kiss on her lips while he waited, the receiver pressed to his ear. "Mmm, yes. Hi." Pulling her against his shoulder he rested his head on the back of the couch. "This is Evan McGrath in Vancouver, B.C. Is Mr. Hunt at home? Good. Yes, I'll wait."

"Evan." Sara squirmed but only succeeded in becoming more firmly pinned to his side. "Let me go. What are you doing?"

"Mark. How are you? How're Laura and that fantastic godson of mine? Good. I've got something to ask you."

"Evan..." Sara's hoarse whisper brought only a grin from him.

"Just a minute, Mark. Sara's here, and she wants a chance to say hi before you and I get too involved."

She glared as the phone was thrust against her ear, then winced. It was the same ear Evan had snagged. "Sorry," he mouthed, and moved the instrument slightly.

"Hello, Mark." She felt like a fool. Mark Hunt was almost a stranger.

"Hi, Sara. Great to hear your voice. Evan sounds like a man with something on his mind. Any idea what it might be?"

Save her from smart men. This one already had laughter in his voice. He knew something was brewing and was preparing to enjoy himself. "Ah, I guess he just wanted to say hello," she said lamely. "Is your family well? Donna talks about Bruce nonstop. If I made her pay for all the calls she makes to him, she'd have no allowance. When you see him, tell him he has my permission to put her off whenever he feels like it."

"Bruce seems to have developed an affinity for babies and young people," Mark said easily. "He thinks the world of Donna. Says she's renewed his faith in the coming generation."

What else was she supposed to say? "Thank . . . ah, thank him for me. And give my best to Laura . . . and . . . kiss little Evan for me. I'll give you back to Evan."

"Okay, just a minute—" he said something she couldn't make out "—stick around after I talk to Evan. Laura'll be down. She's changing his lordship."

Sara mumbled agreement and gave the phone to Evan. He held it high while he kissed her again, then let her go. She narrowed her eyes threateningly and shifted to the far end of the couch.

"Hey, Mark—" Evan watched her, a benign smile on his lips "—remember that favor I did you a while back? Yeah, yeah... I took a trip to San Francisco because no one else was right to be young Evan's godfather? Good choice you made there...." He laughed, nodded, nodded again.

Mark must be filling him in on something, Sara decided. Like "The Infant's" latest miraculous deeds. She felt suddenly rotten, like a mean and jealous child. The Hunts' baby was lovely, and she was glad for them. Within a few months she'd be crowing over her own baby's every move.

"That's great, Mark. This fatherhood thing sounds like a kick. I can hardly wait."

Sara almost stopped breathing.

"Anyway. To get back to why I'm calling.... Sure I wanted to check up on you two... three. Mark, will you shut up for a minute? Great. Sara and I are getting married two weeks from Saturday, and I want you to stand up for me."

She shot to her feet and stood over him, waving her hands. *Two weeks? Getting married? Just like that?* "Evan," she whispered urgently. "Evan, stop."

He smiled sweetly into her eyes. "Thanks, Mark. I knew you would... The noise? It's just Sara. I haven't been able to stop her talking ever since we started making arrangements.... Oh, about two minutes ago. Yeah, I decided to put her out of her misery. Decided I've saved myself long enough. It's time to make some lucky woman deliriously happy, and she happened to be around."

Sara closed her eyes and smothered a laugh. Impossible. He was a wonderfully impossible man. Only two weeks to arrange everything! And Evan would make it all happen somehow. Panic closed in. Donna knew nothing yet, or her own parents, or Ben and Christine. Or Grant. Her chest felt tight. Grant had accepted so much, and he'd become very important to her in a special way. She wanted him to be happy for her.

"Hi, Buff." The change in Evan's tone brought Sara's attention back to his face. The humor had died to be replaced by a softness, even a misty quality in his eyes. "I know how lucky I am. Yes, and I know you told me I would be one day...." He laughed and spread an arm along the couch back, tilting his head to stare at Sara, undisguised love in the set of every feature. "I know I'm getting a bonus. I guess that's because I had to wait a bit longer. God figured I deserved to get a beautiful daughter thrown in, too."

Tears welled in Sara's eyes and she sniffed hard. She'd always known Laura Hunt was a good woman. It had just taken a while to admit it to herself. Obviously Laura was telling Evan how lucky he was to be getting Donna as well as a wife. Sara blinked rapidly. Any minute now, he'd be spilling the beans about the baby and she wasn't ready for that.

"Sara," Evan said very gently. "Laura would like to tell you how happy she is for us." He covered the mouthpiece. "You okay, little one? Are you crying?"

She shook her head and took the receiver. Laura wished her luck, said she knew she was going to have lots of it, promised to be in Vancouver a couple of days early to help with whatever she could. Sara hung up. She'd remembered to invite Irma and Bruce and to thank Laura—hadn't she? *Two weeks. They were going to be married in two weeks.*

"You look tired, love." Evan stood and held her hands. "I know how tough you are, but would it hurt anything if you lay down for a bit?"

She was tired. Her muscles ached, and her eyelids seemed determined to droop. "I'll sit on the couch awhile."

"No you won't." He led her into his bedroom with its huge, low water bed, the bold black and white and mirrored decor. "You're going to bed. I'll call Mrs. Beamis and ask her to stay with Donna as long as necessary. She won't mind, particularly if I make her an accessory. Later we'll talk to Donna together. Before we talk to the rest of your family...and mine."

He waited.

"All right, Evan. If you say so."

He didn't move.

"I'll lie down for an hour, then I'll be fine."

"Can I come to bed with you?"

"You're tired, too?"

"No."

She started to laugh. "You're terrible. Awful, in fact. You pretended you were concerned about my health...and..." Automatically she rested a hand on her stomach. "And this little surprise of ours."

"I am, love. Very concerned. I want to be with you all the time." He pulled his sweater over his head. "I only said I wasn't tired. I'll just lie beside you and watch you sleep—Scouts' honor." The salute was sloppy.

"Were you ever a Boy Scout?"

"No."

The tiredness lifted, wiped away by a tide of yearning that sent heavy heat through her belly and thighs. The white shirt he wore was unbuttoned at the throat.

She longed to feel his naked skin beneath her cheek. Her gaze flickered up to find him watching her and she turned away.

"What are you thinking?" he asked unevenly.

"That you promised you'd call Mrs. Beamis. Why don't you do that? Then, by all means come back and watch me sleep, if you want to."

She couldn't look at him. He knew, only too well, what she was really thinking. He'd be back and quickly.

Evan left her, moved rapidly to the living room to place the call. Mrs. Beamis clucked conspiratorially when he told her he and Sara had made an important decision about the future and needed some time together to make plans. No, she'd say nothing to Donna except that they were delayed. The suppressed excitement in her voice left no doubt that she'd decoded his message accurately.

He hung up and went to the kitchen. He'd seen the tiredness drop away from Sara. She wanted him as much as he wanted her. Soon she'd be his wife, but he couldn't wait two weeks to be with her—totally—again.

They hadn't celebrated. He opened the refrigerator. Beer wouldn't do it. Brandy or a manhattan didn't seem the thing, or a martini. *Hah! He had it.* How could he be so stupid? He assembled a tray with the products of his brain wave, grabbed a bottle in a sack from the back of the refrigerator door and headed for the bedroom.

In the doorway, he hesitated. Only the top of Sara's dark head was visible above his black comforter. Wisps of satiny hair shone against the white pillow. He'd misread her signals. She was already asleep.

"Sara," he whispered, tiptoeing closer. "Sara. I called Mrs. Beamis, and she'll hold down the fort as long as we want. I told her we wouldn't be back until late. She's going to call Anne Parker and explain to her, too. Sweetheart, are you asleep?"

"No. Are you?"

He sighed and set the tray on the bedside table. "Who's a clown?"

"Maybe it runs in families. Donna already says she wants to be one."

He spread her hair carefully on the stark linen. "But first you'll want her to get a degree. Right?"

"Right. Although, at this moment, I don't think I want to think about that."

"What . . . ?" A lump formed in his throat. "What do you want to think about, Sara?"

"Us." She kept the covers over her nose, and her voice was muffled. "Lie with me like you said you would."

The toast would have to wait. With clumsy fingers, he shed his clothes. As a last thought, he picked them from the floor and slung them over a chair, then stepped out of his underpants. The sensation of being watched made him turn sharply toward the bed. Sara's eyes were wide open above the sheet.

"Not so sleepy anymore?" He stood straight, hands on hips. Her gaze traveled slowly over him, and with the visual caress, he felt as if she had touched every part of him. He was instantly aroused. "Did I remember to tell you I always sleep nude? I can probably find some pajamas if that bothers you."

"Yes, you forgot to tell me. And no, I'm not bothered." Slowly she pushed off the covers and held out her arms.

She was naked.

Trembling, he walked into her embrace, stretched his body beside her, rolled onto his back and held her on top of him. Her skin was pale silk, her hair a glossy curtain falling over her face and caressing his. Her breasts, fuller than he'd remembered, molded against his chest. Her belly, slightly less concave, pressed insistently while her thigh separated his. Restraint was unbearable. And exquisite. Just now there was no hurry.

So they didn't. Each brushing kiss, each stroking caress, deepened their closeness. Her skin, his, a million cells awakened and came alive. He brought her to a climax before entering her, knowing her endurance would be longer than his. Watching her face, stark with passion, sent shock ripples up his spine and a sword of pure fire deep into that part of him that would join them again. All the years of his life had been bringing him to this time with Sara and to all the times that lay ahead of them. Their interlude in San Francisco had been planned somewhere before they were born—he would have argued this truth.

Sara lay, facing him, one arm thrown over her head, a breast uplifted. He bent to kiss the nipple, and her slight recoil only urged him to tease more and reach for her other breast.

"Enough," she murmured. "I want *you*." Her leg, raised to clamp his hip, pulled him close. With only a single thrust they were one.

Evan heard their breathing, felt their hearts beat, gave himself to the ancient pattern of movement their bodies knew without coaching. When his release came, he knew Sara was with him, but his voice drowned any sound she made and her arms, not his, held tight, soothing, gentling his knotted muscles until he fell to his back, hugging her to his chest with one arm.

"Okay?" she whispered, her mouth at his throat.

He laughed, and Sara felt the rumble under her cheek. "I'm more than okay, love. I feel wonderful." He sounded sleepy.

"I feel wonderful, too." She managed to prop her head on the heel of one hand. "Are we going to make a habit of going to bed in the middle of the afternoon?" Daylight sent hazy shafts through narrow slatted blinds.

"Absolutely. Any time I can figure out ways to get you there." He arched up suddenly and kissed her, trailed a nipping trail over her jaw and down her neck to the hollow between her breast. "Will that be acceptable?"

"I wouldn't be surprised. What's on the tray?"

He roused and struggled to sit. "Our celebration toast. I thought you were asleep. Then something made me forget."

She laughed softly.

"Here." He reached across her and she kissed his chest, the smooth skin at his side. "Stop that, lady. Or we're both going to get very wet."

"Sorry," she said with mock contrition and sat up, gathering the sheet around her. "I'll try to behave, but it isn't easy."

"A toast to us." He handed her a glass. "To love—the more the better."

Sara laughed as his rough chin grazed her cheek, then stared at the drink. "Milk?"

"Of course," he said, straight-faced. "What else in your condition?"

"Oh, very romantic. Two glasses of milk. Yuck. I hate the stuff."

"Wee-ll. Just this once we'll make an exception." Sitting cross-legged, he produced a bottle of champagne from the brown paper sack and popped the cork. Foam overflowed, and they both tried to catch it in their palms.

Evan tipped the bottle and took a long swallow. "Your turn." He shrugged. "Forgot to bring more glasses."

Sara set aside her milk and put Evan's beside it. She took the champagne bottle and tilted it to her lips to take a tiny sip. Bubbles went up her nose and she laughed. "This is a real class act." She sipped once more and handed back the champagne.

Evan put the bottle on the tray and held her waist, lifting her onto his crossed legs. "I've never been so happy, Sara. I never hoped to be this happy. And I want you to be just as sure of everything as I am."

His eyes told her he meant every word. "I am sure. I'm going back to Jarvis for as long as it takes to find a replacement, and then I'll give all my attention to you and Donna...and the baby. I expect I'll find plenty to do with my time while the children are growing up, then I can think about working outside the home again."

"That may take a while. You never know. This baby business might catch on, and we'll decide to keep doing it."

She turned her face away. "I'm thirty-seven. This is probably going to be the only one. Will you mind that, Evan?"

"Hey," he said, laughing. "We already have one so he can't be the *only* one."

"He, huh?" She smiled despite herself. "And if it's a girl I suppose you'll send her back."

"Naturally." Gently he turned her face to his. "Do you think I care whether we have a boy or girl?"

"Not really. I'm just angling for all the attention I can get. Evan, we can't stay here all day."

Evan frowned. "Let me worry about that for a change. More important. When you decide on a replacement at Jarvis for that Sara Fletcher, make sure she's someone Evan McGrath can work with."

"Don't worry," Sara promised. "*He* will be."

He smiled against her shoulder. "Yeah. You'd better watch me. You know how I play the field."

Sara leaned away and stared seriously into his eyes. "I would never want to tie you down if you weren't ready, Evan. We all need to feel we've had choices and whatever we decide should be something we can live with."

"I've chosen you, Sara. If you want me."

She shivered and Evan pulled the quilt around them like a tepee. "You know the answer to that question," she said. "I'll never stop wanting you."

Harlequin
Superromance

COMING NEXT MONTH

#226 CRIMSON RIVERS • Virginia Nielsen
Volcanologist Holly Ingram knows that it is her duty to
warn plantation owner Lorne Bryant when an eruption
is threatening Kapoiki. And she also knows that this
meeting will bring to a climax the rift that has alienated
them for eight long years....

#227 BEYOND FATE • Jackie Weger
Cleo Anderson thinks romance isn't for her—until she
encounters the charismatic Fletcher Fremont Maitland
at a summer camp in Georgia. Slowly love works its
magic, and the fate that first drew them together
becomes the catalyst for a lifetime.

#228 GIVE AND TAKE • Sharon Brondos
Performing a striptease for a group of women is
embarrassing for Kyle Chambers, but he'll "do
anything for charity." And no one is more aware of this
than Charity Miller. But the marriage and children he
wants to give her are more than she is willing to accept.

#229 MEETING PLACE • Bobby Hutchinson
When an arranged marriage brings the exotically
beautiful Yolanda Belan to a new life in the West, she
quickly discovers that exchanging vows is not enough to
win the heart of her husband, Alex Caine. But her
refreshing approach to life and her smoldering
sensuality soon have him behaving like a newlywed
should!

ATTRACTIVE, SPACE SAVING BOOK RACK

Display your most prized novels on this handsome and sturdy book rack. The hand-rubbed walnut finish will blend into your library decor with quiet elegance, providing a practical organizer for your favorite hard-or soft-covered books.

Only $9.95

Approximately 16" x 8" when assembled

Assembles in seconds!

To order, rush your name, address and zip code, along with a check or money order for $10.70 ($9.95 plus 75¢ postage and handling) (New York residents add appropriate sales tax), payable to *Harlequin Reader Service* to:

In the U.S.

Harlequin Reader Service
Book Rack Offer
901 Fuhrmann Blvd.
P.O. Box 1325
Buffalo, NY 14269-1325

Offer not available in Canada.

Take 4 books & a surprise gift FREE

SPECIAL LIMITED-TIME OFFER

Mail to   **Harlequin Reader Service**®

In the U.S.
901 Fuhrmann Blvd.
P.O. Box 1394
Buffalo, N.Y. 14240-1394

In Canada
P.O. Box 609
Fort Erie, Ontario
L2A 9Z9

YES! Please send me 4 free Harlequin American Romance® novels and my free surprise gift. Then send me 4 brand-new novels as they come off the presses. Bill me at the low price of $2.25 each —a 11% saving off the retail price. There are no shipping, handling or other hidden costs. There is no minimum number of books I must purchase. I can always return a shipment and cancel at any time. Even if I never buy another book from Harlequin, the 4 free novels and the surprise gift are mine to keep forever.

Name   (PLEASE PRINT)

Address   Apt. No.

City   State/Prov.   Zip/Postal Code

This offer is limited to one order per household and not valid to present subscribers. Price is subject to change.   DOAR-SUB-1RR

HARLEQUIN HISTORICAL

Explore love with Harlequin in the Middle Ages, the Renaissance, in the Regency, the Victorian and other eras.

Relive within these books the endless ages of romance, set against authentic historical backgrounds. Two new historical love stories published each month.

Available starting August wherever paperback books are sold.

HIST-A-1